"CAN WE QUIT PLAYING THIS GAME?" CRAIG ASKED IN EXASPERATION.

"I'm not playing a game," Libby replied softly.

"The heck you're not! It's one I haven't seen before and I sure don't know the rules, but you're playing something."

"I don't know what you *want* from me!"

"Don't you?" Disbelief was etched on his weatherbeaten face. The desire in his eyes mirrored her own feelings, and she averted her face, not wanting him to see the naked yearning she felt for him.

"Don't start something you can't finish, Craig."

"So, we're back to promises and guarantees again? Give me a straight signal, Libby. Either yes, it's on, or no, it's off."

"If it's no?"

"I won't bother you anymore."

"And if it's yes?" She could hardly choke the words out.

"You know the answer to that."

CANDLELIGHT ECSTASY SUPREMES

37 ARABIAN NIGHTS, *Heather Graham*
38 ANOTHER DAY OF LOVING, *Rebecca Nunn*
39 TWO OF A KIND, *Lori Copeland*
40 STEAL AWAY, *Candice Adams*
41 TOUCHED BY FIRE, *Jo Calloway*
42 ASKING FOR TROUBLE, *Donna Kimel Vitek*
43 HARBOR OF DREAMS, *Ginger Chambers*
44 SECRETS AND DESIRE, *Sandi Gelles*
45 SILENT PARTNER, *Nell Kincaid*
46 BEHIND EVERY GOOD WOMAN, *Betty Henrichs*
47 PILGRIM SOUL, *Hayton Monteith*
48 RUN FOR THE ROSES, *Eileen Bryan*
49 COLOR LOVE BLUE, *Diana Blayne*
50 ON ANY TERMS, *Shirley Hart*
51 HORIZON'S GIFT, *Betty Jackson*
52 ONLY THE BEST, *Lori Copeland*
53 AUTUMN RAPTURE, *Emily Elliott*
54 TAMED SPIRIT, *Alison Tyler*
55 MOONSTRUCK, *Prudence Martin*
56 FOR ALL TIME, *Jackie Black*
57 HIDDEN MANEUVERS, *Eleanor Woods*
58 LOVE HAS MANY VOICES, *Linda Randall Wisdom*
59 ALL THE RIGHT MOVES, *JoAnna Brandon*
60 FINDERS KEEPERS, *Candice Adams*
61 FROM THIS DAY FORWARD, *Jackie Black*
62 BOSS LADY, *Blair Cameron*
63 CAUGHT IN THE MIDDLE, *Lily Dayton*
64 BEHIND THE SCENES, *Josephine Charlton Hauber*
65 TENDER REFUGE, *Lee Magner*
66 LOVESTRUCK, *Paula Hamilton*
67 QUEEN OF HEARTS, *Heather Graham*
68 A QUESTION OF HONOR, *Alison Tyler*
69 FLIRTING WITH DANGER, *Joanne Bremer*
70 ALL THE DAYS TO COME, *Jo Calloway*
71 BEST-KEPT SECRETS, *Donna Kimel Vitek*
72 SEASON OF ENCHANTMENT, *Emily Elliott*

REACH FOR THE SKY

Barbara Andrews

A CANDLELIGHT ECSTASY SUPREME

Published by
Dell Publishing Co., Inc.
1 Dag Hammarskjold Plaza
New York, New York 10017

Dell ® TM 681510, Dell Publishing Co., Inc.

Candlelight Ecstasy Supreme is a trademark of
Dell Publishing Co., Inc.

Candlelight Ecstasy Romance®, 1,203,540, is a
registered trademark of Dell Publishing Co., Inc.

ISBN: 0-440-17242-X

Printed in the United States of America

First printing—May 1985

For Lou and Lou—
Lucille Stubbe Bogema,
my aunt and first ''heroine''
and Louise Barrows Northam,
for her support and enthusiasm

To Our Readers:

Candlelight Ecstasy is delighted to announce the start of a brand-new series—Ecstasy Supremes! Now you can enjoy a romance series unlike all the others—longer and more exciting, filled with more passion, adventure, and intrigue—the stories you've been waiting for.

In months to come we look forward to presenting books by many of your favorite authors and the very finest work from new authors of romantic fiction as well. As always, we are striving to present the unique, absorbing love stories that you enjoy most—the very best love has to offer.

Breathtaking and unforgettable, Ecstasy Supremes will follow in the great romantic tradition you've come to expect *only* from Candlelight Ecstasy.

Your suggestions and comments are always welcome. Please let us hear from you.

Sincerely,

The Editors
Candlelight Romances
1 Dag Hammarskjold Plaza
New York, New York 10017

CHAPTER ONE

Giant saguaros studded the steep, arid hillsides, their ancient arms pointing at a dazzling blue sky, not a wisp of white cloud invading the domain of the merciless sun. Libby squinted against the glare, half expecting a gang of mounted desperadoes to appear on the far horizon. Her stomach was still queasy after a bumpy descent through a thunderstorm in Denver, where she'd caught her connection to Tucson. The man beside her maneuvered the station wagon around a sharp curve, seemingly oblivious to the sheer drop on her side.

"It's not a very good road, is it?" she asked meekly, not wanting to criticize the driver sent by Millway Productions to meet her at the airport.

"Not too bad," the man said, lifting a massive, overly muscular arm to scratch behind his big right ear. "Twenty minutes and we'll be there."

It was the most he'd said to her since showing his identification card at the airport terminal. Her plane had been nearly two hours late, thanks to the snarl caused by Denver weather, and she wasn't sure whether the eyes shadowed by a huge straw cowboy hat were crinkled in irritation or concentration.

After another hairpin turn, which she endured with closed eyes and clenched fists, she felt the car descending, following the black ribbon of road to the valley floor where the fantastic saguaros grew more sparsely amid a profusion of dusty-dry shrubs. A barrel-shaped cactus, a hundred times larger than the one on the windowsill of her neighbor's New York apartment, was fuzzy-looking with its profusion of spines, and beyond it the tortured, stunted outline of a tree stood leafless on the sandy-tan desert soil. It was the perfect place to shoot an old-time Western movie and less real to Libby Sloan than the stage setting for *Arabian Nights*. Maybe, after a good night's sleep, she'd believe that the palm trees along the streets of Tucson really grew there, but right now she was sure the whole trip was a dream. What was a twenty-eight-year-old struggling actress who'd grown up in Syracuse doing on her way to make a movie in Old Buckhorn, Arizona?

"It's my first time in Arizona," she said to the silent giant beside her, not adding that it was her first trip west of Pittsburgh, where her uncle owned a sporting-goods store.

His answering grunt was noncommittal, as the road they were following ended abruptly at a crossroad. Ignoring the stop sign, he made a sharp left turn and accelerated, shifting his heavy haunches on the gray nylon car-seat. Libby didn't want to know how fast he was driving, but her eyes darted automatically to the speedometer: eighty-two miles per hour.

"Are you a professional chauffeur?" she asked, needing some reassurance that they'd arrive safely at the site of her first movie.

"A grip."

"Oh."

Film making had its own vocabulary, and she'd tried hard to learn something about it from books and friends in the business. Today her mind was blank.

"What exactly do you do?" she pressed.

"Whatever needs doing."

A stagehand? A gofer? She didn't ask. All she really

12

needed to know was her own job, and she hadn't felt so shaky about a performance since playing the wicked witch in a fifth-grade production of *Hansel and Gretel*. What was she doing heading for an Old West movie set to play a wicked saloon-girl?

Fingering the script inside her roomy white corded-cotton bag, made in Taiwan and purchased just for the trip, she still couldn't believe she was there. Actors dreamed that the head of a casting company would see them in an off-Broadway production and offer a part in a movie. She'd always been too practical to believe in miracles. But it had happened to her! Now, months later, after she'd auditioned before a camera and her agent had worked out the details of the deal, the opportunity still seemed too incredible to be real. She wasn't even sure she wanted a supporting role in a made-for-television Western, but the balance in her bank account was healthy for the first time in her career with the rent on her apartment paid through the summer.

Taking the last cigarette from a squashed pack, her uncommunicative driver opened the window and added it to the debris along the side of the road. A wave of heat filled the air-conditioned interior, making Libby gasp for breath. How could anyone work outside when the air was hot enough to sear a person's lungs?

As empty as the road seemed, the desert on either side was littered with cans and bottles, the shattered fragments of glass a glittering mosaic in the sunlight. Apparently not even the desert was immune to the messy hand of man, she thought, fervently wishing she were leaving Old Buckhorn instead of just arriving.

From the highway all she could see was a chain link fence and a sprawling complex of low buildings with pink-ribbed metal sides and flat roofs. The driver, Frank, opened a gate with a flat black control box and followed a winding hard-dirt road past a sign with an arrow that read GENERAL OFFICES.

Ahead a hundred yards or so a surprisingly large building several stories high reminded Libby of a warehouse with huge double doors on the near-end large enough to admit a pair of semitrailers side by side. To her right a high fence of unpainted wooden stakes prevented her from seeing the rest of the site.

"Them campers over there," Frank said, gesturing with his huge hand at a row of white-and-tan mobile homes. "Third from the left is yours. I'll put your stuff there. Door ain't locked."

He stopped in front of a small door to the building that seemed so improbably large in the middle of a wasteland.

"Still be some people on the sound stage this time of day. We been shooting for two weeks already."

He sounded resentful, but she didn't know whether he hated the necessity of talking or blamed her for not having been there the first day.

"I wasn't needed then," she said, a little embarrassed by the insecurity that compelled her to explain. "Thank you for the ride."

He dismissed her with a lazy, one-handed gesture that plainly said it was his job to be inconvenienced by late arrivals. The station wagon pulled away, loosening puffs of dust that powdered the damp, fair skin of her face and tasted gritty in her mouth. The thick blond hair hanging below her shoulders, an inheritance from the Scandinavian side of the family, was hot and heavy on the skin between her shoulder blades. Her coolest dress, a pale-blue cotton halter dress that left one shoulder bare, wasn't comfortable in this kind of sun, and she hurried through the door, wondering if weeks in the desert would leave her as dehydrated as a mummy. She could hardly breathe in the late-afternoon heat.

Inside there were more people than she'd expected to see, all of them busy in the cool, vast cavern of the sound stage. Old Buckhorn, she was greatly relieved to discover, had a very efficient air-conditioning system.

In the theater an actor's first responsibility was to report to the stage manager, usually a very visible person with a clipboard and an air of command. Here, she supposed, there must be an assistant director or production assistant with the job of keeping track of people, but she didn't see anyone in the midst of the working crew-members who seemed even vaguely in charge. Standing well away from the flow of activity, she looked over the open-fronted room settings at the far end, the huge canvas murals hung on the side walls, and an authentic-looking Old-Western saloon not far from where she was standing. Several camera dollies were standing idle, while a slender little man with a bushy black beard spoke into a walkie-talkie. A crew of carpenters were hammering, and rock music was coming from some source she couldn't locate. One thing was certain: They weren't shooting at the moment.

"Can I help you with something?"

The man who approached her was strikingly handsome in the way Douglas Fairbanks had been, a dark, swashbuckling type with a thick black mustache. Libby wasn't addicted to adventure flicks, but she recognized him immediately: Wiley Bails, the star of *Freedom Gulch,* her first movie.

"Mr. Bails, I'm Libby Sloan. I'll be playing Cassandra Rose."

"I knew it the minute you walked in!" He took her hand in both of his, squeezing her fingers until she wanted to wriggle free of his grasp. "Depend on Carl to find the prettiest little thing this side of heaven."

Much to her embarrassment he pulled one of her imprisoned fingers to his lips and kissed it.

"Actually, I've never met Mr. McDowell," she said, knowing the director's name. "My part was filled by a casting consultant, and I—"

"These TV movies," he said, "they've lost the personal touch. If I were directing, I'd personally cast every part down to the old geezer who panhandles in front of the saloon. But for once a so-called expert is right. You *are* Cassandra Rose."

"Well, not quite." Libby could read between the lines enough to know her character was extremely free with her favors. She wasn't.

"With anyone less beautiful, the part would be wasted." The leading man smiled, revealing perfectly capped teeth, and put his arm around her shoulders. "You know, everybody who's anyone in Hollywood has put in some time in the saddle. This could be the beginning of something great for you. I'm talking script now with a highly regarded producer. What he has in mind is a kind of American saga—and he's a producer who listens to my suggestions."

His hand fell to her waist, then roamed over the fullness of her bottom.

"I should report that I'm here," she said, moving away. "The assistant director—"

"The AD, we call him." He closed in again, fondling her upper arm. "The worst thing about being on location is the silence after dark. It's too quiet with everyone holed up in their lonely little trailers. That's when friends make all the difference. I want you to think of me as your friend, Lilly."

"Libby."

"Yes, of course, Libby. Were you named after the actress Libby—"

"I was named for my great-aunt. Is the man in the green shirt the assistant director—the AD?"

"No, that's Bert Halloway, the stunt coordinator. Freeman's probably in his office. Poor kid, I can see you're exhausted. Jet lag. What you need is a tall, icy drink. The bar in my suite is the best-stocked on the lot. Let me make you my specialty, gin and tonic with a twist.''

"Thank you, Mr. Bails, but—''

"Wiley. Call me Wiley. We're all friends here." He patted her shoulder, the bare one.

"I think—''

"You have beautiful hair, Libby. Natural. I can always tell. I'll give our hair stylist the word to let it hang just the way it is. You can't improve on nature.''

He parted his lips, flicking his tongue over first the lower and then the upper. They were too thin, and his skin was sallow, slightly tinged with yellow. The camera flattered him, Libby decided, but that didn't solve her problem. How could she discourage him without making an enemy? She was worried enough about the part without having the star working against her.

"Wiley, the truth is, we had a terribly rough landing in Denver, right through a thunderstorm, and I'm not very good in planes. My stomach is still upset, and I'm not used to this heat either. I was hoping to take some aspirin and lie down for a while.''

"I understand." He smiled benevolently. "You should do just that. The dining hall is just east of the general offices. Chow time is from six to seven-thirty. I usually go late myself, after the cocktail hour. If you're feeling better, I'll show you around Old Buckhorn afterward, then we can have that tall one.''

"Yes, well, thank you. I'll see how I feel after a rest.''

No one else had rushed over to meet her, she noticed. Maybe it would be better to wait until tomorrow morning to meet the AD. She'd feel fresher and more alert after a shower and a good night's sleep. She left the cool interior with a trace of reluctance. The row of mobile homes, parked with rear bumpers pointing toward the chain link fence with five or

17

six feet between each unit, was closer to the office complex than to the sound stage. Apparently most of the cast and crew were housed in the complex of pink buildings, and she silently thanked her agent for securing private quarters, even though she didn't have star status.

The third of the six trailers was hers, which put her in the middle of the lineup. Underfoot, the dirt was hard-packed, but fine powdery dust still covered her strap-back white heels and nylon-clad toes. If her accommodations had a shower and air-conditioning, she might survive.

Her fib about a headache was becoming a fact as excitement, apprehension, and fatigue sapped her energy. The door, reached by three gritty metal steps, was unlocked, and her first impression of the mobile home's interior was one of great coolness. The carpeting was nappy and grass-colored, with honey-gold paneling and color-coordinated furnishings that included a small kitchenette, a booth with seating for four, a built-in plaid couch, and a small TV. The sleeping area was separated from the front by a closed door, and the laconic driver Frank must have stowed her luggage out of sight behind it. Unpacking could wait; all she wanted was water, a cold drink to begin, then a leisurely shower in the tiny but hopefully adequate facility.

Kicking off her shoes, which had started to pinch during her restless two-hour wait in Denver for her connection to Tucson, she turned on the faucet of the kitchen sink and splashed lukewarm water over her face, throat, and arms, not worrying that her travel-rumpled dress got wet. Blotting herself dry with paper towels, she let the water run cold, then drank a full glass, washing away the taste of dust.

All she needed now to be fully refreshed was a shower. Unzipping her limp full-skirted dress, she let it drop to the floor, lifting it on the tip of one toe and tossing it on the couch. She was sliding her half-slip down over her hips when

18

a tiny sound alerted her, making her whirl toward the interior door concealing the bedroom.

"Don't stop on my account."

Pulling up her slip with one hand, she grabbed frantically for her dress to cover her breasts, struck dumb by the sudden appearance of a man wearing jeans and nothing else. He ran his fingers through dark ash-blond hair, sun-streaked above a coppery-tan face and golden-bronze chest, then smiled lazily, revealing square teeth not quite perfect enough to be capped. His lips, full and sensual under a droopy, western-style mustache that curled wickedly on the ends, stretched into a cat-and-mouse grin as he rested his hands on the lean, hard ridges of his hips where faded jeans hung precariously low.

"I wondered who was running water out here," he said. "The other maid doesn't take her clothes off."

"I'm not a maid!" She gasped, unfortunately pulling the dress over her head with the back in front.

"I kind of thought you weren't." He leaned against the door frame, filling the opening with the most attractive chest and shoulders she'd ever seen, the deeply tanned skin lightly sprinkled with pale golden hair between his nipples, down to his navel and the edge of the waistband of his jeans.

Embarrassed by her own reaction, she snapped back angrily, "What are you doing here?"

"Just taking a little siesta," he drawled, "but there's plenty of room back there for both of us."

"There certainly isn't!" All of her premonitions of disaster, conjured up on the trip while she fretted about the movie script, seemed to be coming true; she should have stayed in New York where she knew the rules! "What are you doing in my mobile home?"

"Sweetheart, I had the funniest idea this was supposed to be my pad during the filming."

19

He was enjoying himself too much; his cockiness made her absolutely furious.

"Frank, the man who drove me here from the airport, said the third one was mine."

"Third from the right or third from the left?" He said every word slowly, stringing out his amusement with his vowels.

She couldn't remember! Maybe if this man put on a shirt and some shoes . . . At least there was nothing appealing about his feet, sticking out big and white under his denim cuffs. She riveted her eyes on the floor, determined not to look at that broad, hard chest again. If she were in the wrong trailer . . .

"A little mix-up won't stop us from being friends, will it? Here, let me help you with that zipper."

She'd finally twisted her dress so the front was where it belonged, but the back zipper was stubborn, sticking as she tried to yank it closed.

"I can do it myself, thank you," she said, alarmed when he moved toward her.

"You've caught the cloth, is what you've done," he drawled, stepping behind her and working the material out of the zipper teeth. "I could fix it better if you'd slip out of it."

"Never mind!" She tried stepping away, but he wouldn't let go of her zipper.

"That'll do it." He eased the zipper upward, his fingers trailing over the skin of her back with ticklish lightness. She hoped he didn't feel the little shudder that sparked through her. "Nicely," he added in a purring voice.

Were all the men here predatory? First Wiley Bails had jumped on her, and now this one!

"Stop it," she said angrily, all the day's frustrations coming to a head.

20

"Does that mean we can't be buddies?" He backed away and held out his hands, palms up.

She didn't find his little smirk at all amusing.

"Most likely not!"

She grabbed her purse and started toward the door, not remembering her shoes until her fingers were on the handle. One was lying conspicuously in the middle of the green carpeting, and she quickly jammed her right foot into it, looking around for the other.

"I'm Craig Wicklow," he said, his voice throaty with confidence.

How could her shoe disappear in such a small space? It had to be there! She looked frantically under the table of the booth, getting down on her hands and knees.

"Occupation stuntman," he said in a teasing voice. "Age thirty-three, six foot two and a half inches in bare feet, a hundred seventy-six pounds when I haven't had any beer, single, reasonably presentable, cheerful, kind, considerate. Eagle scout at age fourteen."

"There's no reason to tell me your life story!" She was leaving, shoe or no shoe!

"I'm also good at finding lost items."

Still on her knees, she looked up to see her dusty white shoe dangling from his long index finger.

"You could've told me before I crawled all over the place!" Snatching it away, she mumbled an insincere thank-you.

"You're beautiful on your hands and knees. It's not the best angle on most people, you know."

She was too agitated to think of a snappy comeback, and she didn't want to play games with him. Forcing her foot into her shoe, she stamped on the carpet and again headed toward the door.

"Don't leave angry," he said. "I wasn't teasing about the beautiful part."

"I'm not angry," she lied, "but I would like to know where I'm staying."

"I'll help you find your place," he offered quickly. "Just let me get my boots."

"No, I can find it myself."

"I'll be glad to help," he said, disappearing into the bedroom and giving her a chance to escape.

The door stuck. By the time she figured out that she had to depress a little button in the middle of the knob, he was back, towering over her five foot six inches in high-heeled boots that he certainly didn't need for height.

"Security lock," he said, covering her hand on the knob with his.

He'd pulled on a blue work-shirt but hadn't buttoned it, and she felt uncomfortable having her eyes level with his chest. Feeling silly and girlish, she didn't at all like the way his physical presence overwhelmed her.

"I'll just try the one next door," she said, sure now that she'd goofed and gone into the third from the right instead of the third from the left.

"You haven't told me your name yet," he said, following her down to the desert ground.

"Libby Sloan," she said, hurrying away from him toward the next mobile home.

Practically running, she was slowed by her high heels digging into the sandy surface, but outdistancing him was impossible anyway. He reached the door ahead of her and opened it with a theatrical flourish. Courtly gestures seemed second nature to him as he motioned her to go ahead.

The interior was almost identical to the other mobile home, varying only in the color of the furnishings. The carpet was a deep burgundy-rose complemented by gray paneling that resembled weathered wood and a black-and-white plaid couch. Her three bulky pieces of luggage formed a barrier that trapped her in the front with the stuntman only inches away.

"Your bags?" he asked.

"Yes," she admitted. "I'm sorry for walking in on you."

"Don't apologize; it was my good luck. Let me put your gear back by the closet."

He edged past her, brushing against her shoulder and hips— deliberately, she was sure.

"Thank you, but I can manage."

By hanging the strap of the garment bag on one shoulder and her purse on the other, she'd managed to carry the two suitcases down two flights of stairs, get them into a cab, and lug them herself into the airport. She hardly needed manly assistance to haul them a few feet to the closet.

Ignoring her, he grabbed the two cases, one in his hand and the other under his arm, and pushed open the door. She picked up the doubled-over nylon garment bag just to show him she didn't need a bellhop.

"Blue, your color," he said softly, looking at the shiny coverlet on the built-in double bed. The shade wasn't far from that of her fine cotton dress where it was damp from the water she'd splashed.

"Thank you for your help," she said stiffly, backing out of the pleasantly compact bedroom.

"My pleasure," He grinned again in a way that made her avert her eyes. "You're playing the saloon girl, right?"

"Cassandra Rose, yes."

"No movie experience?" It was a rhetorical question.

"No." Apparently a movie location shared one thing with a theater: Everyone's business was common knowledge.

"You'll love it."

She had serious doubts about that, considering that most of her lines had already been said in a thousand other Western

23

films, but the caressing tone of his voice was soothing and challenging at the same time.

"It pays well," she said, then wondered if he'd think she was mercenary.

Poverty was the common condition of struggling actors, and it felt wonderful to know that she wouldn't have to look for odd jobs for at least a year. For that security she'd force herself to say "Come on up to my room, big boy" with a straight face.

He followed her back to the living area, easing his length onto the couch, his long legs forming a barricade she couldn't sidestep. The choices were to climb over them or sit beside him. She did neither.

"I'd like to take a shower now," she said awkwardly, waiting for him to leave.

"Good idea. I love a cool shower, just enough hot water mixed with the cold so I don't get goose bumps. And someone to scrub my back."

"If you don't mind . . ." She gestured at the door, wondering if she and Sandra Faraday, the female lead, were the only women on location. They couldn't be, of course, but Wiley Bails and this stuntman both acted like sailors on leave, hardly bothering to be subtle.

"Sit down a minute," he said, patting the seat beside him.

"It must be nearly dinnertime," she said, but didn't sit down.

"Where're you from originally?"

"Syracuse. Now, if you'll excuse me . . ."

"How do you feel about making a Western?"

She made the mistake of looking directly into his eyes, colored that changeable shade called hazel, although flashes of green and gold illuminated the irises. They were striking eyes, fringed by lashes that were long for a man's and didn't quite fit the rest of his lean, high-cheeked face. No woman would look at that face and not find it handsome. There was a compelling strength in his chin line and forehead that made Libby uncomfortable. He looked like a man who would have his own way, no matter what obstacles he had to overcome.

The intensity of his stare made her forget his question.

"What?"

"The movie," he said, "you've never done anything like it?"

"No, this is my first film of any kind. The closest I've come to a Western was *Bus Stop* in summer stock."

"If I can help you in any way, let me know."

This was her chance to accept his offer, by requesting that he leave, but instead she shrugged her shoulders.

"Thanks, but I don't know enough to imagine what help I might need."

"Just keep me in mind."

He rose so slowly that he seemed to be uncoiling his body, seeking space in an area that was too confining for him.

"About that shower . . ." he said in a husky voice.

Before she could react he leaned forward and lightly caressed her lips with his.

"I've been told I'm a great back-washer," he murmured.

"Don't!" She pushed him away with both hands, her palms connecting with bare skin where his shirt hung open.

"Welcome to Old Buckhorn," he said, unruffled by her reaction, covering her hands with his.

She snatched her hands away as if they'd been singed.

"You had no right to do that!"

"It was only a sample of Old Buckhorn's friendly ways."

He smiled, and it made her even angrier.

"Friendly! I was hauled out to this desert by friendly Frank, accosted by friendly Wiley, and now you! Western hospitality stinks!"

25

"So, you've met our star already. No wonder you're a little touchy."

"I'm not touchy! Just get out! Out, out, out!"

"Sweetheart, aren't you making an awful big thing out of one little kiss?"

His unruffled calmness only fueled her anger. She could feel tears of rage dampening her eyes and wanted to lash out at the impudent stranger.

"Leave me alone!"

He reached out and caressed her shoulder.

"Sorry you've had a bad day."

He walked out as nonchalantly as he'd entered, quietly closing the door behind him.

His leaving frustrated her too! She should have told him what she thought of macho studs who thought they were the answer to every woman's prayer. She would've let him know . . .

Sobbing and miserable, what she really regretted was having said anything at all. She might look like her mother's stoic Scandinavian ancestors, but inside she had Grandma Sloan's Irish temper. Why couldn't she be cool and sardonic like that darn stuntman? He'd been laughing at her when he left; she was sure of it.

Furious with herself and with him, she peeled off her clothes and dropped them in a heap, seeking relief under the spray of cool water in the tiny shower cubicle. The water ran in rivulets on her face, over her shoulders, and down her torso, and, totally against her will, she wondered how it would feel to have her back soaped by the tall, powerful stranger.

He'd even ruined her shower!

Slipping a short cotton nightie over her still-damp shoulders, she decided she couldn't face any more of the movie-making company that evening. Too tired to eat anyway, she collapsed between pale-blue sheets and let sleep wash away thoughts of her discouraging day.

CHAPTER TWO

Libby resisted coming fully awake, instead burrowing her face into the pillow and resolutely squeezing her eyes shut. In the back of her consciousness there was a vague uneasiness about the way she'd handled herself the day before. Usually she took men's advances as compliments and sidestepped them with good humor. Making a scene with that stuntman—Craig something—wasn't her style at all! His timing had been bad, but he couldn't know that she'd been up before dawn, flown on three planes, gotten airsick, and developed a genuine case of prework jitters.

Did she owe him some kind of apology for having lost her temper? Remembering his suggestive remarks about the shower and his nervy kiss, she felt defensive again. She wouldn't say another word to the man if she could help it. The last thing she needed in her hectic life was to have a cowboy-daredevil underfoot. In the fall, after the filming, she'd begin work on a new Broadway play, a prospect that restored her cheerful disposition. It was only a tiny part, but her list of credits was growing. At least this year she wouldn't have to work at Macy's during the Christmas rush!

Stretching lazily, she enjoyed the luxury of a double bed, appreciating how well equipped her temporary housing was.

A shelf recessed behind the bed held a digital alarm clock whose bold red numerals showed it was only a little after five A.M., an unheard-of time for her to be awake. After having slept more than she usually did in two nights, she was famished. With one last contented stretch, she got up and padded barefoot to the box-size refrigerator. Millway productions, the independent company making the movie, hadn't let her down in the drink department. An assortment of juices, soft drinks, and beer took up most of the shelf space, but she could breakfast on one of several cartons of fresh yogurt without leaving the mobile home. A serving flavored with blueberries took the edge off her appetite, but after a leisurely shampoo and shower, she still felt hungry.

Taking her cue from the people she'd seen yesterday, she donned a pair of white denims and a pale-green top, determined to look casual and at ease if there was a butterfly rally in her stomach. Cameras didn't eat actors, and Carl McDowell was supposed to be a fairly considerate director. What was the worst thing that could happen today? She could be fired, but not without a payoff on her contract. Aside from that, she only had to worry about exposing herself to ridicule, humiliation, and scorn from the more experienced film people, but she knew perfectly well that most of them would be tolerant professionals.

"Oh, stop being silly!" she chided herself aloud, recognizing that opening-night jitters were hitting earlier and harder than usual. She had to relax. She knew her business, and acting was acting, even in the middle of the desert.

Before going outside she patted moisturizer on her face and throat. There was no point in putting on makeup until she found out what the day's schedule was, but her sensitive, fair skin was going to need all the help she could give it in this dry, hot climate. Feeling more like herself, she was becoming excited about her new opportunity.

The temperature outside was surprisingly pleasant compared to the ovenlike heat of the previous afternoon, and she remembered something about the desert cooling rapidly after the sun went down. Across the way a tall man in jeans walked into one of the pink metal buildings, giving her a moment's unease. No, it wasn't the stuntman; he was broader through the shoulders and leaner through the hips. The fact that she'd sized up Craig so accurately was discomforting. Besides running into him accidentally, because they were living in neighboring trailers, she was sure she'd see little of him during the filming. Undoubtedly he'd be in the barroom brawl scene; maybe their paths would cross accidentally, but she didn't need to worry about working with him. His professional duties would keep him outside and away from most of her scenes.

Hoping for some strong coffee and a piece of toast to round off her breakfast, she walked to the door where the man had disappeared and was rewarded by the smell of bacon cooking on a griddle. Even at this early hour a number of people were filling trays at the cafeteria-style line or already eating at tan Formica tables. Feeling very much like the new girl, she was happy when the little black-bearded man left his seat and hurried up to her.

"Libby Sloan?" he asked.

"Yes."

"I'm Freeman Cartwell, the AD. I was going to knock on your door in a few minutes. Glad you're here. I have a copy of the shooting schedule—here. Nothing this morning for you, but you have appointments with makeup and wardrobe. It's all on that sheet. Oh, yes, Carl wants to have lunch with you, then there's a rehearsal at two. How're your lines? John Gardner, our assistant AD, will do some run-throughs with you as soon as he gets a chance."

"Happy to meet you," she said, taking the paper and

offering her hand, feeling a little breathless after listening to the staccato barrage of words that had poured out of the AD.

His hand was damp; she resisted an impulse to wipe hers dry on the side of her slacks after their handshake.

"Nice to have you here," he said briskly, darting away so quickly, she felt slighted.

Telling herself that his job had to be the most stressful in the company, she strolled over to the short line and picked up a bright-orange plastic tray with a knife and fork wrapped in a blue paper napkin. The coffee looked black enough to be a week old, but the toast was golden-brown, unbuttered wheatbread made just the way she liked it, with a crock of berry-filled purple jam near it.

The tables seated eight and several were unoccupied, but sitting alone seemed standoffish. She carried her tray to one where a woman was sitting with two men.

"You must be Libby Sloan. I'm Sandy Faraday." The woman, dark-haired, in her middle thirties, and with beautiful, clear ivory skin, stood and offered her hand, smiling a warm welcome.

"Yes, I'm so happy to meet you, Ms. Faraday." Libby quickly put the tray on the table and met the woman's firm grasp.

"Sandy, and not half as glad as I am to see you. We women are outnumbered about thirty to one here. These Westerns sets are a man's world."

"I had noticed that." Libby smiled at the two men.

"Bert Halloway," Sandra said, "a dear old friend of mine, and you probably know Carl."

"No, I don't."

"Carl McDowell. I've been eager to meet you, Libby. We're nearly ready for you."

Her new director had rusty hair and a face so peppered with freckles that she was reminded of her own nearly invisible sprinkling that tended to show up after too much time in the sun. She visited with the star and director, but it was Bert Halloway, the stunt coordinator, who intrigued her. Brawny and sun-browned with thick salt-and-pepper hair, he dominated the space around him without adding much to the conversation. Was this the true breed of western man, the strong, silent type that was featured in cigarette ads? He'd have to be iron-willed to boss a crew of men like Craig Wicklow.

Surprised that the stuntman's name had come back to her, she missed a question Carl had asked.

"Sorry, my mind was wandering," she apologized, asking him to repeat it.

"I'm not much of a morning person either," he said, "but we try to do the outside shooting before the heat gets too bad. I'll get someone to show you around Old Buckhorn."

"I'll volunteer for that," Craig said, coming up from behind her and putting a tray down on the table beside hers, "if that stagecoach isn't ready yet, Bert."

"Libby, Craig Wicklow. He does most of the stand-in work for Wiley," Carl said.

"Mr. Wicklow." She nodded her head, then quickly drank the last of her coffee, hoping he wouldn't mention their having met the day before. He didn't.

"We're gonna have to reshoot the whole scene," the stunt coordinator said unhappily, "but it'll take 'em all morning to get that wheel ready. More damn holdups on this one. But I guess I say that every time."

"Then I'll have time to show you around after I eat, Libby." Craig piled strips of bacon on a slice of toast, making a thick sandwich of it.

"You got your schedule?" Carl asked her, standing to leave.

31

"Yes, and I'm busy with wardrobe this morning, Mr. Wicklow."

"Let's see." He reached for the sheet the AD had given her before she thought to conceal it.

"You have over an hour before your wardrobe appointment. This town isn't so big that it'll take longer than that to see it."

"See you later," Sandra said cheerfully, leaving with the two men.

Alone with Craig, Libby was upset again, this time at his high-handedness.

"You don't need to show me around."

"I want to." He plunged his fork into a huge mound of scrambled eggs.

"But I don't." She pushed back her chair, starting to leave.

"Libby, let's be friends."

"All right, we're friends." She didn't like the sulky way she felt.

"Then, wait just a minute. You have to know your way around the place, and I'm available. There's no reason why you can't walk around the lot with me, is there?" He stirred sugar into his coffee and drank a big swallow, putting the cup down to smile warmly at her.

He knew that refusing would make her seem ungracious, even rude. She felt trapped, but maybe the easiest thing would be to tour the location and let him know once and for all that she wasn't interested in him.

"Do you always eat such huge meals?" She watched him open two cartons and dump dry cereal into a bowl.

"At breakfast I do." He poured a glass of milk on the cereal and added sugar from a glass shaker. "I burn it off when I'm working."

"I really don't have time to wait while you eat all that."

32

Standing to leave, she accidentally dropped the sheet Freeman had given her.

"Let me." He swooped down on the paper and handed it to her. "You aren't going to let me finish my breakfast?"

"Of course you can. I'll just take a rain check on the tour. I really do have things to do."

"Would avoiding me be on the top of your list?"

"Really . . ." The man was the most maddening she'd ever met.

"You'll be crazy about me when you get to know me," he said teasingly.

"I certainly won't!" She walked away, conscious of several interested glances from a nearby table.

Curious as she was to see where the movie was being made, she preferred hiding in her mobile home to being in Craig's company. He had enough ego for two people, and aggressive, chest-beating males weren't her type. Anyway, she still had to unpack.

Her first suitcase was nearly empty when a loud knock summoned her to the door.

"Ready to go?" Craig asked.

"No." She shook her head. "No, it's not necessary for you to bother."

"You're not afraid of me, are you?" He moved up the steps and filled the doorway.

"Of course not!"

"Good. We wouldn't be off to a very good start if you were."

"We're not off to any start!"

"I can hope."

He arched his brows, giving a little tug on one end of his mustache, a gesture so comical, she had to laugh.

"You're really an actor, aren't you? The stunt business is just a fill-in."

33

"I get a few lines now and then, but I like the way I make my living."

"You like risking your neck?"

"Usually it's not that dramatic, but I appreciate your concern."

He flashed a wicked grin, and she still wasn't sure how seriously to take him.

"I really don't need a guided tour."

"I don't have anything else to do. This is a union film. If I go over and try to help fix the stage wheel, some guy will file a grievance because I'm doing his work. Frank was steamed yesterday because he's not supposed to do transportation."

"He seemed mad at me. I thought it was because my flight was so late."

As familiar as she was with the working of a theatrical production, she had a lot to learn about filming. She just wasn't eager to have this stuntman as a teacher. He was much too sure of himself!

"Let's go," he said.

Deciding it was easier to go with him than to argue anymore, Libby followed him across the open area to the sound stage, ducking under his outstretched arm without comment when he held the door open for her.

"Our sound stage," he announced. "The saloon is a hot set, which means it's been approved for shooting exactly as it is now. Hands off for everyone. Down here is your bedroom."

He led the way to the far end where, the carpenters had been working the day before. The 1880s bedroom was furnished sparsely by modern standards, but blue, fringed window drapes and crudely printed red-on-white wallpaper with a design that looked like upside-down vases made the set seem cheerful in a raunchy way. Libby was glad to be making a made-for-TV movie; she wasn't desperate enough about her career to do an R-rated bedroom scene.

"We do a scene here," Craig said.

"We, as in you and I?"

"You'll like me in a black wig with my mustache darkened."

"You are an actor, then! That's why you have one of the mobile homes."

"Nope. What I do here is take a flying dive out the window for Bails. The mobile units aren't for VIPs. He's staying in one of the inside suites. The studio got carried away when they built this place thirty or forty years ago: sunken tubs and built-in bars for their pampered stars. Millway is renting the whole setup, but they had to bring in some extra housing. That's why the mobile homes are here. Last time I worked here, I had to bunk in the dorm with the crew."

The next set had an outdoor backdrop, romantic with painted saguaros and a luminous moon. Real plants in the foreground made it seem less artificial.

"Have you made many movies?" She was more interested than she wanted him to know.

"Enough to lose count. This door leads to Old Buckhorn."

He touched her elbow lightly, slipping long fingers over the inside of her arm, a gesture that triggered her warning system. She couldn't let his small talk distract her; he was as predatory as Wiley Bails.

They stepped into another world, one so far removed from the artificial sets inside the sound stage that she immediately forgot the modern buildings behind them. Walking between two crudely built wooden structures, they emerged in the West of a hundred years ago.

"It's a real town," she blurted out.

"Sure is. Three saloons, a jail, and a bank that's been robbed about a thousand times. I knocked it over myself last year in *Return of the Restless Rogues*. Terrorized the teller, knocked over a bystander, then took a pratfall off the sidewalk."

"On purpose?"

"Of course." He sounded mildly offended. "Comedy's always the toughest for me. Less illusion. The viewer has to see the injured dignity. Let's go this way."

He only touched her for an instant, but the skin under her thin knit shirt reacted like an alarm, sending signals of sensual pleasure to her brain. Craig Wicklow was, to her at least, more dangerous than any outlaw with a six-shooter.

"This street is wider than most of New York City's," she said, crossing the broad stretch of hard-packed desert sand.

"The whole place is pretty authentic. Land was plentiful out here, so it wasn't necessary to crowd the buildings. They needed a wide street so a team pulling a wagon could turn around."

"Most of the buildings have false fronts," she observed, staring at the weathered board façades to keep from looking at the man beside her. He was wearing cowboy boots, skin-tight jeans, a black shirt open at the throat, and also a white Stetson that added more inches to his already overpowering stature.

"That's not a Hollywood touch," he said. "All the businesses were built that way as soon as they could haul in the lumber. False fronts, sometimes even phony windows."

"Why? Everyone could see what was behind them."

"Looked more imposing, I guess. Sometimes they used them as billboards, like over there at the Dirty Dog Saloon."

He led the way onto a raised sidewalk in front of it. "All the buildings used to have boards in front like this, above the dust or mud."

His boots were loud on the gray boards, and she was aware of his graceful walk, a long-legged stride, totally without posturing or self-consciousness. He moved like a man who owned the town.

"Wide-open spaces, purple hills in the background. I hardly believe I'm seeing this," she said.

He laughed softly. "It grows on you. When I'm in L.A. between jobs, I can hardly wait to get back on location. Maybe someday I'll chuck all this make-believe and buy myself a little ranch."

"And raise cattle?" She peeked through the window of the saloon, surprised to find it complete right down to some poker hands dealt out on a rough board table.

"Quickest way I know to go broke."

"Are all the buildings like this, furnished inside?"

"Most. That's why independent film-makers stand in line to use this place. It's all here: railroad depot, stagecoach office, hotel, general store, sheriff's office, everything anyone needs to shoot a Western movie, TV series, or commercial."

"What's that over there?"

She crossed the street to a building that seemed to be made of mud.

"Adobe schoolhouse."

"I can almost see Loretta Young or Greer Garson flouncing out in long skirts to set some badman straight." She peered inside at the rows of benches and tables that served as students' desks, struck by the meager resources in the room: a tattered map and a few dusty readers.

"The schoolmarm was usually some little thing who could just about read herself," he said. "Teaching was just something to do until a gal got a husband, and there were never enough women on the frontier."

"Well, fortunately those times are gone forever!" she said emphatically, feeling annoyed by his attitude.

"Some things don't change."

She suspected as he was baiting her but decided to ignore his remark and go on to the next building, a sheriff's office complete with a cell for prisoners.

"I'd hate to be locked in there," she said.

37

"It's better than most of the places where people lived, but no one stayed in a town jail long. They either hanged the guilty ones or shipped them off to a territorial prison, if they were lucky enough to get a trial."

"You seem to know a lot about the Old West."

"I've picked up some history here and there."

They weren't alone, she discovered, rounding a corner onto a side street where a camera crew was doing some preliminary work before the morning's shooting. This street was narrow, with crude adobe shacks along one side.

"In the movie this is where Sandy Faraday lives with her drunken father. It's been used as slave quarters and an early Chinatown too. Most of the buildings in Old Buckhorn were built for a specific movie, but they're used over and over."

Words rolled off his tongue, coming out as a shivery drawl, sounding like a different language from that marked by the sharp, clipped accent of New Yorkers. She could listen to him all day, she realized with misgivings.

They made a broad circuit of Old Buckhorn with Craig pointing out locations on the fringes of town where everything from a rodeo to a cattle stampede could be filmed. There was even a mock Boot Hill cemetery, but there wasn't time to see everything before her first appointment. Circling the whole area was a track for the steam locomotive. The chain link fence, Craig pointed out, only provided security where there was access by road. Beyond the town was the vast isolation of the desert. Libby could understand why a woman on the western frontier would have welcomed the protection of a man like Craig, but these were different times. When he put his arm around her shoulders, she shrugged it off.

"Do many of the men bring their wives on location?" she asked.

"No, there's not enough room, and there's nothing to do here. I don't have a wife to bring."

"I wasn't asking that."

"Weren't you?" He laughed softly.

"It's no concern of mine whether you're married."

She sounded snippy, but it was his fault! He made her defensive when she had no reason to be.

"I'm divorced," he said more soberly. "Only once, which isn't a bad record in my line of work. Stuntmen aren't home much. Anyway, it should be against the law for men to get married before they're fifty."

He was arousing her curiosity, but she was too stubborn to let him know it.

"Well, thank you for the tour."

"There's a lot more I could show you."

"Can you tell me where to go for my wardrobe appointment?"

"I'll walk you there."

"I'm sure I can find it myself."

"Back through the sound stage," he said, again taking her arm to guide her.

Remembering what she'd intended to say to him, she pulled her arm away. "I think you should know," she said uneasily, "that I have to hurry back to New York after this to start rehearsals for a Broadway play."

"Congratulations."

"The point is, I'm really not interested in—in getting involved with anyone. My career is just starting to take off, and—"

His low laughter broke into her explanation.

"Sweetheart, you'll never wake up with my brand on your pretty little butt."

"Oh!" In one sentence he'd reduced her to a—to a plaything! Her cheeks, already pink in the open air, flushed scarlet, and she stalked away, so flustered that she forgot which way led to the sound-stage entrance.

"Don't be mad," he said, easily catching up with her, his own mood as mellow as ever. "I think it's good that friends understand each other right from the start."

"I don't like your idea of friendship, and I understand you perfectly!"

"Down here," he said when she started to walk past the alley where she should have turned.

He reached the entrance ahead of her, leaning against the door with one elbow and smiling down on her.

"You'll find out," he said, "that all there is to do on location is work, eat, and sleep. The nearest town's too far away to bother going to. Working on a film is just like being in a play. Everybody gets to know everybody else, and having a good friend makes the time pass more pleasantly." He reached down and lightly patted her bottom. "In a few days I think you'll see what I mean."

"I have an appointment," she said frigidly to show that his little squeeze hadn't fazed her.

She hurried through the cavernous sound stage, pretending she couldn't still feel the memory of his fingers on her rear. Outside the opposite entrance she paused to see where she should go. The wardrobe department was housed in a separate drab, pink building, the metal siding weathered and pitted by sun and blowing sand, but inside it was an efficient operation staffed by businesslike specialists. She had to be fitted for the several costumes she'd wear, and it was a relief to have this routine chore to occupy her.

The costume designer had begun her work when plans were first made to film the script. Some costumes were sewn especially for this production, but most were pulled, which meant they were purchased or rented ready-made. The person in charge on location was the wardrobe supervisor, and Libby was directed to find her in the main room. Here racks of plastic-shrouded costumes occupied three walls. Tables, chairs, and sewing machines were scattered at random throughout the room. Dana Miles was clearly in charge, supervising the repair of a pair of chaps, the handwork being done by a younger woman with a special needle for leatherwork. The traditional cowboy leggings looked worn and authentic with lead discs along the side seams, but Libby wasn't given time to ask any questions about them.

"You're Libby?" the supervisor asked, brushing aside a wave of stark-black hair that didn't flatter her pale, creased face.

Thin to the point of emaciation, Dana Miles obviously stayed that way by expending tremendous energy in her work. Before Libby could blink twice she found herself in a small dressing room, hers for the duration of the filming. standing on a chair in her panties with a modern version of a corset around her waist. Dana's hands, when she adjusted it, were cold, but her running commentary was spicy and interesting, making Libby forget for the moment her skirmishes with the stuntman.

"You're a hurdy-gurdy girl," she explained, "and your main job is selling high-priced drinks in the saloon. You're a cut above the average fallen angel, a kind of frontier geisha. You're supposed to entertain the men with your dancing. Please them, but, most importantly, sell them drinks."

"I didn't read that in the script." Libby didn't say this as a criticism.

"Historically that's the kind of person Cassandra Rose would've been. Of course, all women were either good or bad in those days, but a lot of saloon girls were settlers' daughters who didn't want to spend the rest of their lives half starving in flour sacks, freezing in sod huts if the supply of buffalo chips ran short. It was worth wearing a short skirt to live a

41

little longer and a lot better than their mothers. This will do nicely,'' she said, referring to the corset, which pushed Libby's bust line up unnaturally but was reasonably comfortable.

"Cassandra Rose wants a husband,'' Libby said, slipping a full-skirted, red-striped petticoat over her head at Dana's direction.

"A lot of saloon girls married and became respectable, but until then they had a little independence. That was rare for women in those days. Their own room, money they earned, better food and clothes than a sodbuster's wife would ever see. Here, try this.'' She handed up a slippery green dress, helping Libby carefully ease into it.

"When eastern women saw how things were out West, they liked that taste of freedom,'' Dana went on. "Women's rights first started to get somewhere in the West. Susan B. rode horseback to the Colorado mining camps talking suffrage. This should be a little shorter, I think.''

She tugged on the edges of the hem, reaching for a pin box and inserting the tiny silvery daggers without benefit of a measuring stick.

"Did they really wear skirts this short in the 1880s?'' Libby asked.

"Belva Drake did the costumes for this film. You can bet anything that shows is authentic. Underwear like this built-in bustle has been changed to be more convenient. It would've been worn under the dress, but it's easier to slip it into a sack sewn in the waistline. You wouldn't want to be laced into an antique corset. Women used to cut off their air supply and faint in those things.''

Libby's next costume was rusty-red silk with ruffles on the skirt, bodice, and sleeves. With it she wore a padded bustle tied around her waist.

"This is your street dress,'' Dana said. "Nice ladies tied the bustle around their hips, too, so it wouldn't slip around, but your character wiggles for all she's worth anyway. I'm not sure about this hat."

Libby wasn't either. Hats in the era were small and worn tipped forward, but this one reminded her of a pizza with everything possible on it. A silk flower drooped over one eye, and the artificial butterfly threatened to topple the whole creation.

"I don't think it will stay on. I have to run in one street scene," she said.

"I can pin it to stay, but it definitely needs some rearranging. I was afraid that plume was too squashed when I unpacked the box."

One more feather that size and she could fly down the street, Libby thought, but she was enjoying the costuming session. As a little girl her favorite game had been dress-up. Her mother had saved a trunk of wonderful tulle and taffeta formal dresses from her high school and college "big" dances, and Libby never tired of parading around in them. No one in her family of five was surprised when "little sister" decided to be an actress. Fortunately her parents had always been encouraging and her two older brothers indulgent, even when she recruited them to make a stage setting out of an appliance box or a fairy-princess wand from cardboard and a broken fishing pole.

"This is for your last scene," Dana said, giving her a sleeveless, low-cut yellow garment embellished with a gigantic green silk rose.

"Sometimes yellow is a problem with my coloring," Libby volunteered.

"I was afraid of that, but I can't make costume changes, only adjust them to work. I can call the designer and see if she'll make a switch, but first I'll have to get permission from Carl."

"No, don't do that. I'm supposed to be sad in my last scene. This will work fine."

She had an inherent reluctance to make a fuss. Temperamental actors might be tolerated when they achieved stardom, but Libby envisioned a different kind of career for herself: a long working life in quality stage productions. Offbeat roles fascinated her, and her highest ambition was to experience as many different characterizations as possible. Fussing about costume colors wouldn't gain the kind of reputation she wanted as a conscientious, cooperative performer.

"No trouble. Bails asks for changes in every costume we get for him. If the seat isn't baggy, the shoulders are too tight or the sleeves too short." It was the first time the wardrobe supervisor had sounded less than enthusiastic.

"I guess some people are hard to fit. I'm lucky I can always wear clothes off the rack."

Dana snorted, but Libby knew she wasn't the target of this disgruntled reaction.

"That'll do it for now. You have a morning call, so be sure to report here by six. Darlene will be your dresser. She's new, but she's doing a good job with Faraday. That woman is a lamb. If all actors were like her, my ulcer wouldn't be supporting a medical clinic."

Makeup shared the same building, and Libby wasn't sure why they wanted to see her this morning. She was an old pro when it came to doing her own stage makeup, but Greg, the specialist who consulted with her, wouldn't hear of it.

"It takes a specialist to understand the effect of light on skin coloration," he said a bit self-importantly. "I'm the key on this film."

"The key?" She wouldn't learn film lingo if she didn't ask.

"Key makeup artist. I'll style you now, then have Carl take a look at you."

"I have a lunch appointment with him."

"Good. Let's see."

He got so close to examine her skin that his nose brushed hers. She wished he weren't a heavy smoker, but sweet breath wasn't as important as his technical skill. Craig didn't smoke, she recalled, or at least he hadn't so far. But that fact had absolutely no importance to her!

"A few freckles on your shoulders and chest," the makeup artist observed matter-of-factly. "You'll need some body makeup. Is your face going to burn in the sun?"

"I'm afraid so."

"I'll give you a straw hat. Use it whenever you're not on camera."

He worked quickly with expert sureness, subtly accenting the blueness of her eyes and her delicate bone structure. The shade of lip coloring seemed a little gaudy, but remembering her saloon-girl character, Libby didn't say anything. A runaway from the harsh life on the prairie could be excused for indulging in a scarlet lip rouge. She had to start thinking the way her character would. Psyching herself into a part was the heart and soul of her acting technique, but she wasn't sure how effective it would be in the stop-and-start routine of filming. The weeks ahead could be full of difficulties.

Her makeup passed muster, lunch with the director was fast but profitable in terms of discussing her part, and the rehearsal of her first scene wasn't too traumatic. Wiley didn't know his lines; the rest of them were excused early so the second AD could give him personal attention.

"That's the way it's been since we got here," Sandra confided in Libby as they sat sipping iced tea in the common room that served as a dining room and a place to relax. "We're already running behind schedule, the production manager's having fits over the budget, and I'm dying to get home to my son."

45

"How old is he?" Libby asked, always interested in anything to do with children.

"Seven, and I have to hire a sitter when I'm on location. His father is dead, and leaving Danny is the one thing about this job that I hate."

"I don't blame you." Libby's eyes strayed automatically to the door whenever it opened.

Production work for the day had ground to a halt as far as the actors were concerned, and Craig had been right about one thing: there wasn't much to do except visit with the others. Libby was enjoying Sandra's company, pleased that a veteran player was so congenial and friendly to a novice like herself.

"I know you don't have a tub," Sandra said. "If you ever want a nice, long soak, you're welcome to use mine. My skin couldn't survive all the location work I do without the oil capsules I use in my bath."

"I appreciate your offer, but I won't bother you unless I get desperate."

The temperature was over a hundred, so Libby wore her floppy-brimmed white straw hat for the short walk to her quarters, entering the cool interior with relief. A nap seemed like the only sensible way to end the afternoon, but a warm shower left her too restless to relax on the bed. She tried reading a romance with a western setting to get more in the mood for her part, but today she had too much else on her mind. In spite of everything that had happened since the morning tour of Old Buckhorn, her thoughts kept wandering back to the stuntman who'd been her guide. She was positive he wasn't her type, but then, she'd never met anyone quite like him.

CHAPTER THREE

The desert sunset spread a surreal glow over the landscape, but the cast and crew of the movie ended their evening early in anticipation of predawn wakeup calls. Unaccustomed to the odd hours and too restless to sleep, Libby walked alone, finding another way to reach Old Buckhorn by skirting the long stockade of fence. By herself on the dusty streets, she found the grip of the past even stronger than before, with ghostly gunfighters peopling every corner. A shiver that was part excitement and part fear made her shoulders shake, and she wrapped her arms across her breasts, surprised again that the stifling heat of the day had given way to a temperate breeze that fanned fine tendrils of hair around her face.

In the distance the mountains were deep violet against a glowing orange sky, and her sandals echoed loudly on the boardwalk in front of the Paradise Hotel. One thing Western movies seldom did was dramatize the sheer loneliness of this rugged country, the pathos of a solitary human pitted against harsh and alien elements. Names like God's Country and No Man's Land only began to suggest the overpowering emptiness of the desert.

She forgot that the town was an elaborate movie setting and let her imagination run wild, visualizing a tableau of love and hate, danger and violence, behind every weathered façade. The sun disappeared, and the town was enveloped in a violet haze. Apprehension slowly replaced her dreamy musings, and she felt an urgency to return to the lights and security of her trailer. Looking for a shortcut, she darted between two buildings, searching for the alleyway that led to the sound stage. In the receding light all the buildings looked alike and nothing seemed even vaguely familiar. With her muddled sense of direction, she wasn't even sure where the stockade fence was.

This was a Hollywood-style movie set; there was no reason to panic about being lost. It was laid out in a logical, orderly design, except where new requirements had caused buildings to be built on the outskirts of the original town. All she had to do was find one recognizable landmark, and she'd know the way back. There was no reason to be frightened. Certainly the town was too isolated to have late-night visitors who popped in from the unsecured desert side. The street she was walking down wasn't broad enough to be Main Street; a wagon and team couldn't possibly turn around in the space she'd just crossed.

Was there wildlife in the desert? She wouldn't mind meeting a timid jackrabbit, but what about snakes and lizards and other things that slithered through the dark? Earlier, scaring herself with nonexistent ghosts had been fun, like going through a carnival funhouse. Now she was really alarmed.

What would happen if she screamed? Could someone in the area beyond the bulky hulk of the sound stage possibly hear her? She wasn't quite terrified enough to risk the humiliation of calling for help that way, but probably her voice wouldn't carry that far. Shouldn't she be able to see the roof of the sound stage? How could it possibly grow so dark so quickly?

Half running now, she wasn't prepared for a sudden excruciating pain in her toe, bare and dusty in an old sandal. She'd stubbed it on the railroad track, and that meant she was at the far fringe of the town, alarmingly far from where she wanted to be. At least she knew which way not to go!

She came to a crossing so broad she could distinguish nothing on the far corner, but fervently hoped this was Main Street. A left turn seemed safest, but she wanted the security of being near buildings. Limping because her toe hurt so much, the nail might be loose, she cautiously made her way to the dark outline of a single-story building, welcoming the loud thud of her own footsteps as she crossed a wooden sidewalk. Wary now of what might lie on the ground below the end of the walk, she eased first one foot and then the other onto the ground, blindly stumbling against a solid form.

Her scream was an automatic outburst of sheer terror as strong arms imprisoned her.

"Don't! It's me."

A hard hand muffled her shriek and brought her back to reality struggling for release.

"You scared me to death!" she angrily accused the man who still held her securely in his arms.

"I didn't mean to. I thought you might've gotten lost in here." The voice was Craig's.

"How could I get lost on a movie set?" she asked to cover her embarrassment.

"It's a big place in the dark. I never would've found you if you hadn't made such a racket on the sidewalk."

"Why were you looking for me?" She was too shaken to sound as indignant as the situation demanded.

"I saw you wander out a long time ago."

"I wanted to get a feel for the setting."

"When you didn't come back, I got worried."

"You didn't need to!" She squirmed free of his hold.

"No? If you'd kept going in the direction you were headed,

49

you would've wandered into the corral. We keep real horses there, you know.''

"I get directions confused sometimes," she admitted, only beginning to recover from the shock, managing to add a grudging "Thank you."

"You're welcome. I like being out here at night too," he said. "It gives me a chance to think."

"I suppose it would."

"I'll show you one of my favorite places," he said.

"I should go back. I have an early call."

His arm swept around her shoulders, drawing her so close that their hips and thighs brushed together.

"It's not far."

Her toe was throbbing, sending drumbeats of pain shooting through her foot, but she didn't want to admit how clumsy she was to a man who moved with the grace of a champion athlete.

"Through here," he said, still clasping her against his side as they walked.

All she saw was the bulky outline of a wall, but Craig found a door so low, he had to duck to pass through it.

"This is the Mexican village. There wasn't time to walk here this morning. Wait for me."

He left for a moment; then the area was bathed by greenish light. She was standing across from a replica of an adobe mission church that formed a square with smaller, mud-walled buildings.

"You've probably seen this in dozens of movies," he said, returning to her from the mission.

Again he led her through a narrow entrance, emerging in a small courtyard with a well in the center. It was a step back in time, and she couldn't quite believe she was there.

"If I wanted to build a house, it would have a patio like this," he said. "Pomegranates, ash and fig trees, maybe a

50

fountain instead of a well.'' His voice became harsh, as though he was angry with himself for revealing something too personal. ''But settling down in one place isn't my style.''

''Will it matter that you turned on the lights?''

''No, it won't matter.''

She walked to the well, hip-high and roofed, wishing she had a coin to make a wish. ''Do you have a penny?'' she asked.

''Maybe.'' He slid a hand into his jeans pocket, pulling out some change. ''Will you settle for a dime?''

He held out his palm and let her pick what she wanted. The coin felt warm between her finger and thumb, heated by his body. Standing by the edge of the well, she squeezed her eyes shut, then didn't know what to wish. Important things like world peace and justice for all were beyond the simple magic of tossing a coin into a well. What did she want for herself? Her career was progressing slowly but satisfactorily; she didn't want instant fame or overpowering wealth.

Feeling his hand on her shoulder, she made her wish and let the coin drop. There was no water in the well.

''Can you tell me?'' he asked.

''No, it wouldn't come true.''

She'd wished for a simple thing: love. Didn't every woman want one special man? As dedicated as she was to her career, Libby still wanted to belong to one man, the right man.

''Wishing won't get you what you want.'' He sounded unaccountably disturbed.

''Maybe not,'' she agreed, ''but it's nice to stop for a minute and think about what's important.'' Almost shyly she added, ''It's nice here, but I hope it's not bad luck to wish in a dry well.''

He laughed softly, a throaty sound that she found surprisingly appealing.

''I believe in making my own luck,'' he said.

51

His fingers slid through the hair at the back of her neck, caressing the skin underneath. There was time to stop him, but her backbone turned weak. He was the dashing charro, a Mexican cowboy; she was his woman. He slowly leaned over her, resting his lips on hers and parting them, tasting their sweetness with the tip of his tongue while his fingers caressed her throat, sending waves of sensation through her body.

His kiss became hard, possessive, demanding, all the things she'd been lulled into not expecting. It was an angry kiss, but she hadn't done anything to become the target of his anger. Suddenly aware of their isolation, she was frightened of this man she didn't know. When she tried to break free, his arms held her closer, crushing her against his hard, aroused groin.

Just as abruptly he released her, turning his back and slumping against one of the well supports.

"I owe you an apology," he said hoarsely.

"No." *Only an explanation*, she thought.

"Bad timing, bad judgment," he said. "Forgive me, will you?"

"There's nothing to forgive."

There wasn't; a kiss was only a kiss.

"I don't usually grab and take," he said, sounding very angry at himself now.

"I don't think you do."

"Oh, hell," he said softly.

"You don't have to say any more."

They were walking toward the main square, side by side but several feet apart. She wanted to see his face, to look into his eyes, before he turned off the lights.

"Craig, I can't walk fast."

He stopped and looked at her.

"It's really silly, but I stubbed my toe. On the railroad track. It was dark and—"

"Let me see. Over here."

52

He led the way to a low, thick wall at the foot of some steps that led to a rooftop.

"I imagine this is a good spot for shootouts," she said.

"I've fallen down these steps more times than I like to remember. Let me see your foot."

Feeling foolish now, she stuck out the injured toe, wincing when he unbuckled her sandal and removed it.

"The nail is turning color. You may lose it."

"And I have to dance in some of my scenes!"

"Are you a dancer?"

"I've had some lessons, but I'm not a professional. Anyone can stomp around the way I'm supposed to."

"If anyone stomps on that toe, you'll hit the ceiling. Better put ice on it and see Marty Granger in the morning. He's the first-aid man. Do you want me to carry you back?"

"No! I mean, just walk slower. I can make it all right."

"I could carry you for miles in a fireman's lift."

"What's that?"

"Bottom up, over my shoulder."

Grinning, he was a much more comfortable companion than when he was somber. Or was he?

"I'll walk."

"There are other ways."

"I'll still walk."

He handed her the dust-covered sandal, letting her buckle it while he stepped into the mission to exinguish the lights.

"Stay there. I'll be your guide. I have good night vision."

They walked back without touching or talking, taking a shortcut through a doorless building open at both ends.

"Are these horse stalls?" she asked, peering into the dark and breaking the silence.

"Yes, they shoot livery scenes here."

She knew where they were now. "I feel so dumb, getting my directions confused in the dark."

"Better not wander out here alone."

It was good advice, but hearing it from him was irritating.

"I'll be more familiar with the layout after I start work."

"Don't come here alone after dark anyway."

She bit her lower lip, not quite nervy enough to argue with the man who'd rescued her.

The stockade fence was high and long enough to pass as the inside of an old fort, and it had been filmed as one numerous times. By the time they rounded the end, her toe was hurting unbearably. She couldn't help limping and falling behind.

"This is silly," Craig said unexpectedly. "You can hardly walk."

He scooped her up in his arms with no apparent effort and carried her toward the row of mobile homes. Hanging on to his neck, she felt the hard cords of his throat and the muscular swell of his shoulders. The arm under her legs was as inflexible as a steel bar, and he walked rapidly without breathing hard. She was the one who was short of breath!

"Thank you," she gasped when he'd eased her to the ground in front of her trailer.

"That's okay."

She found herself wishing he'd said, "My pleasure."

"Have Marty look at that toe. He's a licensed trainer who works with Bert. He was a medic in Vietnam."

"I'm sure he's qualified to check toes." She had no intention of making a big deal out of hers.

"Good night," Craig said, hurrying away toward his own door.

Disassociation from reality was what she'd been experiencing since her arrival, Libby decided, as she dangled her toe in an uncomfortably cold pan of ice and water. Everything here was totally different from her normal life, so she had brief flashes when she seemed to be living in a fantasy. Craig had a starring role in this mental extravaganza, but once she settled into her job, he wouldn't seem so heroic and sexy and . . .

Enough was enough! Maybe she had enjoyed his rough kiss, but only because it was part of the Western enchantment she was experiencing. In real life she didn't want an affair without the gentle sharing and caring that came with mutual love. To her that meant commitment, not a tumble in the hay with a macho cowboy!

Using her toe as an excuse, she took two mild pain-killers, hoping they'd relax her enough to sleep, but oblivion was slow in coming. She would have fallen off more easily if she'd found her own way back from Old Buckhorn.

Working in a play, she could dress and do her makeup in less than half an hour. It was hard to believe how long it took a film actress to get ready to perform. Her hair had to be teased into an upswept style that left little spit curls caressing her face and throat, and Greg sent her back to one of his makeup assistants with harsh words about her freckles. Through it all she worried about remembering lines and walking on her painful toe. Fortunately she'd been able to jam it into the soft, high-button shoe called for in her first scene.

They were shooting outside the saloon in Old Buckhorn. Most of the interior shots would be done on the sound stage, although the inside of the sheriff's office, jail, and several buildings would be used too. Wiley Bails, the sheriff, was supposed to be running an easygoing town where cowpokes could carouse and spend their money any way they liked. This suited Cassandra Rose and her boss, Hatchet Jones, who was played by Doug Brickell, just fine. But law and order was coming into the territory, and one of its chief flag-wavers was Abigail Grant, Sandra Faraday, who wanted to clean up the town that had ruined her alcoholic father. The crisis would come with the murder of one of the territory's most

55

important ranchers. Wiley would want to ignore the crime and go on running his crooked little town, but Abigail would inspire him to find the murderers and side with the forces of good. Cassandra Rose, who regarded the sheriff as her "man," would rather have things the way they were.

Even though Sandra's part was a key one, neither she nor the other women were in many scenes. The Western movie still glamorized a man's world, and Libby wasn't sure whether they were reshooting an old script or one adapted from some horse-opera novel of long ago.

Public displays of affection on the streets weren't the norm in Westerns, past or present. The less affection she had to show for Wiley Bails, the better Libby liked it. He arrived on the set wearing a tan leather vest with a collarless dark shirt and, of course, scuffy boots and leg-hugging pants. The sallowness of his complexion was disguised by dark, ruddy-brown makeup that looked as if it would melt when the temperature soared.

Following the makeup artist's instructions, she held the straw hat lightly over her head, hoping her hairstyle wouldn't be ruined. They ran through the brief scene several times with Wiley changing a word or two each time. No one seemed to be bothered by it except her.

By the time they were ready to shoot, her toe hurt almost unbearably, but she'd once finished a third act on a fractured ankle after falling off a backstage platform. Inclined though she was to shriek over the removal of a splinter and cry when her monthly cramps were bad, she was no stoic. It was only the iron discipline imposed by her profession that kept her from tearing off the shoe that was increasing her misery.

As a director Carl was reasonably relaxed. He pushed the cast when they needed it but was realistic in his expectations. He asked about the straw hat Libby kept whipping on and off her head but accepted her explanation without disagreeing.

This scene ended with the arrival of the stage, kicking up a dust column several feet high in its wake. Libby wanted to ask why the driver had to tear down Main Street as if the Apaches were chasing him, but the scene called for her to watch the arrival and say nothing. The stagecoach driver was Craig, almost disguised by a droopy, filthy-looking hat and a layer of dirt-colored makeup. When the cameras stopped, he walked over to her.

"Look at your feet," he said.

She did. Without realizing it, she'd been balancing on the heel of one shoe, taking the pressure off her toe.

"Oh."

"We're gonng have to do another take in case that silly way you're standing shows in the shot."

"I'm sorry."

"Did you have your toe looked at?"

People were beginning to watch them, and Carl was walking in their direction.

"I didn't have time."

"I'll bet it hurts like hell."

"It's okay."

"Problem?" Carl asked blandly.

"No," Craig said. "You'll want another take on that, won't you?"

"Yeah, go a little slower this time. No reason to lather up the horses for a showy arrival," the director said.

Libby managed not to snicker at the chastised stuntman.

"You know us stage drivers," he joked with Carl. "Always showin' off for a pretty filly."

The two men chuckled together; Libby hadn't heard anything funny.

Wiley changed shirts three times, handing over soaked cotton garments to the dresser who worked on the set trying

57

to keep the actor camera-ready. It was a losing battle in the heat.

"Why don't they make this in the winter?" Libby asked Sandra when the crew took a much-needed break for lunch.

"Old Buckhorn is usually booked solid year-round. I imagine we're getting off-season rates. This is a low-budget film."

"Couldn't they save money by using fewer people?" She was walking to the dining room with the actress after both had removed their costumes and makeup. The afternoon would be devoted to line work and rehearsals.

"We practically have a skeleton crew. The unions have contracts that determine how many people work. An electrician can't do sound work. A draper is the only one who can touch upholstery, curtains, canvas drops, anything made of cloth. If a carpenter hangs a net, the whole production could grind to a halt."

"Theater work is like that too," Libby said.

Sandra was too nice to flaunt her experience. In fact, getting to know the TV-and-screen actress was the nicest thing about the filming so far. Not only was she willing to share her experience, she seemed to enjoy talking to Libby.

Stopping for their mail, Libby picked up a scented lavender envelope from her mother. Sandra registered instant pleasure on seeing her single piece of mail, ripping it open to laugh over a red-and-yellow crayon drawing from her son.

"Danny is drawing up a storm," she said, showing the picture to Libby. "This is him with his favorite truck. He plays for hours pushing cars and trucks around the apartment. Lord, I miss that kid! If my agent doesn't get me something in L.A. next year, I don't know what I'll do."

"You must hate missing every single thing he does."

"Do I! I think of quitting to do something else, but acting is all I know. Raising a child is expensive, and someday there'll be college. . . . Hey, sorry, I don't mean to dump my problems on you!''

"You're not! I love hearing about Danny. Maybe someday . . ."

Could the prospect of her twenty-ninth birthday be putting thoughts into her head, daydreams about a husband, a baby? She'd never been particularly domestic!

They filled their lunch trays with shrimp salads and slices of watermelon, agreeing that nothing could taste better than the juicy pink fruit after a long session in the sun. The room was nearly full, but they squeezed in on opposite sides of a table where Wiley was eating with several bit players who doubled as saloon girls and crowd stand-ins. He was the only man at the table, although most had all men.

"Sandra, honey," he said, half rising, "and Lilly."

"Libby," Sandra corrected him.

"I was just telling the girls how you learned to ride a horse for *The Law and Jack Flack.*"

"I'm sure these women would rather hear how you learned, Wiley," Sandra said sweetly.

"I can ride," he said defensively, quickly changing the subject. "Cocktails are on me before dinner. Everyone's invited. My suite."

"I'll pass, thanks," Sandra said. "I want to call home when we're through this afternoon and see how Danny's doing."

"I have to soak my sore toe," Libby said. "Thank you anyway."

"Now, Sandy, honey, don't forget we gotta get together on our big scene, the one before I go after Hank Morgan. You might as well come to my room after dinner and—"

"Sorry, Wiley, not tonight."

Leaving the dining room, Sandra shook her head and said ruefully, "Wiley never gives up."

59

"Doesn't he get mad when you say no?" Libby asked.

"I've said it so often, he'd probably fall off his chair if I said yes."

"At least he doesn't take it personally."

"He doesn't get offended easily, but that's because he can't imagine anyone not admiring him. Anyway, he knows I don't believe in on-the-set romances. It's too easy to fool yourself when you're on location. Everything's bigger than life, and it's an occupational hazard to confuse stage emotions and real ones."

"You don't see actors socially, then?"

"No, I never have. I married a man I dated in high school. Since Brad's death, I go out occasionally with my attorney, but he doesn't want the responsibility of being a father. Danny comes first in my life right now. He has to. There's no one else to take care of him."

"Do your parents live far away?"

"I never knew my father, unfortunately. My mother died a few years ago, the same year we learned about Brad's illness. You don't know how often I've wished she were still here. I use the best agency and they send their best sitters, but it's so hard leaving my son with strangers," she said, shaking her head. "Well, back to work. Thanks for listening to me."

The next day Libby would have seven lines; by dinnertime she felt confident about them. There was a rhythm, a routine, to filming that she was beginning to grasp, although there was still so much to learn that her brain was reeling. Talking to Sandra helped more than anything. She was one of those rare people who knew how to keep things in perspective. She wasn't intimidated by Wiley's frequent and sometimes lewd advances, and in fact brushed them aside as inconsequential. What had she said about romance on location? "Everything's bigger tham life . . . it's easy to confuse stage emotions and real ones." That seemed to fit Libby's situation exactly!

60

Craig Wicklow was part of the excitement and adventure of a new job and a new place. It would be disastrous if she confused her reaction to him with real romance. The best possible thing would be to dismiss him as nonchalantly as Sandra dismissed Wiley. Those two men had one big thing in common: Both wanted a good time and nothing more.

CHAPTER FOUR

His name was Gordon Brandt, but to Libby he was "Eager Eddie." Eddie Garth had been the self-appointed star of her first acting class, the go-getter who always volunteered to be first, who fawned over the teacher and cheerfully stepped on the faces of other students to ingratiate himself with anyone who could further his career. Usually the Eager Eddies of the world ignored her; she wasn't influential enough to help them nor docile enough to nourish their egos. Gordon Brandt was the exception. Cast as a hoodlum gunslinger, he was in most of her saloon scenes, usually without lines, and, oddly enough, he seemed to have a crush on her. Every time she turned around, he'd worked his way to within elbowing distance, using typical Eager Eddie techniques to gain her attention. Worse, he expected her to be grateful.

He was swarthy and superficially handsome; his almost-classic features had just a touch of coarseness that would become more obvious as he aged. His ambition was to revolutionize acting and push aside competition like Dustin Hoffman and Al Pacino. Libby thought he was going to find parts very scarce; too many young men could be typecast in the parts that fit him, and his unbridled self-confidence had to be as annoying to directors as it was to fellow actors.

Sandra's gentle technique for discouraging Wiley was totally ineffective with Gordon "Eager Eddie" Brandt. He buzzed around Libby like a starving mosquito.

Walking back from dinner, tired after a week of shooting that didn't include a weekend break, she wasn't in the mood to fend him off, but there he was, one foot planted on the second step of her mobile home, his elbow resting on his raised knee.

"Hi, babe," he said.

She clenched her jaw, loathing the way he called her "babe."

"I'm going straight to bed, Gordon. It's been a long day."

"That sounds good to me."

"Go away, Gordon." She couldn't say it any plainer than that.

"You don't really mean that."

"I do."

"I thought we could run through our scene together."

He must have been taking lessons from Wiley.

"We don't have a scene together!"

"We'll make one." He kept his foot on the step, blocking her way to the door.

"Please get out of my way." She backed up, refusing to play his game.

"You got a problem here, Libby?" Craig walked around to the front of her unit. "Sorry I'm a little late."

"Oh, I see," Gordon said, removing his foot from her step and shuffling it in the dust.

You don't see anything, she thought of saying, but instead kept quiet. If Craig could get rid of Eager Eddie just by standing there . . .

Gordon left, not graciously but quickly. Her grandmother Sloan's favorite word came to mind: flabbergasted. She was flabbergasted that Craig could discourage the overbearing actor just by standing there.

"Eat supper with me tomorrow," he told her.

It was an order, but she wasn't quite grateful enough to become obedient to the stuntman.

"I really don't think—"

"Maybe you want pipsqueaks like that hanging around."

She giggled, partly because he made her nervous but also because the silly name fit Gordon so well.

"Wait for me. I should be able to come for you by six-thirty."

As unexpectedly as he'd appeared, he left.

After being alone with him in Old Buckhorn, she'd vowed to avoid him as much as possible. It hadn't been necessary; so far the filming had kept them apart, and he certainly hadn't sought her company during their meager free time. This was the second time he'd come to her rescue, and she felt a little ridiculous. If she went to dinner with Craig, she'd be putting herself in his debt. Owing him wouldn't be a comfortable situation.

Much of the next day was spent fully costumed, waiting to be called. Making movies could be terribly tedious, she was learning, and today especially she'd had too much idle time to think. Everything on the set reminded her of the stuntman: the creak of a saddle on a horse's back, the tilt of a Stetson, the clank of boot heels on wooden sidewalk, the male scent lingering in the hot desert air.

At dinnertime, when Craig came for her, she was ready, dressed in a sophisticated, silky-blue jumpsuit with flutter sleeves and tapered, ankle-hugging legs. It was dressy enough for a cocktail party in New York and ultra-flattering with a fabric belt and huge white Art Deco buckle. She wasn't wearing it to impress the stuntman; considering the circumstances, she was overdressed to the point of looking silly, especially when she added white spike heels and a knotted rope of tiny white beads around her neck. What she wanted him to see was how different they were.

Knocking on her door, then stepping back to let her exit, he slowly appraised her with a disapproving frown.

"You're not going to make my job any easier," he drawled.

"I don't know what you mean." She could guess.

"Well, never mind." His attitude said there was nothing he couldn't handle.

The heat always seemed worst at this time of day. Libby inhaled deeply, feeling as though the oven-hot air would suffocate her.

"How's your toe?" Craig asked, ambling slowly beside her toward the pink-shelled dining hall.

The nail was black and ugly, but she kept it covered with a ready-made bandage.

"Fine, thank you."

"Well, how do you like movie-making so far?" As they approached the door, he rested his hand on the small of her back, fingering the silky material covering her skin.

"Please, don't," she said.

"Don't touch you?"

"No."

"I haven't thought about much else this past week."

"I'm sorry about that." Also curious, since he had seemed to be avoiding her.

"Sorry?" He laughed without amusement, then opened the door for her.

Gordon stared at her reproachfully as she entered with the stuntman, but his Eager Eddie cockiness seemed to have drained away. It was hard to believe anything so primitive was happening, but Craig seemed to be king of the mountain in the male hierarchy on location. She sensed that not even the director or the star would infringe on his rights where

65

women were concerned. Walking over to pick up a tray, she caught a glimpse of Bert Halloway, the stunt coordinator. He grinned in her direction, but his smile was meant for Craig, who was standing right behind her. He was the old stag approving of his protégé's selection. Libby wanted to throw her tray at him, at both of them!

Craig quickly decided on a thick slice of rare prime rib, a huge serving of broccoli, and a baked potato the size of a shoe. Libby took the alternative entrée, a baked fish fillet, and a salad. There was one empty chair at the table where Sandra was eating, but Craig was too quick for her.

"Over here," he insisted.

It was a trivial matter, but it irked her to have him deciding things for her. She was mad at herself for meekly following him to a deserted table.

"We could join the others," she whispered.

"How're you gonna discourage that kid if we don't look cozy?"

"Maybe I'm discouraging the wrong person."

"When I make up my mind, I don't get discouraged easily."

Just when she was about to walk away, he smiled, a slow, easy grin that made her melt. He reached across the table and unloaded her tray, piling it onto his empty one and pushing them aside.

"Now," he said, "for some serious eating and some serious talking."

"So much red meat isn't good for you." The eating part seemed safer.

He laughed like a man determined to be entertained. "I work too hard to live on seaweed and alfalfa sprouts."

"I'm not a health-food nut."

"Whatever you're eating, it's doing the job."

The look he flashed at her was so full of approval that she nearly squirmed off her chair.

He squeezed the ends of the giant potato, breaking it open down the middle, and spooned on the contents of a paper cup of thick sour cream. When he added three pats of butter, she couldn't stand it.

"Why don't you get fat?"

"When I'm not working, I cut way down and work out. If I gain a pound, I lose it."

It irked her to have him make it sound so easy. She had to watch every forkful of food.

"Where do you live?" she asked, switching to another safe topic.

"Wherever I happen to be working. My folks live in West Texas. I have a sister in Dallas and a brother in the Rangers, both younger."

"Aren't the Rangers the ones who jump out of planes?"

"Among other things. His unit goes in first when there's trouble."

That figured.

"Were you in the military?"

"No, when I got tired of being a college boy, I worked on a banana boat, then ended up taking acting lessons in L.A. I have a little apartment there, but I don't use it much."

"You do want to act!" She'd felt sure of it; he'd certainly be a more exciting leading man than Wiley Bails.

"Like I said before, I'm satisfied doing exactly what I do now." He sounded a little grim about it.

"What if you get hurt?"

He shrugged and cut off a bite of juicy beef. "Life doesn't come with any guarantees."

His homespun philosophy really was too much. What was she doing, sitting here hanging on every word as though he were some kind of oracle? He said the most commonplace things in a way that made them sound exciting. How could

Carl be content with Wiley Bails in the lead, when twice the man was right under his nose?

Now she was being silly: Craig probably couldn't act worth a darn!

"I'd like to spend the night with you," he said softly.

His directness shocked her. The invitation was there in his eyes and had been since he came for her, but the man had no finesse! What'd happened to handholding in the moonlight and good-night kisses?

"That's surprising." She pushed away her half-eaten salad. "I thought you were busy somewhere else all week."

"No." He looked sheepish. "I guess you spooked me a little. By the well. For a minute there I thought you were seeing a little white house with a picket fence. I hate painting fences."

"Well, you'll never have to whitewash one for me!" She flushed, remembering vividly her wish, but dimes weren't as magical as pennies and the well was dry. "I live in a city apartment—by myself. That's the way I like it!"

"That's there. We're here now."

At least he didn't do any of the obvious things like squeeze her knee under the table or rub his leg against hers. He was forceful, but he wasn't a klutz.

"We're nowhere. I told you how I felt."

"Yes, you told me."

"I'd better go."

"Don't run away from me, Libby. I think we could do a lot for each other."

"The only thing you can do for me is leave me alone!"

She hurried out of the dining room, passing Gordon, who was still morosely nursing a cup of coffee. Before she could cross the dusty stretch to her trailer, Craig overtook her.

"Not now, maybe," he said, "but there'll be other nights."

*　　*　　*

"Craig Wicklow was a friend of my husband's," Sandra said, standing with Libby in the shade of a porch while Wiley swaggered down the street on camera. "I met him in a movie, and they used to work out together at a health club. Brad wasn't too fond of most of the people I worked with, but he hit it off with Craig."

"I think it's even hotter than yesterday." Libby fanned herself with the straw hat, which was no longer white.

"Tomorrow we work inside all day. Paradise!" Sandra pulled a folded letter from a pinafore pocket. Unlike Libby, she wore the drab, traditional cotton dress of the frontier with a pinafore to protect it. "Danny's going to day camp. Here he is, wearing his Indian headband."

Libby was glad to look at the cute little drawing. "Red, yellow, and green feathers."

"The kids earn them. According to his baby-sitter, Danny has to pass beginners' swimming to get a blue one. He loves the water."

"I'm with him," Libby said. "I may take you up on your offer of a tub bath. I feel dry and dusty enough to blow away."

"You really should! Use at least two of my oil capsules. I want to talk to Dana before dinner, but I'll give you my key. There're plenty of towels. Make yourself at home."

"I won't make a habit of it," Libby promised, "but it will feel wonderful to soak for a while."

"Do it!" Sandra insisted. "I won't even be there until after dinner."

Libby intended to hurry, but the warm bathwater nearly lulled her to sleep. Lying back with her head on a little sponge pillow, she could feel the scented oil seeping into her pores, making her skin velvety-soft. She wiggled her toes in contentment and only reluctantly left the porcelain paradise. She was on her knees, scrubbing the tub and letting the air dry her, when there was a knock on the door. It could be Sandra, without a key because she'd given hers to Libby. Making a sarong of a large red-flowered towel, she padded barefoot to the door, opening it only enough to peek through a narrow slot.

"Craig!"

"What're you doing here?"

"Using Sandra's tub."

"I wanted to give her this."

He thrust his hand through the opening, and Libby backed up, unintentionally letting him enter the room.

"It's a Chinese coin, the kind they sell in Chinatown," he explained. "With a little hole in the middle." He held it on his palm for Libby to see.

"Nice," she said, wondering what it had to do with his being there.

She hugged the towel close, aware of the little beads of oily water on her shoulders.

"It's for Sandy's kid," he said, missing nothing, from the moist tendrils of hair escaping the bun on top of her head to her bare toes, the nail of one still discolored. "I won it in a poker game last night," he explained.

"So that's how you spend your free time."

"It's not my first choice." He closed the door, looking at her with obvious enjoyment.

"Are you good at it?" *Bad question, Libby,* she quickly told herself, watching a satyr's leer spread over his features.

"Sometimes I hit a losing streak, but I more than make up for it when my luck changes."

"Well, leave the coin. I'm sure any little boy would be thrilled with it."

"It was the gaffer's lucky piece."

"Gaffer?"

"Electrician."

70

"Oh, of course."

"Do you know what feels good after a bath?"

"No! I mean, I don't want to know."

"I give great back rubs."

"I'll take your word for it. Now, if you'll leave so I can get dressed. . . . You can put the coin on the table. I'll tell Sandra you left it."

"Do that." He moved a step closer and she retreated two.

"Well, good-bye."

"Aren't you going to eat?" he asked.

"Yes, but I'm not ready."

"I'll wait for you."

"No, you don't want to do that."

"Yes, I do."

He walked in his lazy, loose-jointed way to one of the two chairs beside a low coffee table. "If we're going to make it to supper, you'd better put some clothes on."

Heat rushed to her cheeks, but she knew he was right. His lap was too inviting, and saying no was getting harder all the time.

"Has that actor kid been bothering you?" he called through the bathroom door while she dressed.

"No."

She couldn't bring herself to thank him for discouraging Gordon. She'd escaped a mosquito to face a mountain lion.

At dinner she avoided being alone with Craig, and afterward she slipped away before he could offer to walk back with her. Something spooky was happening: the West was casting a spell, firing her imagination more with every passing day, and at the core of all her daydreams, all her fantasies, was the rangy blond stuntman, his mustache waxed to dagger points and his eyes green crystals in a suntanned face. She felt doubly vulnerable because nothing seemed quite real.

One of her biggest scenes was scheduled for the sound-stage bedroom, ending when the sheriff crashed through the window to a horse supposedly waiting below. Stars didn't leap through windows, not even artificial panes with inflated landing pads on the other side, so Craig had to work with her that day. Libby couldn't believe how lighthearted and giddy this prospect made her.

Her costume for this scene was the red-and-white-striped petticoat with only the corset on top. Away from the seclusion of her dressing room, she wasn't enthusiastic about having her breasts pushed up to look like two cantaloupes, but it was fun having her waist feel tiny under the elastic cincture. In this, her big moment, she would try to persuade the sheriff to stay with her instead of riding off on a dangerous search. When his enemies blocked the hallway, he would narrowly escape with his life by crashing through the window. They rehearsed it over and over, wanting the take to be perfect when Craig did his dive.

From the rear the stuntman could pass as Wiley. The fringe of his hair, worn long over his collar, was darkened, and so was his mustache, although his face would never be on camera. On the set he was all business, treating Libby as professionally as any actress could wish. Before making his leap for Wiley, Craig had to push Libby onto the bed, presumably out of the path of stray bullets. He patiently taught her how to fall naturally without hitting any part of her anatomy on the bedposts. Their bit together was filmed so smoothly, the director congratulated both of them, but to Libby it meant the end of her working time with Craig. The only other scene they shared was a free-for-all saloon fight where she mainly cowered in the background. Libby couldn't understand why women in Westerns never picked up a bottle and put a bad guy out of action. Calamity Jane wouldn't have waited to be rescued; Cassandra Rose shouldn't, either, if she was the kind of woman Libby imagined her to be. But if there was one thing she'd learned about this movie, it was that she was playing a type, not a person. As long as the story moved along, no one was interested in a saloon girl's assertiveness. Without long blond hair and satisfactory curves, she would never have gotten the part.

The empty hours between dinner and bedtime were hard to fill. Libby didn't want to play cards, and there were very few chores to do, since the production company provided daily maid and laundry service. She was tempted to walk alone through Old Buckhorn again, sure that the streets were familiar enough that she wouldn't get lost. Putting on jeans and sensible running shoes, she was ready to leave when a rap summoned her to the door.

"Do you ride?" Craig stood hatless below her door, one booted foot on the bottom step.

"Horses?"

He shrugged. "What else?"

"I took lessons once—only six. I'm not very good."

"Let me decide for myself whether you are."

"You mean now—ride now?"

"Sure, you're dressed for it. I don't suppose you own any boots?"

"No, but—"

"Come on. We'll be bending the rules a little, but the head wrangler is a friend of mine."

When they reached the corral, her second thoughts were all negative. She didn't ride well enough to take a strange horse out in the desert.

"Craig, maybe I'd better not go."

"You're not afraid of horses?"

"No."

"I've had Sneaky Pete saddled for you."

"Old Dobbin would be more my speed!"

73

"Don't let the name bother you. Sneaky Pete is the horse Bails rides in the closeup shots. He's a lamb in horse's hide."

"Where will we ride?"

"Just around. It's good for the horses."

"For them, maybe!"

She followed him around the circle of plank fencing to the barn, where her nostrils told her the animals in the cast were stabled. Unfortunately his good friend the wrangler had kept his word: two horses were saddled and ready to ride. With a show of bravado she took the reins of the larger but more docile of the two beasts, tried desperately to remember which side to mount, guessed correctly which stirrup to use, and threw her leg over the saddle.

"It's the wrong kind!" she said.

"Wrong what?"

"Saddle. I learned on an English saddle. Maybe we'd better just forget—"

"Won't matter. A western saddle's easier riding. How're the stirrups?"

She wiggled in the saddle, finally centering herself somewhat comfortably. "Too long, but I don't think I can ride in these shoes. The heels don't catch."

Rising in the saddle, she tried for a graceful dismount, but the horse was so tall, she sat down in the dirt, trying to free her foot. Only her pride was injured.

"This isn't a good idea," she moaned.

"Ben!"

His call brought a skinny man in a worn denim jacket ambling toward them.

"Got a pair of boots you can loan the lady?" Craig asked.

"What size?" The man held a cigarette to his lips between two outstretched fingers.

"Why don't we just forget this?" she said. "I wear an unusually narrow size seven, and—"

74

"Seven," the stuntman said.

"Maybe we could do this another time," she went on. It's nearly dark, and—"

"Try these," the wrangler said, ducking in and out of the barn in a flash.

There was nowhere to sit, so she leaned against the fence, letting her seat slip through the wide span between boards. The boots stuck going over her heels but were loose and sloppy when she got them on.

"Okay?" Craig asked, standing so close, her cheek brushed the worn cotton of his sleeve when she straightened.

"I guess."

"Anything she needs to know about the horse, Ben?"

"Naw. That one's a sleepwalker. Fall asleep and she'll walk ya right home."

Libby clenched her teeth and half stood to be sure her feet were firm in the stirrups. The ground seemed perilously far away, but Craig was so close on his mount, their legs touched for an instant.

"Thanks, Ben. We won't be gone long."

He led the way, keeping his friskier horse at a slow walk, then dropping back beside her when they passed the last building on the outskirts of town.

"Should we be riding in the desert at night?"

"It's the only time to ride in the desert." He sounded relaxed and amused. "Nice, huh?" Craig asked.

Something marvelous was happening in the sky surrounding them as starbursts of light appeared, miniature stage lights for an incredibly large, creamy-yellow moon still low on the horizon. Silhouetted against this full moon, Craig became the spirit of the land, the personification of all the cowboy heroes of the West. Libby loosened her grasp on the reins and stopped fighting the rhythmic slapping of the saddle, enchanted again by the wonder of the landscape.

"Can we ride to the mountains?" she asked.

"No, they're farther away than they look. We'll just circle around and come in on the other side of town. How's it going?"

"Fine," she could honestly say. Old Sneaky Pete hadn't sprouted wings yet; in fact, he seemed to think that just lifting his feet was work enough.

"I never did show you Boot Hill," he said. "Over here."

Her horse followed his, stepping a bit more lively and bouncing her in the saddle. Craig secured his horse on a low fence and walked over to help her dismount, tying the reins of her horse too.

"It seems like a real cemetery at night," she said.

Under the illumination of the moon the rough rock slabs marking imaginary graves were as chilling as any real tombstones, making her grateful for the presence of the tall man beside her. She had too much imagination to visit graveyards at night.

"It's hard to believe this is only a movie set," she said, welcoming the arm that circled her shoulders.

"It's hard to believe you're here with me."

His kiss was gentle, slowly descending on parted lips, then roaming over her face, brushing her closed lids, and teasing the corners of her mouth. Burying his fingers in her flaxen hair, he caressed the back of her head and neck, bending to move his mouth over the smooth column of her throat. His breath tickled, and she laughed, reaching out to touch him as she had so often in her daydreams. Bathed in the magical light of the full moon, he was her phantom cowboy.

On tiptoes, clinging to him, she returned his next kiss, covering his mouth with hers, experiencing the sweetness of this fleeting moment. They shared hard, hungry kisses, locked in each other's arms, swaying and clinging together. His tongue explored her mouth as she melted against him, arms locked around his hard torso.

"Libby," he whispered into her hair, as he slipped his hands under her loose jersey, finding the smooth flesh of her breasts and holding them like fragile treasures, his gentleness as thrilling as his urgent kisses.

She wanted to be handled and hugged and held. Shivering under the electrical touch of his fingers, she reached out to part the buttons on his shirt and touch the warmth of his chest.

"Come back with me," he pleaded.

She didn't answer, wanting to prolong the enchantment and their closeness under the star-sprinkled sky. Instead she rubbed her cheek against his chest, encircling his waist with her arms.

"You're in terrible danger," he warned.

"I don't believe that."

"Always believe me," he said seriously.

"You always tell the truth?" She pulled his face to hers and teased his lips apart, muffling his answer.

"Sand makes a poor bed," he threatened when she let him speak.

Moving her foot, she brushed it against one of the mock tombstones and remembered where she was.

"Let's go back." His voice was hoarse with longing.

He helped her mount, slipping her foot in the stirrup, sliding his hand over her thigh and resting it between the saddle and her crotch.

"Oh, no." she moaned, shaken by a reaction so raw and powerful, she quivered.

Her whole life seemed to be racing out of control. She laced the reins around her palm and gripped the saddlehorn as though her life depended on it, stunned by the depth of her longing. Bouncing helplessly in the saddle, she tried to make sense of her feverish attraction to Craig. She'd never wanted a man more nor been so afraid of having her wish fulfilled.

He expected her to make love, and she'd given him every reason to believe it was what she wanted too. Minutes ago it had been. Now she was frightened, unsure of her feelings and of his. Craig wanted a temporary playmate; it was one role she didn't know how to play. She had to care about a man to make love, and she didn't often risk rejection.

Tormented by growing doubts and reluctance, she kept her eyes on the tall figure riding easily in the saddle ahead of her. He was beautiful, wholly true to his masculine image, but he wasn't for her. She was already in too deep, promising more than her cool, rational self would allow her to give.

There was no future in being the temporary mistress to a fun-hungry stuntman.

Scampering off the horse before he could help, she remembered the borrowed boots, impossibly loose for running away.

"You can change your shoes," he said, finding them where they lay by the fence. "I promised to unsaddle the horses. Wait here for me."

The boots were off before he disappeared into the stable, lit by one small bulb. She rammed her feet into her own shoes, tied hasty knots so she wouldn't fall over the laces, and ran. This time she knew where the stockade fence was, and nothing tripped her in the dark. She reached her trailer before Craig missed her, turning on all the lights so he wouldn't think she was lost again, then sinking down in misery on the couch, too drained to begin her bedtime routine.

His knock came sooner than she expected. At first it was soft, then sharp and demanding. He said her name loudly enough to be heard, but he was too proud to persist. After a minute that lasted an eternity, he left.

She could imagine the horrible things he was thinking. Men hated teases, and she was worse than one, responding with genuine longing and not hiding it from him. Running away didn't even make sense to her, but the compulsion to flee had been so strong, she couldn't regret it. Her own safety and welfare demanded that she get away from him. She could not make love with Craig Wicklow.

Pacing the length of her confining quarters, palms pressed against the sides of her head as though she could push away her feelings, she admitted the truth to herself: The stuntman was more than she could handle. She truly regretted having let something start that couldn't have a happy ending.

CHAPTER FIVE

Beginning the day with dread, Libby knew that sooner or later she'd come face to face with Craig. Would he be cold and scornful? Or would anger make him vocal? She could imagine some of the things he might say about her abrupt disappearance. Last night running had seemed the only way to avoid involvement in a no-win relationship, but she wasn't proud of having disappeared without a word. Even Eager Eddie deserved to know where he stood.

The schedule called for a full day of shooting in the sound-stage saloon, a big set with a polished wooden bar and whiskey barrels behind the counter. There were kerosene lanterns mounted on the walls, a shelf of old brown bottles, a wooden staircase that led nowhere, and plenty of tables for drinking and gambling. Libby had three lines to say in the scene, but she had to stand around all day to get them said. A lot of bit players were involved, and she expected Craig to appear at any moment. She felt anxious all day for nothing. He didn't come near the saloon set.

She'd skipped breakfast, and for lunch she'd grabbed a quick sandwich on the set between takes. Hungry and tired, she forced herself to go to the dining room for dinner. She couldn't hide from him for the duration of the filming. It was

80

inevitable that they would meet sometime. Too agitated to care about food, she pointed numbly at a pan of veal cutlets, forgetting to tell the server not to dump a mountain of mashed potatoes beside her meat.

"Now who's eating enough for a linebacker?" Craig intercepted her at the end of the line, taking her tray and carrying it to an empty table. Watching dumbly while he unloaded it, she noticed that he didn't have any food himself.

"Go ahead and eat," he said, sitting down on the opposite side of the table. "I'm through. I was waiting for you."

Picking up her fork like an obedient child, she tried scraping the sticky potatoes away from the meat, certain she wouldn't be able to swallow a bite.

"Libby, look at me." There was no harshness in his voice, but his words were a command. "Now."

She searched his face for signs of anger, but what she saw only puzzled her.

"Sweetheart, it's okay."

"You're not mad?" She didn't quite believe him.

"We all get cold feet sometimes."

"I didn't plan things to go the way they did."

"I know." He reached across the table and took the fork from her limp fingers, covering her hand with both of his. "If you have that many doubts, it was best to run away."

Breathing deeply, she had to blink back tears of relief. "It's not my style, really."

"I never thought it was. Eat your dinner."

He broke off a small morsel of tender veal with the fork and held it to her lips.

Feeling a little silly, she took it from him, chewing slowly, finding it delicious. When he offered another, she took the fork from him.

"Are you going to eat all those potatoes?" he asked.

"None, probably." She speared a small mound and offered it to him, sliding the fork carefully between his lips.

"Fresh-cooked, not those powdered things."

"We can't complain about the food," she said.

"No. I need your help."

"More potatoes?" She offered him the fork again, feeling a little self-conscious about doing it in a room where other cast and crew members were still eating.

"No, thanks. What I need is a good envelope licker."

"That doesn't sound like a hard job."

"It is with the number of letters I have to sign, fold, and seal."

"What are they?"

"Fund-raising appeals for an environmental group. It's like tryin' to build a dam with little twigs, stopping people who want to turn this country into one big garbage heap. My batch of five hundred goes to people in the movie business. Will you help me?"

"All right, but you have to do some of the licking."

"I've got a sponge."

She hesitated for a moment when they reached his door, and he noticed.

"Tonight is all business," he reassured her.

Libby nodded her head, wondering why she trusted him when she didn't trust herself.

The letters and envelopes were neatly stacked, and he'd made a start on signing them. She could see why the work went slowly; on almost every letter he added a few personal words.

"Do you know all these people?"

"Not all are personal friends, but I've worked with most of them. You can start folding these."

The folding and sealing went faster than his signing, and she fixed cups of coffee, sitting across from him in the booth

82

as he labored over the appeals, adding a plain, legible signature with a fine-tipped felt pen.

"What will the money be used for?" She moistened a flap, then smoothed it down.

"Mostly political action projects. Trying to buck the spoilers without the right legislation is like spitting in the wind."

"Do you do much volunteer work?"

He smiled a little sheepishly. "Everybody needs a cause."

Stealing glances at him, watching him frown as he stuck with the task, she had more questions than answers about this man.

He smiled at her and flexed his fingers. "I guess my hands aren't in shape for this kind of work. I'd rather spend twenty-four hours in the saddle."

Libby remembered their brief ride together and got up to rinse their cups, feeling troubled by the vivid memories she'd tried to shove to a far corner of her mind. Only a few more signatures, and Craig's job would be done. Could he possibly be as understanding as he seemed? Did he expect her to stay after the last envelope was sealed?

"That's it," he said, passing her his final letter and standing to stretch his whole body. "Do I hate desk work!"

In flexing his arms and shoulders he pulled his gray cotton shirt loose, making his jeans slide down to the ridge of hip bone that held them on. Libby looked away, fighting an urge to touch the fine hair below his navel.

"I'd better go. Those early calls are doing me in," she said.

"I love sunrise when I'm camping," he said. "Everything's so clean and fresh, I forget the world's turning into a garbage pit. Ever camp out, Libby?" He perched on the edge of the table looking down on her.

"I went to drama camp in the Catskills."

He laughed softly. "That's not quite the same thing as

83

waking up in the mountains, taking a bath in a stream with rocks underfoot as cold as ice cubes. Fixing coffee and beans for breakfast. Climbing all day till I can look down on a valley all purple and green with wild brush and trees.''

She held her breath, seeing a new side of Craig and one she liked very much.

"Do you camp alone?"

"Sometimes, but two in a sleeping bag is more fun."

"I should go now."

"Yeah, you should." He stepped back, letting her pass him and move toward the door. "Thanks for helping."

"You're welcome. I can see it was for a good cause."

"Good night." He didn't follow her. "And thanks again."

"I was glad to help." Her hand was on the knob.

"I'll walk you home."

"No, you don't need to. It's so close."

"It's the least I can do." He was volunteering, but he wasn't pushing himself on her.

"All right. It is dark."

He stuffed the bottom of his shirt into his pants and followed, staying two feet away until they reached her steps.

"Good night," she said, turning on the second step.

For once she was nearly eye level with him, but his face was a shadowy mystery under the starlit sky.

"How do you feel about a good-night kiss?" he asked, keeping his voice teasingly casual.

"Friends do that sort of thing, I guess."

He leaned so close, she could feel his breath on her face.

She closed her eyes, trying not to feel disappointed when he barely brushed her lips and stepped back.

" 'Night, sweetheart."

For a long while she sat in the dark on the edge of her bed, fingers intertwined on her lap and legs clenched together, wondering whether a woman's sexual yearnings were a gift or a curse. How could she feel so drawn to a man like Craig,

84

when the only thing they had in common was chemistry? Why had his casual little kiss been such a letdown? How could she be on location with him for weeks without totally losing her head?

Much later she fell asleep without a single answer.

The next evening Libby hurried to dinner, trying to arrive at at the time when Craig usually ate, but was disappointed not to find him there. Lingering over a third cup of coffee, a guarantee that it wouldn't be easy to fall asleep, she was one of the last to leave the dining room. He never came.

Wandering the desolate streets of Old Buckhorn had lost its thrill. The crude, weathered buildings might be authentic, but the magic had faded. The place was just a movie set; she'd been foolishly romantic to see it any other way.

One of the old plank-seated chairs in front of the Paradise Hotel was occupied. Moving closer in the dusk, she recognized the man who was constantly in her thoughts.

"I told you not to walk here alone after dark." Craig stood at the end of the wooden sidewalk, hands resting on his hips, looking like a gunfighter poised for a shootout. The image only annoyed her.

"I'll walk wherever I choose."

"I don't think so." He stepped to the ground but didn't look any less imposing.

"Are you ordering me out of town, sheriff?" She stood her ground, hands on hips too.

"By sundown," he said with mock seriousness.

"Over my dead body."

"You wanna do this the hard way?" He took a long step forward, looking genuinely menacing.

"You stop right there." She backed up two steps.

"I'm calling your bluff, Sloan." He started walking toward her.

"Now, stop, Craig!" She couldn't back up as fast as he came forward.

With a grunt of satisfaction he bent forward and swept her over his shoulder, imprisoning her legs and letting her head and arms dangle ignominiously. She pummeled his back with her fists, squirming impotently and yelling.

"Put me down!"

"Stop hittin' me or you're goin' over my knee."

"You have no right—"

"You women always talk rights when you're wrong!"

"Oh!"

She was ready to explode with anger when he stopped and dropped her roughly to her feet, catching both her hands in his and backing her against the stockade fence.

"I told you it was dangerous to be out here alone."

"I don't believe you! There's nothing to be afraid of!"

"There's this!" He crushed her against him, punishing her with a kiss that lasted until she had to fight for breath.

"I came out here to avoid you," he said angrily, taking her head between his hands and soundly kissing her for the second time.

"Is that why you didn't eat dinner?" She pulled at his hands until he dropped them to his sides.

"When did you start keeping track of my meals?"

"One thing is sure. You're grouchy when you don't eat!"

"Grouchy? Is that what you think I am?"

"Well, you're not nice like you were last night."

"Last night!" He sounded overcome with disgust.

"I thought you were nice—then," she said meekly.

"Nice!" He walked away, then returned with quick, angry steps.

"Working for the environment—at least I thought you cared about something besides yourself."

"You think whatever you like, lady!" He did walk away this time, heading back toward the hotel where she'd found

86

him. "Get out of here! I'm not in the mood to go looking for you."

The last place she wanted to be was alone in Old Buckhorn with a crazy stuntman! She ran all the way back to her temporary quarters, fervently wishing she could be on a plane home at the crack of dawn.

"Another slowdown!" Sandra wailed over lunch. "Can you believe they drove Wiley into Tucson for an allergy shot?"

Libby hadn't been needed that morning; she'd spent the long hours working on her lines, which she already knew so well, they were boring to her.

"I thought people came to Arizona to get rid of their allergies."

"Leave it to him to have some freakish one!"

"Maybe dust. It's so windy today."

"Yes, and it's supposed to get worse. We could have a windstorm, and that'll cost us more time. At this rate Danny will be back in school before I get home!"

"Did you find the Chinese coin? Craig brought it for him."

"Yes, he told me. There's a man who hasn't been himself lately?"

"Oh?"

"You've gotten to know him, haven't you? I've seen you eating with him."

"A few times," Libby admitted.

"Surprising."

"That he'd eat with me?" Libby felt a little hurt.

"Oh, no, not that exactly." Sandra seemed uncomfortable.

"What, then?"

"Well, Craig usually likes women who are fluffs, pretty but easily forgotten. You don't fit the pattern at all."

"I wouldn't try. We'd be an impossible mix. The men I like are . . . well, they're much different."

Without Wiley on location, Libby was temporarily unemployed. She wandered into the sound stage, watching Sandra do a brief take that had her searching the saloon for the sheriff. Something she was doing didn't please the director, and they went over and over the sequence until Libby totally lost interest. With time heavy on her hands, she went outside, holding her hat on her head as she walked aimlessly through the town. The wind was blowing sand, and she pulled down the straw brim to protect her eyes, deciding Old Buckhorn wasn't the place to be.

Hurrying now, she followed the stockade fence to go to her trailer, a little alarmed because the swirling grit stung her cheeks and arms, forcing her to cover her eyes with her hands.

Running blindly, she passed the end of the fence, bowing her head and squeezing her eyes shut against the driving force of the stinging wind. Her unit had to be close, but she hated to open her eyes, risking instead just a glimpse through the separations in the straw brim. She couldn't see any of the bulky mobile homes. Jerking around, feeling like a leaf in a hurricane, she realized that she'd been running in the wrong direction. Ahead of her was a scenery dock at the rear of the sound stage, but she didn't know whether to try for shelter there. If the dock was deserted, if the doors were locked . . .

"Libby!" Her name came to her as a muffled shout, then the decision was taken from her. After an instant of temporary sanctuary under Craig's sheltering arm, she was propelled into the wind, led blindly but trustingly to safety.

"Thank God I saw you! Didn't you know a dust storm was coming?" Craig held her close after securing the door, taking her forlorn hat and brushing sand from her hair.

Dust and fear made her mouth and throat ash-dry, and she barely choked out an answer. "How could I know that?"

"They announced it to everyone in the sound stage. Where the devil were you?"

"Out there." She gestured limply, knowing how it felt to be scoured by sand.

"Let me get you some water."

She hung over a sink, rinsing her mouth, taking cautious swallows, beginning to realize that she must look like last season's scarecrow.

"Are you all right?" He hovered over her, not scolding her anymore for being caught by the storm.

"Dusty is all." She could finally drink without swallowing grit. "How did you find me?"

"I was running for shelter myself when I saw someone going in the wrong direction. The doors by the docks are locked when no one's loading or unloading. You couldn't get in that way."

"You saved my life!"

"I didn't save your life," he said. "Look, there's still some visibility, but it's getting worse. I'm afraid you're stuck here until it dies down."

They were in his trailer, the green-and-gold oasis where she'd accidentally invaded his privacy when she'd first arrived. She wasn't any more comfortable about being there now, and she looked a whole lot worse, wind-battered and disheveled.

"I'd better get home before it does get worse."

"It's not worth the risk. A sand storm isn't anything to fool with."

The sand and wind were battering the metal exterior of their shelter, telling her he wasn't exaggerating. Leaving would be foolhardy, but staying wasn't safe either.

"I feel like I've got sand inside my clothes," he said,

sitting to pull off his boots and shake them over a paper basket.

"You're getting sand everywhere."

"Sand is everywhere. You can use the shower first." He peeled off a thick white sock, brushing at his foot with it.

"I can wait until the storm's over."

"Don't be silly. I'm offering to let you use it alone."

"My clothes are too sandy to bother."

"I'll find something for you." He walked barefoot into the bedroom, coming out with a folded cotton shirt. "I don't bother with pajamas and robes, so you'll have to settle for this."

She took the garment but didn't move.

"I'm taking my clothes off." He started unbuttoning his shirt. "You can stand there and watch me or use the shower first."

The bathroom lock worked the same way hers did: not very well. She played with it, wiggling and shaking until it finally clicked into place, knowing he could hear and would know how anxious she was to secure the door.

Blessedly free of sand after showering, she made a neat pile of her gritty clothes and, satisfied that the long-sleeved brown-and-yellow plaid shirt was suitably concealing, went back to the main room.

The storm worsened, enveloping the mobile home in an unnatural dusk and lashing it so the floor shook underfoot. Craig was waiting on the couch, one leg spread out on its length, shirtless but still wearing jeans. He looked much as he had at their first meeting: a golden legend become flesh. Then she'd only been attracted to him; now she felt a stirring so deep and powerful, it hurt.

"Aren't the lights working?" she asked.

"I didn't try them."

"Do storms like this last long?"

90

"Long enough."

He rose slowly and brushed past her. She didn't hear him coax the lock into catching.

They couldn't go out for dinner, so she explored the refrigerator and cupboards, setting out a plate of crackers and cheese and a jar of peanuts.

She heard him leave the bathroom but didn't look up, pretending to search the cupboard for a second time.

"You've fixed dinner," he teased, standing beside her with a yellow bath towel secured around his waist.

"I guess it's all we'll get. I hope it's enough for you."

"It will be." He tossed a handful of peanuts into his mouth, slowly chewing them. "Did you find the wine?"

"No, I thought you'd like beer."

"Not tonight." He located the chilled bottle and a cork-screw, slowly extracting the cork from an imported German wine.

"It's a rumor that only the French make good wines."

"I didn't know you were a wine expert."

"I'm not, but I trust my own taste. The company slipped up: no fancy goblets." He handed her a water glass filled to the top with pale golden liquid, toasting her with his eyes.

"How long do dust storms last?" she asked.

"Didn't you ask me that once before?" He sipped the wine, standing beside the counter where she'd laid out the food.

"I guess I did."

"You look good in my shirt."

"I hope it's not your last laundered one."

She tried to avoid looking at him, but the clean scent of his skin was perfume to her nostrils, and she was close enough to touch the sprinkling of damp hair on his chest. He ran his fingers over the ends of his wet mustache, shaping the points that gave him a devilish look.

91

"You are so beautiful." He ran one finger under her chin, tipping her face toward his.

"I'm only here because it's an emergency." Her voice sounded feeble.

"It's been an emergency for me since I first saw you."

"Craig . . ."

His kiss tasted of wine, sweet and fresh, and his lips moved over hers, gently nibbling their softness.

"You're always hungry," she said breathlessly, pulling away. "This won't be much of a dinner for you."

"I only care how it will be for you."

He held her at arm's length, massaging her shoulders with his fingers, riveting her in place with his eyes. Almond-shaped and heavily lashed, they were the most extraordinary eyes she'd ever studied. She regretted the dimness of the room.

"Do you get tired of being told you're beautiful?" he asked, tracing the outline of her mouth with one finger.

"I haven't heard it often enough to—"

"Come here," he commanded huskily.

Without consciously moving she was in his arms, her lips pressed against his chest, betraying her real feelings by kissing the little peak of his nipples. His towel touched her bare leg as it fell, enveloping her toes in a terry-cloth heap, but he lifted her free of it.

His bedspread was folded down, and Libby knew no maid had uncovered the sandlewood sheets. While she'd showered he'd been making plans to seduce her.

"Craig, I'm not ready for this!"

"That's all right. We have plenty of time." He lowered her to the bed, stretching out beside her and unbuttoning the top button of the borrowed shirt.

"I don't want to sleep with you!" she lied, trying to convince herself.

"We won't sleep." He unfastened the second button and ran his fingers over the hollow between her breasts.

"You're impossible!"

"Anytime you want to walk out to the other room," he drawled in a husky voice, "I won't stop you, and I won't follow you."

"Do you mean that?"

"Yes." He opened the last button, touching her so lightly that butterfly wings seemed to be caressing her breasts.

The bed shook under the impact of the wind, and he slid the shirt from her shoulders, touching her smooth skin.

The light in the room had a vaguely green tint, and in her heart she believed it was an enchanted glow radiating from the depths of his eyes. She reached out and traced the sandy line of his brows and the prickly fullness of his mustache, fingering his face with awe.

"Have you always had a mustache?"

"Not in grade school."

He nuzzled her, tickling her nose.

"Do you wear it to get jobs in Westerns?"

"No, I could paste one on."

He kissed her throat, sliding his lips along the hard ridge of her collarbone. As he leaned over her breasts she could see the long expanse of his back, tapering down to pale, rounded buttocks. She ran her nails lightly over his shoulders to the knobby length of his spine, letting her fingers creep down to the dimpled hollow at the end.

Her breasts ached with pleasure as he gently suckled them, running callused palms over her torso until the tiny tremor deep inside grew to earthquake proportions. If just once she could make love with him and give free rein to the passionate impulses he inspired in her, it would be enough. She could be her own sensible, controlled self again and forget the daydreams that tormented her. For once in her life reality

93

would be better than fantasy. Craig was the man who could make it so. She wasn't afraid now, not of him, not of what was building between them.

"Beautiful, beautiful Libby." His words were a languid caress, as unhurried as his lovemaking, making her feel wonderful about herself, about being with him. She wasn't thinking straight, wasn't thinking at all, until he backed away for a moment, asking his question urgently: Was she protected?

"I never thought . . . when I came, I didn't expect . . ."

"I'll take care of it," he said.

The magic was slow in returning; she couldn't believe how heedless she'd been, how utterly careless of consequences. But he caressed her and told her how good it would be, how it should be between a man and a woman, until finally she believed what she heard, clinging to him while wave after wave of sweet contentment rippled through her.

Later, when the wind died down, they awoke from a deeply restful doze to eat cheese and crackers in bed and sip wine from a shared glass, then made leisurely love with the ceiling light glowing brightly above them. She loved his legs, long, powerful, and supple, and his arms, the veins standing out on steely muscles. She kissed his scars, a surgical crisscross of white hollows on his knees and ankle, souvenirs of stunts gone wrong, feeling a little weepy over all the pain he'd suffered.

He laughed at her, showing a pleased, indulgent humor that made her feel like a little girl—until he kissed her in his special way, crushing her against him because no degree of closeness was quite enough for either of them.

For the first time she didn't hate awakening in the early hour of dawn. When his clock, identical to the one in her trailer, began its annoying beeps, she felt him stir beside her and reach out, not for the off button but for her, raining playful kisses on her face until she tickled him in self-defense.

94

Watching him get up and cross the room, she felt her heart bunch into a hard knot, so full of emotion that the rhythm of its beat went haywire for a moment. Instead of feeling fulfilled, her passion spent and her mind clear for other things, she felt possessive and selfish, not wanting him to return to his life, not willing to share him with the world outside his trailer.

Was this love? Could two people who were totally wrong for each other everyplace but in bed look forward to anything but disappointment?

Naked, he came back into the room, drying himself with a towel as he walked, totally unselfconscious, smiling at her as she pulled the sheet to her chin.

"Shower's yours. Hurry up or we'll miss another meal."

"Give me your towel."

"There're plenty of clean ones."

"Please."

"Okay," he said, smiling, "but this is one morning I hate to go to work."

"I thought you enjoyed your job." She made a tent of the sheet and wrapped the towel around her, knowing that her sudden attack of modesty was ridiculous.

"I do." A shadow passed over his face, and he turned away, letting her get ready without saying anything else.

If this was love, it wasn't the storybook kind that brought a glow to a woman's cheeks and a twinkle to her eyes. For the rest of the day she went through the mechanics of doing her job, completing a scene after a maddening number of takes, but she was troubled for obscure, elusive reasons.

Did she want to be in love with Craig? From the beginning he'd made himself clear: he only wanted her as a diversion on location. Last night none of his endearments or sexy little compliments mentioned love. He wasn't going to fall in love with her. If she tumbled for him, she could only be hurt.

95

Now was the time to forget Craig. There was no future for a serious actress and a stuntman. He certainly wasn't interested in more than fun, but could she handle that? Did she have a choice?

CHAPTER SIX

"Why can't I convince you this is no place for a lady after dark?"

He'd found her sitting in front of the Paradise Hotel, gloomily watching the sun disappear behind a jagged mountain that looked like the head of a prehistoric monster.

"Why do you want to?"

"It'd save me the trouble a' fetchin' ya back all the time."

"I don't want to go back just yet."

"Wanna tell me why not?"

"No."

"I'm supposed ta guess?"

"Your accent is thicker than usual tonight."

"I took lessons to get West Texas outta my talk. Sometimes I don't give a damn."

"What times are those?"

"When I have more important things on my mind," he said, speaking more crisply.

"Like what?" she challenged.

"Those hills out there." He stood beside her, both hands jammed in his jeans pockets.

"Aren't they mountains?"

"I won't quibble about it."

"The one on the right is shaped like a monster."

"It is a monster!" He said it so emphatically, she was startled.

"Why?"

"That's where I tore up my knee, doin' some fool stunt that looked easier 'n it was."

"How did it happen?"

He shrugged and was quiet for a long time.

"You don't have to tell me." She walked to the edge of the sidewalk, feeling slighted and sulky.

"No big deal. The script called for a flying leap down about eight feet. The ledge crumbled under my foot when I started to jump. Threw my timing off and kept me out of work for three months."

"Not exactly your lucky mountain, huh?"

"We're shooting there tomorrow."

"What do you have to do?"

"The gunfight."

"Where Wiley catches up with the murderers? That won't be dangerous, will it?"

"If there wasn't any danger, the company would let their star do it."

"Now I am scared."

"Don't be." He put his arm around her. "I know my business, and I don't make the same mistake twice."

He never mentioned his marriage; was that another mistake he didn't intend to repeat?

She was wearing a full cotton skirt, the design made up of artist's palettes dabbed with bright colors. Bought on impulse several years ago because the sale price was such a bargain, she'd never enjoyed it until now, standing in this desert setting, feeling the breeze move it against her bare legs.

98

"I feel like dancing!" She slipped away from him and twirled on the sidewalk, letting her skirt billow out.

"What will you use for music?" He propped one foot on the edge of the raised walk, leaning on his knee.

"You'll have to sing for me."

"You don't even know if I can."

"I'm sure you can."

"You may not like my kind of music." He hummed a few bars she couldn't identify.

"Something lively!"

"All I know is country-western."

"Anything!" She kicked up her heels, doing the saloon dance she'd been practicing for the movie.

"Now, Clancy was a family man, he loved his wife so well." He tapped his foot and clapped his hands in a fast tempo. "But Nancy was a bloomer gal who—"

"I've never heard a song like that!"

"Folk song. I just made it up—the song, not the bloomers. They were the Barbary Coast version of bunny tails."

"I thought suffragettes wore bloomers."

"They probably did."

He swung her around in a high-stepping stomp that left her breathless with laughter.

"Come here," he said, grabbing for her and missing, giving her a chance to dash to the other end of the street.

Her sandals slapped the dusty street as she raced full speed through the ghost town, turning a corner, letting her mock panic become real as she searched for a place to hide. He was behind her, not really trying to catch up, playing her game with the knowledge he could easily overtake her whenever he chose.

She reached the livery stable, the one without real horses, and ducked into the entrance, picking a stall as a hiding place. He walked through, not hurrying, whistling softly to

99

himself. Counting to a hundred slowly, she crept out the way she'd entered, her heart racing with excitement, right into the arms of her pursuer. Her shriek sounded louder than a fire alarm in the total stillness.

"You lose!" he said, flicking her over one knee and planting a noisy swat on her rear.

Her wail was one of sheer indignation. "Leave me alone!"

"That's not why you led me on a chase all over town." He easily kept up with her furious retreat.

"I wanted to get away from you!"

"You wanted to test me!"

"Test you! That's macho nonsense!"

"Only snooty little girls think *macho* is a dirty word."

"If that's what you think of me . . ."

"What I think of you is, you spend too much time trying to make everything fit your own little set of rules."

"Well, that makes me sound boring!"

"No, you're certainly not boring." He grabbed her hand and backed her against a rough wooden post supporting a roof overhang.

"I can't stand men who flaunt their physical strength!"

"Do you want me to pretend I weigh one twenty and can't open a pickle jar?"

"You're making fun of everything I say!"

"No, I'm not. I just don't want you to be so uptight about a little simple, honest sex."

"I'm not!"

"You're not what?"

"Uptight!"

"About what?"

"About a little . . ."

"See, you don't even want to say the word. You're trying to make sex into some big dramatic deal."

"Thank you, Dr. Freud. I'm sure you have all kinds of

evidence to support that." She pushed on his chest with both hands, but he wouldn't budge.

"I know I spend more time chasing around this lot at night lookin' for you than I do workin' here in the day."

"*Chasing* and *looking* are words that end in *ing*," she said distinctly. You're a trained actor. You don't have to talk like a man with a mouthful of mush."

"So you think I'm a phony? That makes your hangups all right?"

"This is the dumbest argument I've ever had! I don't even know why we're fighting. After last night . . ."

"I thought you'd come to me tonight. I can't depend on sandstorms all the time!"

"Just because something happened last night . . ."

"Sex happened."

"Just because I did a dumb thing last night doesn't mean we're going steady!"

"Going steady!" He stepped back and laughed without amusement. "Next you'll want my class ring!"

"I didn't mean it that way!"

"I know what you meant." He sounded weary and indifferent. "You want a relationship that has a name, that has rules and conditions. We're back to that."

"I don't want anything from you." She walked away, and this time he didn't follow.

"You do, but you're not honest enough to admit it to yourself."

Alone in bed, she was still so angry, she sat bunching the top sheet in her fists, wishing she'd never met Craig. She could forgive a playful spanking that no one saw; maybe she had provoked him to see what would happen. She would never forgive the terrible things he'd said! She had a right to organize her life any way she pleased. If she liked having things spelled out . . .

Hot, angry tears rolled down her face. Craig had to perform the most dangerous stunt in the movie tomorrow. Was that why he'd been so cruel to her, saying unforgivable things? No, she wouldn't make excuses for him! He was the one who'd pushed his way into her life, trying to pretend he had no past and no interest in the future. All of a sudden she felt homesick for New York. The sooner her western exile ended, the happier she'd be. What were a pair of broad shoulders and a golden-haired chest compared to the excitement of a Broadway opening? She'd wipe the stuntman out of her mind as soon as she left this make-believe place.

Filming schedules weren't made for the convenience of supporting players. She was facing an idle day, so there was no reason to refuse the invitation Carl made at breakfast.

"Ride along in the Jeep with me," he said. "You might as well see some action shooting while you're here."

She agreed, not sure why she hadn't slept instead of rising so early on an off day. There must be something in the air that woke her at dawn.

They made a strange caravan crossing the roadless desert: a truck with camera equipment, horse vans, a modern-day chuck wagon, the caterer's van, four-wheel-drive vehicles, and the air-conditioned station wagon for Wiley so his allergies wouldn't flare up. Bert had gone ahead with his stuntmen to do some preliminary work. Libby was the only woman from the cast who was there, but no one paid much attention to her. Since Craig had shown interest in her, men had stopped pursuing her. She thought of demonstrating that the cowboy had staked his claim prematurely, but flirting didn't appeal to her.

The mountain was a forbidding hunk of rock with only sparse patches of scrubby vegetation. Up close the romantic deep-violet shading became a drab brownish-gray, and the prehistoric head appeared to be nothing but a steep, hostile peak. She hung back in the shade of the Jeep when the others

102

started doing their jobs. Seeing Craig in the distance with two other men dulled her interest in action filming. He might assume she was there to watch him. Worse, he might think she was worried about his dangerous stunts.

He looked in her direction but didn't acknowledge her. Maybe he resented her presence.

Tired of being alone, she located Carl and stayed as close to the director as she could without getting in his way. At least that would tell Craig she was an invited guest; the danger of his stunt had nothing to do with her being there to watch.

The scene was a shootout, such a requisite part of Western films that Libby thought they might as well reuse a scene from some old movie. When she saw men moving like mountain goats on the treacherous peak, she was troubled by the risks they were taking. The general plan soon became clear: The sheriff was alone and outnumbered, cornered by the murderers who wanted to kill him. His only escape route was the sheer, hostile face of the cliff. His horse was conveniently grazing below it. All he had to do was use his cowboy rope to descend from the jagged cliff where he was trapped and make his way down a series of steep drops. That was all, only Wiley wouldn't be hanging on the rock wall on a puny cord. Craig would.

Her heart was in her throat as she pieced together what was expected of the stuntman. This was no trick, no illusion. He wouldn't be diving onto an air mattress or doing a practiced roll down steps. He could be seriously hurt dangling on the rock wall or darting from one precarious foothold to the next. Rattlesnakes could be lying in wait in hidden crevices, or hidden faults in the mountain could split apart, sending Craig crashing to his death.

Forgetting her anger, she walked as close as she could without becoming a nuisance, holding her straw hat on her head and not noticing the sandy grit working its way between her toes and into her sandals. Already her blue silk blouse, which she wore with her white denims, was sticking to her back in the heat, and she could imagine how much hotter it must be on top of the cliff where Craig was standing, dressed in clothes identical to Wiley's: a heat-absorbing black shirt, tight pants, and the suede vest that was the sheriff's trademark.

He looked in her direction, taking off his hat and waving it. She took off hers and waved back, hoping he could catch the good-luck wish she was sending him.

No wonder he'd been edgy the night before! There were no gimmicks on this stunt. Once he started down the side of the cliff, he was on his own, completely dependent on his skills and athletic ability.

She was squeezing the edge of her hat, turning the straw into damp shreds, not wanting to watch but too worried to look away. Her sunglasses weren't enough protection to keep her eyes comfortable in the burning glare, and she didn't envy the men on the mountain who couldn't wear modern sun shields on camera. She hoped the wide-brimmed hat Craig was wearing protected his eyes.

Impatient with herself for fretting over a man who would probably hate her protectiveness and concern if he knew about it, she distracted herself by helping the driver of the catering van fill small water jugs from one of the twenty-five-gallon water containers. Technicians were swarming over the western slope of the mountain, the easily accessible side, setting up the shots for the shootout. Lunchtime arrived, and still Craig hadn't made his dangerous descent, although the noisy crack of guns firing blanks told her that the fight was in progress.

Food and water were carried up to the men on the cliff, but their break was a short one. Unable to stand the suspense, Libby climbed up to where one camera crew was working, finding the ascent far from easy. Suspicious of every cranny and rock, worried that they concealed dangerous reptiles, she didn't pay enough attention to the rugged path underfoot, slipping and landing on one knee. Embarrassed but not hurt, she brushed stones and dirt from her knee and found an incline where she could watch without being in the way.

The sheriff knew he was trapped; he didn't have a chance of shooting the bad guys hidden behind rocks, and they were slowly closing in. After taking a series of closeups of Wiley, the camera crew seemed to tense up, speaking in sharp, hushed tones and moving their equipment. Their attitude warned Libby that the dangerous part would begin soon, and her heart was in her throat. Wiley pased her, free now and going down for a cold drink; he wouldn't be needed until Craig was safely on the desert floor. Libby followed him. In order to see Craig, she'd have to stand on the ground below the perilous side of the mountain.

He was standing on the highest peak, on the horn of the monster's head. The question of whether this was a hill or a mountain was answered in her mind. Hills were green and rolling, pleasant swells that invited hikes and cycling. The beast Craig had to conquer was jagged and barren, no place to play games or make movies. She felt a little queasy but blamed it on the heat. Why should she be sick with worry over a man who only saw her as a bedtime playmate?

There he was, silhouetted against the sky, crouched and waiting, looking down at the desert far below him. He saw her, and she was embarrassed to be caught staring anxiously up at him. At least the stuntman couldn't know that fear was tying her intestines in knots and triggering little twitches in her arms.

No one could clamber down the side of that mountain with only a short length of cowboy rope. Experienced climbers would use all kinds of special equipment: hammer, nylon rope, mountaineering boots. And no one could leap from the last narrow ledge to the back of a horse! Where did screenwriters get crazy ideas like that?

Several cameras were in position to film the sheriff's escape from different angles. There wouldn't be any retakes. A coiled rope went flying to a jagged outcropping of rock, and Craig yanked on it for the cameras. The rock's soundness had been tested and retested under the supervision of the stunt coordinator, but Libby didn't trust a sliver of rock when a man's life was at stake.

Craig was poised on the edge. In an instant he'd make his move, and it would be too late to stop him. She wanted to scream, to beg them to cancel the dangerous stunt, sure that she was experiencing a premonition of disaster. Then he started down the rope.

Something was going wrong! A boulder came loose, but Craig must have heard a warning sound. He twisted violently to his right, propelling himself out of the path of the falling rock but slamming his side into the solid wall.

With blood pounding in her ears, Libby barely heard the stir of concern, the muffled oaths, from the men on the ground, but she knew Craig was in trouble. He came to the end of the rope too quickly, kicking out to drop to the ledge but landing on his knees instead of his feet. Bert Halloway was just off camera, shouting at Craig to stay there, but the stuntman gave no sign that he heard. For a moment he seemed dazed, then he started the hazardous downward trek, scrambling from precarious foothold to foothold, poised at last on the ledge above the waiting horse.

"Damn!" Bert cursed loudly, gesturing at Craig, who still didn't seem to hear him.

Obviously favoring one side, Craig made the final leap, landing awkwardly facedown over the horse's mane.

"Cut!"

Men were racing toward him, shouting, carefully pulling him off the horse to lie flat on his back on the desert floor while Bert and Marty Granger examined him.

Bert was chewing him out the way a proud father yells at his son for making the winning touchdown his own way instead of the coach's. Marty was flexing Craig's knee, cutting up the length of his pant leg. Someone splashed water on his face and cradled his head, holding a cup to his lips. She wanted to be there with him, but her pride kept her away.

Freeman wandered over to her, moving at what was a leisurely pace for the AD, and talked for a minute, offering to give her a ride back now that the day's shooting was a wrap. Craig was standing now, limping but shrugging off help, the cowboy wounded but triumphant. When he looked in her direction, she pretended not to notice.

Libby rode back in the air-conditioned station wagon, listening to Wiley complain about the dust clogging his sinuses. Freeman Cartwell was stewing about budget overruns, broadly hinting that Millway couldn't afford any more allergy delays. Libby closed her eyes and pretended to nap, thoroughly tired of movie making and all that it entailed, especially dangerous stunts performed by daredevil stuntmen.

When she saw Bert fill a tray with enough turkey, dressing, and mashed potatoes for two people, then cover it with metal food warmers and leave, she worried even more about how badly Craig was hurt. Being served dinner wasn't his style.

Bert was leaving Craig's unit as she returned to hers. She smiled and waved at him but hurried inside without talking. There was no way she'd ask about that macho stuntman! If he wanted to make a living risking his life, it was his business. Never again would she stand by in terror waiting to see if he broke his neck. If she ever fell in love again, it would be with a stockbroker or a banker or some other man who worked in an office and came home in one piece every evening.

Fall in love again! She wasn't in love. No way! Not with Craig Wicklow.

No matter how hard she tried, Libby couldn't keep her thoughts off Craig that evening. The memory of him slamming against the wall of the mountain and landing awkwardly kept replaying in her mind. Remembering the deep scar on his knee, she worried that he was suffering a lot of pain. Would he have his dinner delivered if he weren't? Washing her blouse in the kitchen sink, she saw one of the other stuntmen leave Craig's trailer. Did that mean he wanted to sleep? Maybe he was taking pain pills that made him groggy.

Finally she admitted to herself that she wouldn't be able to sleep until she knew if he was all right. A visit to a sick co-worker was a perfectly innocent gesture. The worst Craig could do was throw her out. If he did, it would be good shock treatment to help get him out of her system.

Checking her image in the full-length mirror attached to the closet, she wasn't pleased. Her hair was dry-looking, and it took a vigorous brushing to bring crackling life to the thick swirls on her shoulders. The lavender wraparound skirt made her waist look tiny, and her breasts were full and erect under a sleeveless white cotton knit shirt. She changed to old brown shorts and a loose-fitting tan cotton blouse. Craig didn't need to think she'd dressed up just to see how he felt.

There was no response to her knock. After psyching herself up to come this far, she wasn't going to leave without learning how he was. Feeling sneaky, she turned the knob, finding the door unlocked. If Craig were sleeping, possibly drugged by pain pills, she could see how he was and leave undetected. Moving as silently as possible, she stepped inside, easing the door shut. The main room was empty, and there was no sign of the dinner tray. Where did cat burglars get their nerve? Walking uninvited into another person's home, even a temporary one like this, made her as jumpy as auditioning for a big part. Her own breath seemed as loud as a trumpet fanfare, and she was poised for flight if her reception was anything but friendly.

Tiptoeing even though the carpeting muffled her footsteps, she approached the half-open bedroom door, slipping through without having to risk a creaking hinge. Craig was lying in the middle of the bed, one knee propped up by a pillow with an ice bag resting against it and leaking onto the pillowcase, making a big wet patch. His eyes were closed, and he didn't stir. He certainly wasn't one to relax in pajamas, but at least he was sleeping in Jockey shorts, not his usual habit, as she remembered vividly. A sheet was draped over the side of his body that lay away from her.

If the melting ice pack stayed where it was, he was going to have a damp bed. The least any good neighbor would do would be to take it away. She had to lean over part of the bed to reach it, and his sudden move made her cry out.

"You scared me!"

"Sneaks deserve to be scared!" He had seized her wrist in his hand.

"I'm not a sneak. Your ice bag is leaking. I was going to take it before the whole bed gets wet."

"You just happened to be passing by my bed?" He lifted his knee from the damp pillow, wincing just a bit.

"I saw you get hurt. When you didn't come to dinner . . ."

"You were worried," he said softly.

"No! I mean, I thought you might need something."

"I do." He pulled her down beside him and managed to kiss her ear before she wriggled free.

"Don't do that!" She sat on the far edge, her wrist still captive.

"Oh." His groan was involuntary.

"Are you all right?" She slipped away and turned on the overhead light, even though it wasn't quite nightfall.

"Yes, but you can do me one favor. Get that tray out of here." He gestured at the partially eaten meal on the bedside stand. "And take the ice too."

"You didn't eat much."

"I'm more thirsty than hungry."

"I'll get you some water."

"A beer would be better."

She took away the damp pillow with the ice bag and tray, returning with a glass of apple juice.

He drank it down and then complained, "That's not beer."

"Apple juice will give you pink, healthy cheeks."

"Your cheeks are pink enough," he said.

"I'm a little sunburned."

"Why stand around in the desert all day?" He propped up a pillow and sank back against it, moving with the exaggerated care of someone who's hurting.

"Just curiosity. I didn't have anything else to do." She was standing beside the bed, wishing she hadn't turned the light on as she tried not to look at his lean, outstretched length.

"Don't do it again." He sounded weary.

"What?"

"I don't want you around when I'm working."

"You don't need to worry about having me around anytime!" She tried to leave but he grabbed her arm, tumbling her down beside him none too gently.

"I'm not saying that to hurt your feelings."

"You can't hurt my feelings, Mr. Wicklow."

"I did last night, and I'm sorry about that." She could tell by the way he said *sorry* that it wasn't a word that came easily to him. "But I don't want you hanging around when I have tough jobs to do."

"I wasn't hanging around you!"

"No?" He shifted to imprison her against his chest, moan-

110

ing slightly. "Anyway, you raised havoc with my concentration."

"Are you blaming me because you got hurt?"

"No, I'm blaming myself," he said harshly, holding her in the crook of his arm in spite of her resistance. "Damn it, stop thrashing around!"

"I didn't touch your knee."

"My knee is the least of my problems."

"Where else are you hurt?"

"My shoulder and arm."

She freed herself and knelt beside him, carefully slipping aside the sheet he'd pulled up with uncharacteristic modesty. She gasped when she saw that his upper arm was a mass of bruises and lacerations, the skin angry purple and red.

"It looks worse than it is." He impatiently pulled the sheet over it, making a loose toga.

"Did the rock hit you?"

"You saw what happened."

"How do you know I did?"

"Damn it, Libby, if I hadn't been so worried about where you were, this wouldn't have happened."

"You *are* blaming me!"

"No! When the boulder fell, it surprised me. I was showing off instead of concentrating. My timing was off. I didn't need to slam into the wall that hard. Then the pain clouded my mind for an instant. I hit the first ledge wrong and twisted my knee. I screwed up, and I paid for it."

"Is that why Bert was yelling at you?"

"No, he thought I should've let someone else make the last jump to the horse."

"Because you were hurt! Will you be leaving tomorrow?"

"No." He sounded surprised by the suggestion.

"You can't finish the movie."

"I'll be back to work tomorrow. These are just bruises."

She didn't want to believe him. "Shouldn't you see a doctor or go to a hospital?"

"All I need is your attention." He pulled her to him, cradling her head on his uninjured shoulder.

"Craig, I just came here to—"

"Nurse me back to health?"

"No! To see if you needed anything. I can refill the ice bag."

"You can stop moving around so much. Honey, right now my shoulder hurts like hell." Admitting it was a big wallop to his pride.

"I'm sorry." She tried to lie absolutely still, resting her head on his good shoulder.

"This is nice," he said huskily, brushing a lock of hair from her forehead. Libby murmured her agreement. Right now she wasn't in a hurry to have the filmmaking end. Craig didn't initiate lovemaking. Just holding and being held was enough for the moment.

She didn't understand the glow of contentment that washed over her, but he seemed to feel the same way. It was the most natural thing in the world to slip down so that they were lying against each other and fall asleep.

His groan woke her. The overhead light was still on, but the room had the yellow glow that heralded the rise of the sun over the desert. She was beside him, her cheek pressed against his uninjured arm. The annoying beep-beep of the alarm told her he'd set it, perhaps before she came over.

"Sweetheart, will you do me a big favor?" He was talking up to the ceiling, not moving.

"If I can."

"Go make me a pot of coffee, nice 'n' strong. Then run along back to your place." He shifted his knee but didn't otherwise move.

This request wasn't what she'd expected or wanted. She

112

felt so close to him, so protective, that the urge to communicate was as powerful as sexual longing. They needed to talk! Something special was happening, had happened already. She didn't move, hoping he'd say something about their peaceful night together.

"Please." There was an undertone of irritation in his voice now.

"If that's what you want."

She'd slept all night in tennis shoes. Her feet felt hot and grubby, and her cheeks were prickly from sunburn. Feeling as droopy as a dirty sock, she went out to start a pot of coffee in the automatic maker. If Craig wanted strong, he'd get strong. She doubled the usual amount of grounds and added another scoop for good measure. Watching the dark-brown liquid trickle into the glass pot, she waited until it was full and switched off the brew button.

Craig was watching her from the bedroom door, his hair uncombed and his eyelids still heavy with sleep.

"Thanks, babe," he said softly, "and not for the coffee."

The bedroom door closed between them before she could say anything. There was nothing to do but go.

CHAPTER SEVEN

Craig's abrupt dismissal didn't change the way Libby felt. All day she carried a warm glow in her heart, knowing that, for a short time, he'd needed her as a person and welcomed her concern. She did hate having him return to work so soon. He might minimize the extent of his pain to others, but she knew a day of work would mean agony for him. The stuntmen were scheduled to do a chase sequence on horseback, and she was positive he should take a few days off.

Cassandra Rose was facing a confrontation with her rival that day. It was a meaty street scene with name-calling, pushing, and shoving, one of Libby's big moments in the film. The writing was better than in most of her scenes, showing some sympathy for the saloon girl whose love was simpler and less manipulative than that of the crusading character played by Sandra Faraday. Libby thought her own grasp of the scene was good, but Sandra kept flubbing cues and forgetting lines. It wasn't at all like her, and at noon they still didn't have a good take.

"Libby, I'm sorry." Sandra joined her during their brief on-set lunch break. "My mind just isn't on this scene. I'll try to do better."

"I'm sure we'll get it soon. Did Danny get his blue feather?"

"Yes, he passed swimming with flying colors." Her brief smile faded. "But day camp ends for the summer tomorrow, and I have a problem."

"Oh?"

"My sitter's mother is critically ill. She has to leave to be with her. Tomorrow's her last day, and that means Danny has to get used to another stranger. I hate hiring someone sight unseen."

"School hasn't started yet?"

"No, not for weeks. He'll be confined in the apartment with someone he doesn't know." Sandra pleated folds of calico through her fingers, unconsciously creasing the skirt of her costume.

"Bring him here," Libby suggested.

"How can I? It's just not done!"

"You're the star. You should have some privileges besides a bathtub."

"Carl would love a curious little kid underfoot!"

"He wouldn't be in the way." Libby was excited about the idea now. "Listen, this is the last scene we do together. That means one of us will always be free with nothing to do. I'll take turns watching him for you. I've been dreading all the time I have to wait around to do what little is left of my part. I'd love to get to know Danny."

"You make it sound so possible."

"It is possible!"

"I'd have to talk to Carl."

"Talk, but be insistent. Tell him you can't concentrate because you're so worried."

"That's certainly true!"

"Won't Danny enjoy being here! He can play cowboy in Old Buckhorn and ride the horses and—"

"Libby! I'm not sure I can swing it! And I don't have time to go home and get him."

"Airlines are wonderful with kids. He'll get VIP treatment all the way!"

"I suppose his sitter could put him on a plane before she leaves."

"And the flight attendant will deliver him to you in Tucson."

"I'll explain to Carl that this is an emergency."

"It is! You can't leave your son with just anyone."

"Well, it won't hurt to ask." Sandra looked a bit skeptical but considerably more cheerful. "I guess we'd better do our scene right this afternoon."

At dinner Libby didn't have a chance to find out if Sandra had gotten an okay. She waited until she saw Craig limping toward the dining room, then hurriedly caught up with him. For once she could move as fast as he did.

"How was your day?" she asked, reading the answer in his frown.

"Fine."

"It couldn't have been! You're limping and—"

"Drop it, Libby." He opened the door for her but stayed behind to talk to one of the other stuntmen.

Feeling slighted, she went ahead and filled her tray, looking without interest at the section of roast chicken on her plate, carrying it to an empty table because she was too disgruntled to make small talk with anyone. Craig didn't have to eat with her! Let him sit with his good-old-boy buddy, if that's what he wanted. She picked at the awkward portion with her fork, then decided to forget daintiness, going at the chicken with fingers and teeth.

"That's the way you should eat chicken." Craig took the seat across from her, unsmiling but less grouchy-looking.

"I'll be done in a minute if you'd rather sit with someone else."

"I'd rather eat with you or I wouldn't be here."

116

"I'm honored," she said sarcastically, wiping her fingers on a napkin.

"Just don't start on my accident, okay? I'm fine."

"It's no concern of mine if you want to pretend your arm doesn't hurt. And your shoulder. And your knee."

"I don't need mothering."

"Pardon me." She brushed her lips with the napkin and pushed her chair away from the table.

"Stay here."

"I have things to do."

"They'll wait."

"You can't give me orders, Mr. Wicklow." She took a nervous sip of water.

"I sure as hell don't feel like chasing you around Old Buckhorn tonight."

"In your condition you probably couldn't catch me."

"Don't count on it." His eyes were mesmerizing, the gold-flecked pupils holding her there against her better judgment.

She felt a little tingle of excitement and disliked him for it. She didn't deserve the effect he had on her glands—and her heart.

"All right. I'm here. Shall we talk about your day?"

"No, yours."

"I finished the fight scene with Sandra."

"How'd it go?" He was tearing chicken apart with more gusto than necessary, as though he were deliberately showing her how a real man wolfed down food.

"Fine."

"I would've changed the script. Made it more physical. When two women fight over a man, they can get pretty rough."

"Are you speaking from experience?"

117

He ignored her question. "A little hair-pulling and slapping would have made a better scene."

"Why not eye-gouging and kicking?" she asked sarcastically.

"Women are more apt to scratch when they're mad."

"Oh, that's too much!" She got up and flounced away, sure that he was deliberately trying to shock her.

He caught up outside the door. "Don't you know when I'm having fun with you?"

"I imagine your idea of real fun is having two women pulling hair over you!"

"No, my idea of a good time would be getting into your panties." He reached down and fondled her bottom.

"Stop that!"

She was hot, and embarrassed to be manhandled in the open yard. Putting space between them, she half ran to her own door but didn't manage to unlock it before he lifted her off the steps into his arms.

"Put me down!"

"Come over to my place."

"No!"

There was nothing seductive about his expression. He was testing her, not propositioning her. For one blinding moment she saw him through a red haze, hating what he was doing. Then he put her down and kissed her roughly, scratching her face with the prickly beginnings of a beard.

"You need a shave!" She ran the back of her hand across her mouth as though she could wipe away his kiss.

"I have to look scruffy for the rest of the film." He touched his chin, running one finger over the sharp little bristles. "It'll soften up in a couple of days."

"I don't care if it does." She held her key like a lance, determined not to put up with his heavy-handed tactics. "I'm going in now."

"Have it your way." He took the key and unlocked the

door, handing it back to her and planting a light swat on her backside.

"Your keep your hands off me!" She was angry enough to cry, but her pride wouldn't let her do it in front of him.

He shrugged indifferently and left.

She knew what he was doing, but understanding his behavior only made her angrier. Last night he'd been vulnerable; he'd needed her. Tonight he was putting up new barriers, telling her that nothing had changed. The he-man in him was willing to make love, but he didn't want her to get close to the person he really was.

Clenching her fists in frustration and sobbing until her throat ached, she let bitter tears of unhappiness run down her face. She couldn't let herself fall in love with the crude, macho man who'd just left her. Even though she could see through his act, she didn't know how to get through his defenses. If he didn't trust her with any of the important parts of his life, there wasn't any hope that they'd ever be close. That was the way he wanted it.

Exhausted from crying, she went to bed early but lay awake in wide-eyed misery, wishing she'd never seen the tender, loving side of the stuntman. She could cheerfully hate him if she hadn't.

The knocking was persistent and urgent. Libby checked the clock and reluctantly got up, knowing her alarm would ring in a few minutes anyway. Whatever Craig had to say to her at this time of morning, she really didn't want to hear it. Slipping into her pink cotton robe, she padded unwillingly to the door in bare feet.

"It's all set!"

Sandra's face told it all: Danny was coming.

Libby smiled, trying not to feel disappointed because her early-morning visitor wasn't Craig. There was really nothing more to say to him anyway.

119

"Wonderful! When will he get here?"

"The plane will be in Tucson at eight-seventeen this evening. Craig agreed to drive me to the airport in the station wagon, but I want you to come too. I'm eager for you to meet Danny. I'm so glad you talked me into having him here."

"I can hardly wait, but you should meet him alone. He'll want to be with his mother the first night."

"Not with Craig along. Danny used to follow him around like a puppy dog when he came over to see Brad."

"All the more reason to give him a chance alone with the two of you."

"Oh, I'm afraid Danny's hero worshiping is one-sided. Craig doesn't take to children very easily. I've often wondered . . . Of course, he was divorced before we knew him."

"Wondered what?"

"Nothing really. Are you sure you won't come?"

"I'll meet Danny tomorrow. It'll make my day. Have some coffee with me."

"No, I have a long day. That's why I had to catch you before I went to work. I noticed you're not on the schedule today."

"No, another day with nothing to do. I'll be delighted to have Danny to play with!"

"I can't thank you enough."

"You don't have to try. I'm the lucky one, getting to know your son."

Her day wasn't quite as free as the schedule made it seem. She had a rehearsal and a hair appointment. The wispy hair along her forehead, too fine to be called bangs, needed trimming, according to the company's hairstylist, and she wanted to work out in the weight room, a back corner of the props warehouse with a few exercise machines for the cast. Her thighs could use some time on the bike.

The warehouse was windowless and just a little spooky, deserted as it was in the middle of the afternoon. Libby turned on all the lights and decided to start by walking on the treadmill, not her favorite exercise but one she needed. She was sorry she hadn't thought of using the machines sooner. The treadmill was a lot safer than walking alone in Old Buckhorn when Craig was around to follow her.

A window unit provided the only air conditioning, and the partitioned-off exercise area was warm. Libby's hands were slippery on the metal sidebars, and she could feel perspiration soaking her running shorts and tank top as she walked at a fast pace. Even with her hair tied up in a long tail and a sweatband around her forehead, moisture was rolling down her face. Mopping herself on a towel, she turned to the exercise bike, deciding to do some stretching exercises first.

"I thought I'd be alone now."

Angry at being startled, she turned to confront Craig, seeing him in shorts and athletic shoes for the first time. Bare-chested with a white towel hanging around his neck, he looked cool and composed, exactly the opposite of the way she felt.

"So did I . . . expect to be alone. Why aren't you working?" she asked.

"Time off for good behavior."

"Unlikely!" She snorted, hiding her face on the towel as she tried again to dry off.

"Libby . . ." He seemed about to say something but changed his mind.

She felt red-faced, sweaty, and uncomfortable, but darned if she'd let him scare her away! Plopping down on the bike seat, she attacked the pedals, watching the speedometer climb to ten, fifteen, twenty miles per hour. Her calves were stiff, and cycling when she was tense made them tighten more. Craig was on his back on the weight bench, and she tried to

121

ignore him, failing utterly. Even with her eyes lowered she caught glimpses of his torso, glistening now as he lifted. Hard knots in her legs made the usually pleasurable exercise a chore, but she wasn't expecting the sudden stab of pain in her right calf. Crying out and stumbling from the bike, she tried to hobble around to ease the severe cramp but instead doubled over in pain. Craig was by her side before she was aware of his movement.

"What's wrong?" he asked frantically. "Cramp?"

"Yes." She tried to put weight on her right leg but it hurt so much, tears came to her eyes.

"It's okay, sweetheart!"

He bent and took her calf in both hands, slowly kneading the knot of pain. He was faultlessly gentle, but this kind of cramp was hard to relieve. She was crying without realizing it, resisting his help because her leg hurt so much.

"Lean on me and walk slowly."

With his arm around her for support, he made her circle the exercise area until the cramp gradually subsided, leaving her leg sore.

"Drink your milk," he said, kneeling again to rub the aching muscle.

"I don't like milk."

"Naughty girl. That's your trouble. Better get some more calcium and potassium in your diet."

"Now you sound like my father!"

"No." He straightened and looked down at her, his face grim. "I'm not applying for that job."

She was hot, damp, and miserable, in no mood to be kissed. He was just as warm, perspiring heavily from his weightlifting. His first kiss was totally unromantic, a squishing of lips, an angry joining of their mouths. She didn't want it to happen, and his low curse told her he didn't either. Gathering her against him, he assaulted her mouth until she gasped, swept up by the warmth of his body and the passion of his kisses. She wanted to be ravished and possessed! It had to be the heat making her so crazy, but she still did nothing to stop him when his hand slid under her shorts. All she could hear was the pounding of her own heart and his labored breath. Pressed against him, she ran her hands down the length of his back, digging her fingers into his hard, clenched buttocks.

"What are you doing to me?" His mouth was near her ear and the words were puzzled and anxious.

Wrapping his arms around her, he made answering impossible. His beard wasn't soft yet, but she hardly noticed, losing herself in the barrage of kisses. She was caught up in his urgency, not thinking, only feeling.

"Sorry, I'll come back later," a man's voice said.

It took Libby a moment to realize that the voice came from an intruder.

"No, Marty, it's okay," Craig said.

"I thought I'd see how your knee's doing."

"Not good on the leg lifts."

Craig released her, continuing a casual conversation with the man who served as trainer to the stuntmen. How could he sound so cool and objective when only moments ago they'd been lost in each other's arms? Wasn't he at all uncomfortable?

She was embarrassed enough for both of them, slipping away before either man said anything to her. What would've happened without the interruption? There was a gray mat folded against one wall; if Craig had carried her there . . .

Her face was burning with humiliation. Public exhibitions weren't at all her style! Craig was so wrong for her, but when he touched her, she stopped thinking about consequences.

Her evening was free of temptation. Craig was driving Sandra to pick up her son at the airport. When, late at night, a soft rap sounded on her door, she didn't answer.

Her part for the day consisted of some spirited dancing and a few words of enticement to the harried sheriff, which he ignored. Her minute on-camera meant a day on the sound stage, but she had one pleasant distraction. Sandra brought her son to the set.

Libby offered her hand to the young boy, and he took it without hesitation. "Danny, I'm so glad to meet you," she said. "Did you like flying on the plane?"

"I sat in the pilot's seat."

"Did he show you how to steer?"

"No." He stared at Libby with large, serious brown eyes. "But he gave me these." He pointed proudly at a pair of silver-colored wings pinned on a yellow T-shirt that said CAMP ARAPAHO.

"Pilot's wings. Do you want to fly planes when you grow up?"

"No, I'm going to ride horses like Craig."

"We have to let Libby go back to work now, Danny," his mother said. "Maybe she'll eat dinner with us."

"You can count on it," Libby said.

Libby was in love! She couldn't wait to finish work so she could see Danny again. His face, just beginning to lose its baby-roundness, was grave under a mop of dark, tousled curls, and she was dying to see him smile, to do something to make him laugh.

Dinner was fun. Sandra beamed with pleasure at having her son with her, and Libby coaxed him into eating his meat loaf, sympathizing because it was one entrée she could do without herself. Craig came into the dining room late and didn't sit with them, even though Danny waved hopefully at him.

Afterward the three of them wandered through Old Buckhorn. Seen through Danny's eyes, it became a playground. Wooden rails were bucking horses, an old barrel was a mountain to be climbed, and the livery stable was perfect for a shrieking, laughing game of hide-and-seek. Libby tried not to think of the time she'd hidden there from Craig.

"Look at this, Mom. See this, Libby!" He'd found a battered old wagon to climb, calling out with excitement.

Libby was as tired as Danny after a frantic romp through the town, but she left Sandra and her son with the warm feeling of having made a new friend. Tomorrow Danny would be her responsibility, and she could hardly wait.

No one knocked on her door that evening.

Entertaining a young boy all day proved to be a challenge. Danny was interested in everything, but no one thing held his attention for long. He quickly tired of watching his mother and Wiley repeat their scene, and most of Old Buckhorn was off limits as some busy street activity was being filmed. Danny spotted Craig driving the stagecoach and waved enthusiastically, giving Libby a hard time when she wouldn't let him run over to him.

"The cameraman is taking his picture," Libby pointed out, although this wasn't entirely true at the moment.

The men were taking a break, but Craig only acknowledged Danny with an offhand wave. Libby was annoyed; it wouldn't cost him that much time or effort to walk over and say a few words to the boy. She gestured at him, but he ignored her, turning his back on both of them.

Sandra met her and Danny for dinner, and Craig came through the line shortly after they were seated. One thing was becoming clear: He wasn't going to come near Libby while she was with Sandra and Danny.

"I thought Craig was a friend of yours," she said softly to Sandra while Freeman explained to Danny, not too successfully, why there were no Indians in the movie.

"Just a friend," Sandra reminded her. "For some reason

kids make him uncomfortable. Don't bother about us if you'd like to go over and join him.''

"No! I wouldn't think of it!" Libby's protest was a little too vehement, but her friend let it pass without comment.

Danny was determined that Freeman's bushy black beard had to be fake. The AD was patiently letting him "test" it.

"He's been suspicious of beards ever since he figured out that the Santa Claus who visited his school had a cotton one held on by strings."

"Ouch!" Freeman called a halt to the beard testing, and both women congratulated him for being a good sport.

Libby welcomed some time to herself after a hectic day of watching Danny. A quiet hour or two of reading was very appealing. How could mothers take care of two or three or even more young children all day without being totally drained? However trying to the day had been, she'd had a marvelous time seeing things through Danny's eyes. She didn't at all regret her offer to help take care of him.

Craig came out of his trailer and waited by her door, watching with narrowed eyes as she approached.

"How was your day?" he asked.

"Lovely. Danny and I had a great time."

He was frowning as if he didn't like her answer.

"Do you want to take a walk?"

"No, I did enough walking today."

"You might be interested to know that the letters you helped me send out are already bringing results."

"Oh, the environmental fund. Well, that's nice."

"It was nice of you to help."

No matter how friendly he seemed right now, she wasn't going to ask him in.

"Come ride with me," he said, sounding a little put out.

"Not tonight, Craig."

"Okay." He started to leave, then turned back. "Tomorrow's our scene together."

"It is, isn't it? What would a Western movie be without a fight in the saloon? Danny will enjoy watching it."

"Good night," he said, leaving abruptly.

Sandra brought Danny to watch the mock fight, and Libby joined them for a few minutes, helping her friend explain that the men were only pretending.

"The bottles they're breaking are made of sugar," Libby assured him. "They don't hurt anyone."

"And the blood isn't real either," his mother said. "You know about fake blood, Danny."

"It's like ketchup, only they make it special," he said.

"Never hit your friends with anything," Sandra said. "What the men are doing is like a game. The chairs are made to come apart. They're hitting each other with Styrofoam, like that white stuff that came in the box with your tape player."

"Only colored brown," Danny said to show his understanding.

Craig was in the scene, scruffy-looking with his beard coming in darker than his mustache and hair. He was playing one of the battling poker players, not standing in for Wiley, who would enter at the end of the scene to restore order. Libby didn't think the brawl added anything to the story line, and cowering against a wall all day wasn't her idea of acting. She still thought Cassandra Rose should swing a few bottles herself.

She lost track of Danny and his mother, but she rather envied them their freedom. The staging was complicated, with all the stuntmen and bit players involved, and most of the men were sweating profusely. The set was rank and stifling, and the three saloon girls were little more than backdrop for the big fight.

Craig was busy in the center of the action, but even when

127

the camera wasn't rolling, he ignored her. Were his feelings hurt because she hadn't wanted to walk or ride with him? Libby wondered if she'd ever understand him.

Sandwiches and iced tea were served on the set, but all Libby wanted was some air that wasn't heavy with the odor of men's sweat.

Outside it was hot, and she was glad she wasn't going to be in Arizona long enough to get used to the dry, burning heat of the desert. Spotting a slice of shade beside the scenery dock, she wandered to it, staring at the barren sand and gritty pink buildings that made up the behind-the-scenes world of movie making at Old Buckhorn.

"Pretty hot out here." Craig stood twenty feet away, legs apart and hands on hips.

"You look like you're ready for a shootout." She watched him walking closer.

"No, just a little fresh air."

"You should be used to the scent of battle."

He shrugged. "It's a living. You're getting a nice tan."

Compared to his sun-bronzed face, hers was pallid.

"At least my burn has faded."

"I kinda like pink cheeks on you."

He was close now, as sweat-stained and deliberately grubby as any of the men inside, filling her nostrils with an intoxicatingly masculine musk. Instead of being repelled, she wanted to hug him close and feel the power of his arms around her.

"How are your bruises?" As a defense against her own feelings, she asked the question most likely to make him withdraw.

"You can see for yourself, if we ever get done with that mob scene inside."

"Your word is good enough for me."

128

"My arm looks worse than it feels. My knee feels worse than it looks." For him this was quite an admission.

"Maybe if you took a few days off . . ."

"Libby . . ."

"What?"

"We aren't gonna be here forever. Can we quit playing this game?"

His eyes held hers, and she parted her lips nervously.

"I'm not playing a game," she said softly, not meeting his gaze.

"The hell you're not! It's one I haven't seen before, and I sure don't know the rules, but you're playing something."

"I don't know what you *want* from me!"

"Don't you?" Disbelief was etched on his face, making him look weather-beaten and older.

The desire in his eyes mirrored her own feelings, and she averted her face, not wanting him to see the naked yearning she felt for him.

"Don't start something you can't finish, Craig."

"So, we're back to promises and guarantees again?"

"We should go back to work."

"They can't start without me." He ran his hard fingers under her chin, forcing her to look at him. "Give me a straight signal, Libby. Either yes, it's on, or no, it's off."

"If it's no?"

"I won't bother you anymore."

"And if it's yes?" She could hardly choke the words out.

"You know the answer to that." He turned and walked away.

Her head was pounding, and it took her last ounce of professionalism to return to the sound stage. The rest of the day was a nightmare. Of course, she wanted Craig, but not after he'd delivered his ultimatum. He was so unfair, wanting things his way or not at all. Did he expect her to be on his

129

doorstep at nine P.M., all powdered and perfumed and ready to hop into his bed? He was a throwback to the days of the frontier. A hundred years ago men like him probably raped Indian squaws and stole the wives of Mexican landowners. Didn't he realize that women weren't chattel anymore? She didn't exist to give him a good time. She had an interesting life of her own that didn't include him.

Interesting! Of all the bland, nondescript words to apply to her own life, this was the worst. She couldn't even remember how it had felt to be Libby Sloan before meeting Craig Wicklow.

The mock fight that went on all around her that afternoon was tame compared to the battle in her mind. Craig set up barriers, not letting her get close to him as a person, at the same time inflaming her senses and seducing her with his overpowering masculinity. She wanted to be alone to sort out what she felt. Raw sexuality was second nature to Craig, but to her it was novel and confusing and more than a little frightening.

Danny insisted on eating dinner with her, and again Craig refused to join them. Sharing this normal, happy time with Sandra and her son was an interlude of sanity after a day spent in the midst of crashing chairs and flying fists. She still didn't know how everyone got through the brawl without injuries. Even close up, it looked as if the stuntmen were really hitting each other, and when Craig went flying over the bar, she was sure he'd be hurt again. This was definitely her first, last, and only Western. She told Sandra this.

"They grow on you," she said, laughing. "Look on the bright side. The men do most of the work, and you don't have to take your clothes off in front of the camera. I've made over twenty action flicks, and an infected hangnail was my worst injury."

"I don't know," Libby said doubtfully. "You have more faith in the stunt coordinator than I do."

"Bert's the best. I've worked with a few who aren't nearly as cautious or clever as he is. He only hires top men like Craig."

"Will Craig take me for a ride on a horse, Mom?" Danny could seemingly ignore a long conversation and still catch anything that interested him.

"I don't know, honey. You'd better not plan on it. The horses are just for the cowboys to ride."

"I'm a cowboy," he insisted, plopping on the straw hat his mother had made him remove for dinner.

"You're a great cowboy," she agreed, "and maybe Libby will take you to see the horses tomorrow while I'm working."

"You can count on it, pardner," Libby said.

She knew what she would tell Craig if he came to her that evening. Nervously fretting in her trailer, she did her nails and wrote hasty notes to her parents and her brothers' families. Waiting was almost as hard as facing him would be.

He didn't come, and she hated him for agitating her. Why give her an ultimatum if he didn't intend to hear her answer? Why let her build up courage if he didn't intend to confront her? Anger kept her awake long past midnight, but no one knocked on her door.

CHAPTER EIGHT

"I need to get away from this place. Come into town with me tonight." A red-eyed, weary-looking Craig cornered Libby at lunch.

"What town?"

"Does it matter?" He scratched his thickly bristled chin.

She shrugged. "Does your beard itch?"

"Yes, and I've got a blister on my heel. Otherwise I'm sound as a dollar."

"No one says 'sound as a dollar' anymore."

"Yes or no, Libby?"

"I'd like to get away from here for a while."

"Damn it, you're still doing it!"

"What?"

"Sending fuzzy signals! You can't say a simple yes. That'd be admitting you want to be with me! You have to make it sound like you'd just like a change of scenery."

"What do you think you do? Forget it! I don't want to be with you."

"A minute ago you did!"

"That was before you started yelling at me," she said, lowering her voice to a whisper, conscious that they weren't alone.

"I've got the company wagon lined up. We'll leave at six and have supper in a little town about an hour from here."

"Why do you bother to ask me? You don't listen to my answer!"

"Which one? I can't stand here all day waiting for you to make up your mind."

"I have made up my mind," she said firmly, walking away from the dining room so no one else would hear what she'd intended to tell him the night before.

He followed, stopping when she did. "Well?"

"I like you." That was an understatement.

"Thanks a lot," he said wryly.

"But I can't do things the way you do."

"What things?"

"I want to be your friend. I'd like to go tonight, but I don't want to go to bed with you."

"You're saying no sex?"

"Yes."

"Hell, I was only gonna buy you a hamburger anyway. Be ready at six." He tousled her hair, making her feel like a pet Pekingese, and left.

Craig never did what she expected! Sometimes he melted her resistance; other times, like today, he was as kind and indulgent as a big brother. Could she trust him when he wasn't making demands or issuing ultimatums?

Mule Creek started as a watering hole and never progressed much beyond that, seemingly in existence only to sell gas and hamburgers. Unlike Old Buckhorn, it didn't have any kind of sidewalks, only strips of hard-packed dirt and a few random slabs of blacktop.

"How do people make a living here?" Libby asked, sitting across from Craig in a wooden booth in the Longshot Café.

"I imagine they just get by." He didn't seem too interested.

"Every town has some economic base."

133

"There's an Indian reservation nearby. Maybe they do a little trading. What do you want to eat?"

She glanced over a one-page typed menu in a plastic holder. Next to each item at least three price changes were penciled in.

"We know what their prices were in 1970," she said.

"All I promised was a burger."

She thought he was overplaying the part of the laconic cowboy.

"I'll try a garden burger."

"Drink?" he asked.

"Coffee."

"Too much makes you jittery. Better have milk."

"I don't like milk."

"Do you like leg cramps?"

The waitress had a tiny pug nose and cheeks rouged to look like two apples. She was either an early-blooming twelve-year-old or a painfully shy teenager. Craig's pleasantries gave her a bad case of nervous giggles.

"You scared her half to death," Libby said when the girl scooted off to place their order.

"She's just discovered that men are men." He grinned, studying Libby intently with half-hooded eyes.

"I can't believe you said that!"

"Just because you're not interested in me doesn't mean—"

"Oh, stop it! I know what you're doing."

"What am I doing?" He was wearing a black shirt open at the throat. All he needed was a suede vest to double for Wiley on camera.

He was confusing her, making her feel like a schoolgirl with a mad crush on a movie idol, but she couldn't tell him that.

"You're trying to make me feel guilty," she said instead.

"Guilty of what?"

"Not being suitably appreciative of this meal you're buying me." She gestured at the nearly empty café, the tables covered with black-and-white oilcloth and the chairs an odd assortment of "early attic." They were sitting in one of only three booths, and she couldn't find a place to put her legs without touching his.

An older woman who had to be their waitress's mother brought Craig's beer, a dark-brown draft in a glass mug. Craig went out of his way to be cordial to the mother, sending her away with a broad grin bunching up her cheeks.

"Why did you want to come here?" Libby asked.

"I didn't especially. I found it on a map. Didn't think there'd be many crowds in a town called Mule Creek."

"You don't like crowds?"

"Do you want me to say I wanted to be alone with you?"

A familiar warmth made her feel vulnerable.

"I meant what I said, Craig. I don't want to—"

"Yeah, I believe you."

Her hamburger came on a platter big enough for a Thanksgiving turkey, the oversize bun crowded by finger-thick potato sticks deep-fried without peeling the skins. Craig's double burger was about six inches high, and she wondered how he'd tackle it. Surprisingly he took small bites, chewing them thoroughly, paying more attention to her than his food.

"Tell me about your Broadway play," he said.

"It's about a tenth class reunion. The leads went together in high school, and now they're both divorced."

"And they want to get something started again?"

"They give it a try."

"But the old magic isn't there?"

She wasn't sure whether he was poking fun at the play or her.

"No."

"Sounds like it's been done before."

"It's almost as original as *Freedom Gulch*!"

"Good point!" He laughed. "What part do you play?"

"One of the classmates on the reunion committee."

"Many lines?" He drained his beer mug.

"No, but I'll take anything I can get on Broadway. What will you do after this?"

"Go back to L.A. and see what turns up."

"Do you visit your family in Texas very often?"

"Once in a while."

"What do your parents do?"

"My mother's a postmistress. My father runs a livestock auction. He could retire, but he wouldn't know what to do with himself."

Craig usually avoided personal questions, so she was pleased to hear him talk about his parents.

"Were they surprised when you became a stuntman?"

"Not much, I guess. What about your family?"

"My parents are retired in Florida. My brothers still live in Syracuse."

"How old are you?"

"Twenty-eight." She felt strange, answering such a basic question after all that had happened between them.

"I'm thirty-three." He motioned to the waitress to refill his beer mug.

"You told me the first time we met."

"Maybe I came on a little too strong," he mused.

"A little!" She sipped her water, ignoring the tall glass of milk he'd ordered for her.

"No dessert if you don't drink your milk." He grinned, but he wasn't teasing.

"Do you always rush the first woman you see on location?"

"I got here a couple of weeks before you."

"That's no answer!"

Her water glass was empty, and the olives in the garden

136

burger made her thirsty. The older waitress brought another mug of beer for Craig, and Libby pushed the glass toward her.

"Could I have some more water, please?"

"Never mind," Craig told the waitress. "She can drink her milk."

"That was embarrassing!" Libby hissed. "You can't treat me like a baby."

"You don't want to be treated like a woman."

"Just because I'm not swooning at your feet—available when you wiggle your little finger . . ."

"You just can't handle that three-letter word, can you?"

"Did you ever, just once, stop to think that it might be you?"

"That you can't handle?" He took a long swallow of beer, draining half the glass and leaving a trace of foam on his mustache.

The urge to lick away the tiny bubbles above his lip made her mind go blank. He wiped them away himself on a paper napkin, not taking his eyes from her face.

"The film isn't in the can yet," he said, reverting to his deepest drawl.

"My part is nearly done."

"I checked the schedule. You'll be here until the end. So will I."

The end of the movie would be the end of them. Thinking about it was so dismal, she drank some milk without thinking.

"Good girl," he said softly, momentarily dazzling her with a smile that turned his eyes into deep green pools. "I still think we could do a lot for each other."

What he was doing to her now should be illegal! Every nerve in her body was standing at attention. She curled her fists into a ball on the lap of her white cotton skirt and groped for something to say that would break the spell he was casting. He was deliberately trying to make her regret refusing him, and he succeeded with only the effort it took to twist his lips into an omniscient smile. He knew she was fighting herself.

"If you're done, I'm ready to go," she managed to say.

"I'm through eating." His tone warned that he wasn't through with her.

In profile his face was somber, the high cheekbones accentuated by lean cheeks and jaw. In the twilight his beard looked like a shadow on the lower part of his face, and she wondered if it was long enough to be soft.

This stretch of road was deserted, cutting through largely uninhabited scrubland with only an occasional solitary, tile-roofed house to be seen. A sign with the name of a ranch burned in the wood marked a trail to the right, but Craig kept going straight ahead, driving at a moderate speed, once in a while making a remark about something inconsequential. Libby was getting a little tired of the strong-silent-hero side of his personality.

"How long have you been divorced?" she asked impulsively.

"Some years."

"That's not an answer."

"I don't keep track like it's some kind of anniversary," he said impatiently.

"You must know whether it's been two years, six years, ten years!"

"It's been about five. Why does it matter?"

"I suppose it doesn't."

He made her feel like an intruder prying into his private life, but a compelling need to know more about him made her ignore his reluctance.

"That's about the time you met Sandra, isn't it?"

"I think we did a picture together shortly afterward."

"She said you and her husband were good friends."

"I suppose we were. I only knew him for a couple of years. Why dig up the past?"

"I didn't know yours was classified information!"

"Don't get huffy." He reached over and squeezed her thigh, more a diversionary action than a sexual one. "You have nice legs."

"So do you," she said dryly, pushing his hand away.

"I had no idea you'd noticed."

"It seemed polite to say so."

After a silence that seemed long to her, she said, "I've never been married."

He laughed.

"Why is that funny?"

"Thinking you had to tell me is funny."

"You don't know much about me. You don't want to!"

"That's not true."

"It is! If you knew me as a person, you'd see me as something besides . . ."

"A sex object?" His voice was expressionless.

"Yes!"

He took a deep breath, and his knuckles went white on the steering wheel.

"That's some opinion you have of me," he said.

"Isn't that what you want me to think?"

His silence angered her more than any answer could.

"You only like mock fights," she accused him.

The car skidded onto the shoulder of the road so abruptly that sand billowed against the windows, but Craig was in control, braking to a stop and turning off the motor.

"Why did you stop?" she asked angrily.

"Libby, what are you trying to prove?" He turned sideways on the seat, switching on the dome light and staring her down with eyes as cold and forbidding as a northern forest.

"I'm trying to understand why you act the way you do."

"If I wanted to be analyzed, I'd pay a professional."

"I suppose that's not your style."

"Not at all. Let's not make things complicated, okay?"

"For me they already are," she said hesitantly.

"For me they're not!" he said a little too emphatically. "You're a beautiful woman. You have a fantastic body. I'd like to make love to you, but if you're not interested, I'll have to live with it."

Compliments had never sounded less flattering. At this moment she didn't even like him.

"Can we go now?" she asked quietly.

He started the car without answering, driving back to Old Buckhorn in silence.

Danny was becoming her best friend. They played games inside during the hot early-afternoon hours and built a truck from interlocking Lego pieces. His sitter had been wise, packing more games and toys than clothing for him to bring.

"Can we go see the horses now?" he asked, reminding her for at least the twentieth time of her promise.

"Sure, let's do it, pardner," she said, deciding she might as well get it over with.

The stuntmen were shooting outdoors today, but there might be a few horses left for Danny to see. Wiley was working inside, so old Sneaky Pete should be in his stall.

The walk to the corral seemed exceptionally long today, but it wasn't Danny who was sapping her energy. She just wanted to go home to New York and forget she'd ever met Craig Wicklow.

"Remember," she warned her overly eager companion, "the horses are just for the cowboys. I can't give you a ride."

"I know," he said impatiently, climbing up and down on a section of corral fence just for the fun of it.

The crude but clean barn was silent, but she was right about Sneaky Pete. He was one of several horses left behind.

"Here's my favorite," she said. "Sneaky Pete."

She patted the horse's face and lifted Danny to do the same, letting him feed the animal an apple he'd saved from lunch. The big teeth that took the fruity offering scared her just a little, but Danny was enthralled.

"He likes it," he said with awe.

"Sure he does. You picked the best one, didn't you?"

"I wish he had his saddle on."

"Well, horses only wear saddles when they're going someplace. We'd both be in big trouble if we tried to ride Sneaky Pete."

"I could ride him alone."

"Sorry, honey. Only big cowboys can ride here."

They both turned to look when a man leading a horse came into the stable.

"Craig! Hi, Craig." Danny raced toward him before Libby could stop him.

"Craig, can I ride Sneaky Pete? Will you take me for a ride?"

"Sorry, I can't do that, Danny." He led the pinto to its stall and shooed the boy away, seemingly oblivious of his disappointment

Danny insisted on hanging over the gate of the stall while Craig unsaddled the horse.

"I didn't know you were a wrangler. Won't some union object if you do the work of one?" she asked.

He flashed an impatient glance over his shoulder. "I wouldn't ride an animal if I didn't know how to take care of it."

"Of course not!"

It was all she could do to keep Danny from plunging head-first into the stall.

"Get down before you fall," Craig ordered.

Danny obeyed immediately, but his face was puckered with disappointment.

The head wrangler came through the door, talking to a man leading another horse. Apparently Libby's timing had been bad. A group of hot, weary men descended on the barn, bringing their mounts back. Danny left without protest, quietly agreeing to watch the return of the horses from a perch on the corral fence. Libby felt as disappointed as the boy looked. Craig could have shown him some small kindness! Just sitting on a horse's back for a few minutes would have been a tremendous thrill for the boy.

Anger stayed with her through the dinner hour, which she spent recapping the day's activities for Sandra. Libby didn't mention Craig's rejection of Danny to his mother, but she thought of little else. At the first opportunity she was going to tell him what she thought of the way he'd treated Danny.

Leaving her door open, she finally saw Craig walking toward his trailer. She stood in her doorway and waved to him.

"Can I talk to you?"

"You don't need an appointment," he said in his usual lazy drawl, smiling easily.

She backed up and let him enter, confronting him immediately.

"You were mean to Danny!"

"Mean? What was I supposed to do, let a horse trample him?"

He slammed the door shut behind him, standing three feet away and regarding her with barely contained hostility.

"What would it hurt to give him a short ride on a horse?"

"They're not my horses!"

"You use them whenever you feel like it."

"Riding myself is different."

"You took me out on one, and I'm a terrible rider."

"You're an adult."

"You just don't want to have anything to do with Danny!"

"Be reasonable, Libby. I can't be responsible for the kid. Horses are unpredictable. What if he got hurt?"

"How could he get hurt if you were holding him?"

"You don't understand about insurance. There are rules."

"I don't think that has a thing to do with it. You just don't like Danny."

"That's ridiculous! Why wouldn't I like a little kid?"

"I don't know, but you go out of your way to avoid him."

"Now you're being silly. Just because I don't want to be a surrogate father . . ."

"His father was a friend of yours. You could at least be nice to him."

"And have him following me all over like a homeless puppy? What happens when the movie's over? Do you want me to marry Sandra so I can play daddy?"

"Marry anyone you like! I just think you're mean to Danny!"

"You don't know what mean is!"

"I imagine you could show me!" She backed away a step.

"No, you're not my responsibility either!"

"You don't care about anyone but yourself!"

His face had the shocked look of a man who's just been slapped, and he seemed to shrink a little in front of her eyes.

"Is that what you really think?" His voice was chillingly quiet.

"I don't know what to think when you treat Danny—"

"Forget Danny! I don't think we're arguing about him."

She backed up two more steps, realizing that the open door of the bedroom was just behind her.

"I don't want to argue about anything, but it wouldn't hurt you to give a little boy—"

"Libby!"

143

He said her name so harshly, she hardly recognized it.

"Don't . . ." she whispered, not knowing what it was she didn't want him to do.

She was in his arms without knowing how it happened, dizzy with excitement. He covered her mouth, overwhelming her until she clung to him, feeling as though a blast of desert air were stealing the air in her lungs.

The force of his kisses carried her backward into the bedroom, and she dug her fingers into his shoulders, forgetting Danny and horses and angry words. No one had ever aroused her the way Craig did, his arms holding her now with a strength great enough to keep a rein on his own savagery.

Their anger was spent in grasping caresses and punishing kisses, until nothing existed but a clamoring need that sent them sprawling on the bed, locked in each other's arms. She bared her breasts for him, tearing a buttonhole on her blouse, touching her own nipple to offer it.

His knee was between her legs, his lips on her throat, and she wrapped her arms around the hard, sinewy muscles of his back, losing her own identity as a storm of passion demolished her will.

A flash of insight told her this was her own doing as much as his, but she was beyond the point where she wanted to control herself. Everything about him felt so good; his still-prickly beard, the compactness of his body, his urgent caresses, his arousal pressing against her. As she reached for him, her nails scraped on heavy denim. The metal button at his waist came loose under her groping, but when she tried to force the heavy zipper downward, it stuck.

His hand covered hers, and he rolled to the floor with a gasp of agony.

"We can't do this here." He groaned, slumping like a man who's just been punched in the stomach.

"Craig?" She was stunned by his sudden withdrawal.

He pulled himself to the edge of the bed, sitting with his back to her and his head drooping.

"What're you thinking of?" He sounded angry, and she didn't know why.

"Nothing." Nothing but him, she meant.

"You can't possibly be as naive as you act! Are you trying to get pregnant?"

"No, of course not. I just didn't think . . ."

"I have no intention of becoming a father." He stood and secured his jeans, not looking at her, buttoning and tucking in his shirt like a fireman answering an alarm. "Come back to my place."

If he'd faced her, if he hadn't sounded so mad, she would have gone.

"No," she said quietly.

"More mixed signals?" he asked sardonically.

"Not intentionally." She covered herself with the blouse.

"That makes it all right?" He did look at her then, but there was no warmth in his face.

"I'm sorry." She was expressing her regret, not apologizing. "I shouldn't have said anything about Danny."

"You're making a big thing out of nothing," he said, sounding less sure of himself.

"I won't mention it again."

"Thank you."

For an instant she read something new on his face, but it vanished before she could guess what his strange expression meant. He paused, looked down at her, then left without another word.

Nothing like that had ever happened to her before. She didn't know whether to feel embarrassed, relieved, or astonished. Sitting motionless, waiting for the trembling to stop and her pulse rate to slow, she was staggered, more than anything else. She couldn't explain or justify the way Craig made her act. Hopeless frustration was all she felt at the moment.

Why was he so tense about children? Did he have a family somewhere he'd deserted? Sandy would know something that important, and she'd never even hinted at it.

Lying on her back on the bed, Libby pressed her palms on her stomach, wondering how it would feel to swell with new life, to have a tiny human with fluttery legs and arms inside her body. She adored children, but giving birth was always something she envisioned for the future. First she had to find a special person, the phantom man she'd tried to conjure up in a dry wishing-well. Sometimes she thought Craig might be the one, but she couldn't let herself love a man who disliked children.

She knew so little about him. He worked hard, had friends, showed consideration in small things, and made her feel fantastically erotic. On the flip side, he was unwilling to share his feelings or accept her as a person. He was also handsome, seductive, and self-assured, but, in his case, she wasn't sure if these were assets.

Sandra said he liked "fluffs," women who were pretty but certainly not demanding. Imagining Craig with another woman caused her unbearable pain. She hoped he wouldn't find someone before she left.

"Oh, Craig!" She said his name aloud in angry frustration, wishing she could erase him from her mind this very minute, wishing even more that he were beside her.

CHAPTER NINE

Poised on the bottom step of the saloon staircase, Libby looked woefully at Wiley, who expectantly returned her gaze, waiting for her to say something. The cameras were rolling, it was their umpteenth take, and Libby's mind was a total blank. She couldn't remember her line!

"Cut! Take ten," the director yelled.

Seventeen actors and extras relaxed, some wandering off for a smoke, others sitting down to rest. Libby felt frozen on the step, waiting for a reprimand that she thoroughly deserved. This had been the worst morning of her career. On a day when practically everyone was involved in her scene, she was doing a terrible job.

Carl didn't yell much, but when he walked in her direction, she knew his patience was exhausted.

"What seems to be the problem?" he asked.

"Just having an off day. I'm really sorry, Carl."

"Well, loosen up. We really need to wrap up this scene today. Do you have your line now?"

"Yes." It had come back as soon as the cameras stopped.

Leaving the set to get a drink of water, she caught a glimpse of Craig standing by one of the exits, looking in her direction. If he had nothing better to do than watch her make mistakes, why didn't he pay some attention to Danny? Seeing him brought out some of the anger that was seething deep inside her, but she didn't want to confront him again. The days since he'd walked angrily out of her trailer had done nothing to help her forget. When she looked away deliberately, he didn't approach her.

Everyone was in place, and she stood on the steps facing Wiley. He delivered her cue, and she responsed, but her words were about as exciting as wet newspaper.

"Cut!"

Please, let her never hear that word again! Movies were crazy! They didn't shoot things in order. Here she was, in the middle of the story, and they'd already filmed scenes that followed it.

"You're supposed to be mad, Libby!" Carl said sharply.

Any other time his tone would have lacerated her pride; today she just felt defeated and ashamed of her performance. The clapper was poised to record another take, when Craig walked up to Carl and said something she couldn't hear.

When the stuntman came over to her on the set in front of curious cast and crew members, she wanted to hide.

"Look," he whispered softly, "you're a professional. You're wasting too much time and money here. Do it right this time."

No director in the world could have called forth more of her anger than Craig did. On the next try she snapped off the lines to Wiley with more spirit than Cassandra Rose had shown in the whole film. This didn't change the way she felt about Craig's little pep talk. Everyone would think he'd pulled her strings. Or worse, they'd assume her poor showing had been due to a lovers' quarrel! When she was done for the day, she couldn't get away from the set quickly enough.

Sandra hadn't seen her terrible string of goofs; she and

Danny were the only ones Libby wanted to be with that evening.

The next day they had to redo one segment of an earlier scene because of a minor rewrite later in the movie. Libby would be on camera for less than a minute, doing a rowdy stomp with one of the saloon's customers when the sheriff came in and asked a question. For this bit of work she still had to go through hairstyling and makeup. Her partner in the dance was Gordon, still stung by her rejection, and he acted in a typical Eager Eddie way, shrewdly taking advantage and upstaging her for all he was worth. This didn't delay the shooting as much as her flubs had the day before, but it again brought her into disfavor with the director. Finally finishing, she'd never felt so unhappy with her work. Cassandra Rose was a potentially complex, sensitive character. Libby was sure her interpretation was as bland as three-day-old meat loaf.

She was alone in her little dressing room, removing her makeup and feeling very sorry for herself, when Craig came to her.

"Aren't you working today?" she asked, trying to sound casual.

"I've been at it since five A.M. If that's not working, I don't know what is."

"My mistake, I'm sorry," she said stiffly.

"Want to talk about it?"

"What?"

"Your part."

"There's nothing to say."

"Libby, up until the last couple of days you were doing a fantastic job."

This was the first time anyone had complimented her on her film work. She felt a little better in spite of her resentment toward Craig.

"Thank you. Movie making seems so chopped up. I don't know what I'm doing."

"The last scene I saw was lousy."

"Carl seemed satisfied."

"He doesn't have time to be dissatisfied, but you know you're letting down." He stood behind her, looking at her mirror image, the top of his head too high to be seen in the reflection.

"You're giving my confidence a wonderful boost."

"I shouldn't need to. You're good, and I think you know it."

Until the last few days she had thought her work was more than adequate for the TV Western.

"What do you want from me, Craig?"

"I don't want it on my conscience that I ruined a promising career."

She whirled around angrily, confused to see him smiling.

"You've got to relax," he said firmly.

"I don't know how."

"Let me help."

"I don't think so, Craig."

They couldn't be casual friends; the past weeks had proven that.

"We'll just talk about the part a little." As usual, he wasn't paying any attention to her objections.

Craig as a counselor was a person she hadn't met before. He waited outside while she changed into white shorts and a navy top, then walked with her back to her trailer. Sitting on one side of the kitchen booth while she sat on the other, he read through her remaining scenes, cueing her, making small jokes about the different characters.

"Have you seen Wiley on a horse yet?" he asked.

"Only sitting still, not riding."

"I shouldn't laugh. If he were good, I wouldn't work as much."

"How's your shoulder?"

"Fine. And my knee is as good as it gets." For once he sounded matter-of-fact instead of irritated.

"When are they doing your next scene?" he asked, after satisfying himself that she had a good grasp on the rest of her part.

"Thursday."

"I can switch my schedule around to be there."

"No, don't do that."

"I'm going to. It's my fault you got off track. I'm seeing that you finish like the pro you are."

No one had ever taken charge of her in quite this way, and she didn't know how to react.

"You might make me nervous."

"I won't be there to criticize, only to help if you need me."

"Craig . . ."

She couldn't tell him what she really needed: to know and understand him better. The way he was being right now, she'd choose him as her best friend any day. It was only when they tried to have a deeper relationship that everything went haywire.

True to his word, he was on the set, an interested spectator to another of her scenes. This time she didn't embarrass herself by flubbing lines or failing to follow directions. She felt more at peace with herself and more relaxed about her part. Craig hadn't said or done anything special to bring this about; he'd just been there. She didn't want to think about him much more until the film was finished. Another day of shooting and it would be all over. Instead of relief or regret Libby felt emptiness, as though seeing the last of Old Buckhorn would leave a great void.

Craig seemed to have slipped out of sight. After giving moral support when she needed it, he just eased himself out of her life. For several days she caught only glimpses of him, and they didn't speak.

A bit envious of Sandra because she had Danny, Libby left the two of them after dinner, deciding to take one more nostalgic walk through the Western town before dark. Now she had real memories to associate with the movie location; the dusty streets weren't peopled with ghosts anymore. If she could lay to rest one more haunting image, her wish at the well, maybe she could forget Old Buckhorn. The town was deserted; most of the company saw enough of it during the day. At best it was hot and dusty with no tall, cool drinks available in the mock saloons. Libby had it to herself, except in the corral where the head wrangler bedded down near his horses.

Her white tennis shoes got scuffy with dust, but the air was cool enough to feel good on her bare legs below a pair of red nylon running shorts. Her T-shirt was a souvenir of a summer internship with a stock company: Sister Lake's Playhouse.

The best place to watch the sun go down was the porch of the Paradise Hotel, but sitting there alone made her melancholy. Craig had said they could do a lot for each other. She believed him, but not in the way he'd meant it. His strength was like a magnet, attracting her against her will. But if they joined forces, combining his power and her intensity, they could be awesome. Why didn't he see how right they could be together?

This line of thinking did nothing for her peace of mind. Craig had never let her hope there could be anything for them together. His honesty was one of the things that intrigued her. He didn't lie because he felt no obligation to explain himself.

The sun disappeared behind the monster's head, the mountain that had jinxed Craig, and she realized she was seeing everything in relationship to him. He controlled the focus button in her mind, and images associated with him were sharper and clearer than all others. Without him in the picture, the view was fuzzy and blurred. She'd even lost her excitement over acting in a Broadway play.

Measured in terms of minutes, the day was nearly over; soon it would be dark. She wouldn't get lost again, but the town was too much a part of the desert for her to feel comfortable alone at night. Still she didn't leave. When she saw the solitary figure approaching, she knew why.

"Libby."

Craig stood in the middle of the street in his gunfighter's stance, the Stetson hiding most of the top of his face, thumbs hooked in his belt loops.

She wanted to say something trivial like "Surprised to see you here," but her tongue felt glued to the roof of her mouth. She nodded her head and watched him move toward her with long, lazy strides.

"I thought I'd find you here," he drawled.

The only truthful thing she could say was: "I was waiting for you." Instead she kept quiet.

"It's nearly dark," he added softly.

"I was just leaving." She stood to convince him that this was true.

"There's no hurry now." He stepped closer, leaning his arm on a post with only a few feet between them.

"Now that you're here to protect me, you mean?" she asked wryly, trying but failing to make the idea seem ludicrous.

"No, now that I'm here to be with you."

His voice sent little shivers down her spine.

"You were waiting for me, weren't you?" he asked.

"No!" The denial came automatically.

"How was your day?" It was a bland, conventional question, but he made it sound extraordinarily personal.

"I'm nearly done."

"Yes, we all are. Are you glad?"

"I've learned a lot, but I don't think movies are what I want to do."

"That's not what I asked." His voice was mildly mocking.

"Of course, I'll be glad to get home," she said defensively.

"Tell me about home." He put one foot on the raised boardwalk and leaned on his knee.

"Everyone knows about New York City."

"I don't."

"You've never been there?"

"I've passed through the airport a couple of times going on location, that's all."

"You really should see it sometime."

"One big city is just like another, I guess. Noisy and crowded."

"But there's so much to do! The theater, first of all. Museums, concerts . . ."

"You." He stepped up beside her, his face masked by the wide hat-brim and a scraggly growth of beard.

"I'll be glad when you shave," she said impulsively, then remembered that she might never see him clean-shaven again.

"Will you? Why?"

"I didn't mean it that way. I just meant that you look better without it."

"Do I?" he asked indifferently. "It's getting soft."

He took her fingers and guided them to his face, forcing her to feel the springy, almost downy, growth.

She pulled her hand away but not before reacting to the lean firmness of his cheek.

"It really will be a good thing when you shave."

"Good for whom?"

His question hit a sensitive spot. Of course, he'd had women in the past, and he'd find others, maybe even one special lady, in the future. She wouldn't be the one to enjoy

154

his freshly shaven cheeks, fragrant with a splash of the spicy aftershave he sometimes wore.

"For yourself, I suppose," she said sharply.

"I'm only sorry I can't get rid of it right now—for you."

"Craig, you know how I feel."

"No, I only know how you say you feel." He rested his hand on the side of her throat, caressing her ear with one finger.

"Craig . . ."

"I've tried avoiding you. It doesn't work."

"I know," she admitted meekly.

"Libby . . ." He rested his chin on her head, touching the gold-tinged waves on her shoulders as though they were spun-glass angel hair, beautifully filmy but dangerous to handle.

His skin was sprinkled with golden hairs where the top buttons of his shirt gaped open, and she rubbed her hand over it, loving the grainy texture of the seductive warmth. Resting her palm over his heart, she counted the strong, rhythmic beats, feeling as though the pumping were keeping them both alive.

He was going to kiss her, and every second that passed made her more eager to feel his mouth close over hers. Tipping her head in anticipation, she wasn't disappointed. He nibbled at her lips, toying with their tenderness, then gnawing more hungrily, a strangled sound in his throat betraying his urgency. Every kiss in their pasts had been practice for this one.

Women sell their souls to the devil for lesser men; Libby wasn't sure what else Craig was, but he was her demon lover, starting something that had to be finished. Her thighs were throbbing as though she'd run a long race, and her whole body was straining to uncoil.

His kisses covered her face and throat, and nothing less

155

than an earthquake could tear her from his arms. He wasn't going to ask permission for anything tonight.

Lifting her in his arms, he carried her through the town that had seen so many staged dramas, but both of them were oblivious to it. Tonight they didn't need fantasy.

Clinging to his neck, nuzzling the hollow above his collarbone, she felt deliciously dizzy. The scent of his skin reminded her of well-oiled leather, strong yellow soap, and camping beside a mountain stream, and it seemed natural for him to carry her the length of the town, as though she weighed no more than an inflated plastic doll. His door wasn't locked, and he didn't put her down until he'd kicked it shut behind them.

"Now." He sounded as decisive as any general who ever gave an order to charge into battle, tossing aside his hat and gathering her against him.

"Now," she echoed, so filled with love that any other response would have been sheer hypocrisy.

His hands made lazy circles on her back, sliding under the T-shirt to massage the smooth skin of her back. Loosening her bra, he kept rubbing until she tingled, then slid his fingers beneath her elastic waistband to discover the fine, almost invisible hairs at the end of her spine. His touch on this feathery down was ticklishly light, but it sent waves of pleasure rippling through her.

Pulling her even closer, he kissed her with undisguised longing, slipping his tongue past the ridge of her teeth to caress the inside of her mouth.

From the bedroom the dim light of a small dresser lamp glowed enough to illuminate her beauty when he slowly peeled off her shirt. The unsnapped bra fell to the floor, revealing rosy brown nipples that grew hard under the gentle caress of his thumbs. He knelt in front of her, stripping off

156

her shorts and shoes, then slowly lowering her panties, trailing kisses from the crease of her leg to her knee.

She crushed his head against her, sliding to her knees into an embrace that took their breath away. The fine cotton of his shirt was soft against her breasts, but she wanted to feel his hair-roughened skin.

"Take off your clothes," she whispered.

"No, you do it."

He stood and led her to the bedroom, his face so softened by passion that, for a heart-stopping second, he seemed a total stranger. Her unsteady fingers fumbled with the buttons of the yellow plaid shirt.

"I once saw a magician steal a man's shirt without him knowing it," he mused, looking down on her efforts with emerald eyes, the intensity not shadowed by his long lashes.

Running her hands over his shoulders, she pushed the garment to the floor, marveling at the perfect form of his upper body. Gently touching the bruises still visible on one arm, she bent her head and kissed the inside of his elbow, following the curve of his bicep with eager little kisses, nipping the softer skin on the underside of his arm until he lifted it, letting her finger the long, silky hairs underneath his arm.

"How many ribs do you have?" she teased softly, pretending to bite his side.

"The standard number." His voice was hoarse as she opened the top of his jeans, pulling down the zipper with difficulty.

The jeans stuck on the top of his boots, and she insisted on pulling off the stiff leather footwear, turning her back to brace herself and tug. She'd never suspected undressing a cowboy was such hard work.

"There," she said, dropping his last sock, collapsing against him as he rose to take her in his arms.

His beard tickled her face, and the silky hairs on his chest gave her goose bumps as she rubbed against them, tucking one knee between his legs.

"Aren't you forgetting something?" he murmured.

"Pardner, this is a stickup," she said teasingly, poking her finger at his navel. "Drop your drawers."

"You've been watching too many Westerns." He took her in his arms, flicking his tongue over her eyelids, kissing each as he filled his hands with her warm mounds.

"You're asking for a showdown," she warned him.

"Maybe." He kissed her soundly, then held her away at arm's length. "You're so beautiful, so special."

Earnestness wasn't what she had expected from him, and his smile melted her heart. He buried his face in her hair for a moment, then turned his back to slip out of his shorts and yank the bedspread and covers into a heap on the floor.

Taking her hand, he led her to the bed, lying beside her and drawing her into his arms with so much tenderness that her eyes grew misty remembering the night he'd been hurt.

Time after time she was sure their lovemaking would soar to a conclusion, but Craig seemed never to tire of caressing her body, savoring the salty-sweet tang of her skin and exploring the center of her femininity. She learned that the lightest stroking under his arms tickled him and that bumping his knee caused him pain. He taught her to caress the places that stirred him erotically and made her tell him what gave her the greatest pleasure. His patience and caring was a constant revelation, warming her inwardly and outwardly. Only once did he spoil the mood.

"I told you we could do a lot for each other," he said.

"No one likes an I-told-you-so!" She pinched his hip and was punished with a hard kiss.

Weak with anticipation she felt secure and cared for when he took precautions.

The void was gone; he totally filled it, leading her on a path to the stars. Their frenzied rocking was like another storm, this one contained within the metal shell of their shelter, and through it his breathless endearments made her feel wonderfully cherished. For a long, naked, dazzling moment they knew each other completely.

Sometime in the night he opened the window, letting the desert air blow over their bodies, coaxing her to sleepy awareness, then wide-awake exhilaration. Being apart from him was unbearable. She couldn't live without the throbbing, coursing excitement he generated. The pursuit of giving him pleasure and pleasing herself were inseparable. Even the little tingling ache that remained was a pleasurable reminder of having been loved long and well.

When they awoke again, it was the dawn of their last day. Craig groaned sheepishly, a lover conscious of overindulgence but still far from satiated.

"Bert will have my hide if I'm late this morning," he murmured against her ear, fingering a lock of silky hair.

"Do you plan to be late?" She teased his navel with the tip of her little finger, keeping her mind blank to preserve the wonderful feeling of well-being.

"Will you write him an excuse?"

"No, but I'll give you one."

He led her to an armless rocking chair, one of the few homey touches in the impersonal trailer, taking her on his lap facing him. There, with her head on his chest and her hands delighting in his wonderful muscles, they rocked their way to a trembling, bittersweet climax.

"What plane are you taking?" he asked.

"It leaves about nine tonight."

"A night flight," he said morosely.

She'd been in such a hurry to get back to New York that she'd booked the first available flight. Now she couldn't remember why. Clinging to him, she knew he could keep her from taking that plane, but he was silent, as uncommitted as ever.

Knowing this was all they'd ever have didn't make her accept it. He stirred, thinking now of going to work, but she couldn't let him go, not yet, not after all that had happened during the night.

"Will we ever see each other again?" she asked.

"It's a small world." He stood, shaking her off as easily as he would a pesky kitten that was napping on his lap.

As if to compensate for his flip answer, he patted her bottom and kissed her lightly on the cheek. "You're one terrific woman."

She didn't take his remark as a compliment. It was the wrong time to tell her she was good in bed.

There was little for her to do, but she had to be in costume to be shot in a group scene, her last in the movie. Wandering off when a break was called, she saw Danny standing by the steps in the adobe village, the ones Craig had tumbled down so often in gunfights. It wasn't until she got close that she saw Craig, but he didn't see her.

"Can I fall down the steps?" Danny was asking him.

"Don't try it. You'll get hurt," the stuntman warned sternly.

"You do it." Danny was never easily dissuaded.

"I'm bigger than you, and I know how. Terry!" He yelled at another stuntman on the other side of the square.

"Do you want me?" The younger man was as scruffy as Craig, with a patch of stubble on his face.

"Take the kid off my hands," Craig said in a voice low enough so Danny couldn't hear.

Libby did hear.

There were so many good-byes to be said that Libby didn't have time for dinner. Now she was packed and ready to leave, one of several people scheduled to leave that evening. Only one good-bye remained to be said.

Craig found her alone, putting a few last-minute things in her suitcase.

"How long before you leave?"

His face betrayed him; he really wanted to know whether there was time for a quickie before she left.

"Almost immediately."

"I thought you weren't leaving for another hour."

"I have some more packing to do."

He looked at her pile of luggage. "I see. Well, good luck on Broadway."

"Thank you."

"I'm glad you were here."

"I was a big help licking envelopes, wasn't I?"

"That wasn't quite what I meant."

"I know it wasn't."

"It is a small world," he said.

"I guess so."

"Have a good flight."

"Thank you."

"Good-bye, Libby." He bent his head and kissed her, catching only the corner of her lips because she turned her head.

"I could load your suitcases in the station wagon for you."

"I wouldn't want the union filing a grievance against you."

He shrugged. "I guess you don't need me to carry them."

"Good-bye, Craig."

He looked uncertain for a moment, then pulled her into his arms and kissed her again, this time right on target with quite a bit of gusto.

"You'd better go," Libby said miserably.

He looked at her for a long moment, then left.

* * *

The saguaros looked like primitive candelabras, black against the shadowed hills of late evening. Taking a night flight was inconvenient with tedious stopovers, but she'd booked it expecting to be eager to get home. Two other cast members were being driven to the airport, in the same car, by a crew member who seemed to enjoy the job, chattering easily with the two men who'd played the murderers in the movie. They politely tried to include her in their conversation, but she didn't care who was leading the National League.

What had she expected from Craig? Their affair had no place to go; he'd never suggested they be more than casual lovers. He'd never mentioned love, not even when their lovemaking reached the height of intensity. She certainly couldn't claim he'd deceived her.

Getting to the airport was a relief; boarding the plane was a welcome escape from an alien climate with bizarre vegetation and painful memories. The key to forgetting Craig was returning to her normal life. Libby was sure the spell would wane once she put enough distance between them. A cowboy! She'd never been at all attracted to the pseudo-western men who'd roamed the streets of New York when boots and cowboy clothes were a fad. Nothing could be more illogical than trying to rearrange her life to include a reckless stuntman. She had a part in a Broadway play waiting for her.

Safely in the air, hoping the trip would be smooth and storm-free, she let herself think about the good times with Craig. The memory of hiding from him in the livery stable still brought a little stab of excitement, and she'd never forget his thrilling, sensuous lovemaking. Knowing there was no future for them added a bittersweet poignancy for the short time they'd been together, but she had to be brutally honest with herself. Not until Craig let her go tonight had she really

162

believed their parting would be so emotionless, so final. When he said good-bye, he'd killed her hope.

Before she got home, her sadness was mixed with anger. Craig was selfish. He wouldn't even spare a few minutes for a fatherless little boy who idolized him. It wasn't surprising that he let her leave without any signs of affection or regret. She was the one who'd made the serious mistake, hoping for more than Craig was prepared to offer.

Their careers alone were enough to doom any relationship. His base of operations was Los Angeles; his agent, his opportunities, and his interests were there. She was more determined than ever to succeed in the theater. Movie making was profitable but not what she wanted. Sandra seemed to like the rough-and-tumble, chase-and-shoot type of film, but it didn't hold much appeal for Libby. Even with rubber bullets and fake fights, it seemed like a hazardous life for actors and stuntmen. Being a starlet was equally unappealing, and R-rated movies weren't for her. She was firmly rooted in the East, and long-distance love affairs were usually more painful than successful. She should be congratulating herself on a narrow escape! That's what her head told her all the way home, through three changes of planes.

Nonetheless, her heart was hurting. She might mean nothing to the stuntman, but Cupid was a careless little devil. If pain was any indication, she had an arrow firmly embedded in a very sensitive spot. She was very much afraid she was in love with Craig Wicklow.

CHAPTER TEN

Rehearsals for *Most Likely to Succeed* began on a note of quiet optimism; everyone hoped they had a winner, a meaningful contemporary drama. Libby wanted it as much as anyone, but she kept hearing Craig's words: "It's been done before." In fact, his laconic remarks on all kinds of subjects seemed to pop into her mind with disturbing frequency.

The biggest criticism she had of the play was that it didn't excite her; she could say the same thing about her life since her return from Old Buckhorn. The little things that used to be fun were flat: she felt silly eating a dill pickle on the street, and her favorite fruit-seller had retired and turned the business over to his son. The Labor Day party was canceled; her friends were too busy with their careers or too involved with their personal lives to carry out a tradition started in acting school. Her days were full, but her thoughts were disquieting. Craig didn't fade into the backdrop of her life; instead, whenever she was alone, he was with her in spirit.

Still counting on time to make the hurt go away, she kept frantically busy. For the first time since she'd moved to New York she could afford to do something with her small studio apartment, a third-floor walk-up where she lived alone. After rehearsals she would paint her apartment and her Salvation

Army furniture, but no amount of redecorating in the world could make her feel happy. She still wasn't over Craig.

She could call him, but what would it accomplish? The first week home she'd gone as far as getting his phone number from the information operator in Los Angeles. It was still on her message board in the little alcove that served as a kitchen, held in place by a ladybug magnet. She'd looked at it enough times to memorize it but had never even dialed the area code. There was no reason to suppose Craig wanted to talk to her. Even if he was congenial and pleasant, what could she say to him? Wild professions of love would only embarrass both of them.

Cool and sunny with just a touch of early gold in the trees, it was a day to be outside. She put on persimmon wool slacks, pleated at the waist and tapered at her ankles, a white broadcloth blouse, and a long, pocketed, Shetland wool sweater, the cobalt-blue making her eyes look vivid. She'd take a long, long walk, then drop in on a friend or see a double feature, anything but sit around moping over a man who might, after all, be entirely different from how she saw him in her fantasies.

Old Buckhorn seemed far away; she could hardly remember the dazzle of the sun on weathered wooden buildings or the deep violet shadows of sundown. Someday, she fervently hoped, memories of Craig's long, lean body and his lazy, taunting smile would seem just as distant.

Grabbing her everyday camel-colored shoulder bag, she checked to be sure her key, money, and other essentials for a day-long jaunt were in place. On her way out the phone rang, but she almost didn't answer it. On the fifth ring she relented; her parents liked to call on Sunday, and they'd try all day if she didn't answer now.

"Hello," she thrilled cheerfully, knowing from experience that her mother would turn into a combination investigative-

165

reporter-psychiatric-counselor if she detected a note of unhappiness in her only daughter's voice.

"Hello. You sound happy today."

She didn't need to hear a name to identify that easy drawl.

"Craig!"

"How are you, Libby?"

"Fine. Are you calling from L.A.?"

Her heartbeat was racing, and she felt like a schoolgirl getting her first call from a boy.

"No, I'm here at Howard Johnson's."

She had a wild, fantastic hope that he'd come to see her, but it was dashed a moment later when he said, "I'm on my way to Spain."

"On vacation?" She wasn't a good enough actress to keep the disappointment out of her voice.

"No, I'm playing the lead in a spaghetti Western."

"Well, that's nice for you. An acting job."

"The voice will be dubbed in. I'll be doing what I always do."

"It's a boost for your career, anyway."

He laughed softly, a familiar throaty sound with the same tingling effect it had always had on her. "I kinda doubt that, but the money's good. I didn't call to talk about my job. Are you free today?"

He could have called ahead of time; it would be his own fault if she said no. But if she didn't see him now, the chance might be gone forever.

"Yes, I can be."

"Maybe you can show me a little of this big city you were bragging about."

"What would you like to see?"

"You, mostly. I'll come over, and we'll talk about it."

She knew what the chances of talking were if he came to her apartment.

"I have an errand. Why don't I meet you?"

"How about lunch? Tell me where."

"All right. Do you like Chinese?"

"Not much. I like to know what I'm eating—not have it all mixed together."

"A steak house?"

"Sounds good."

"I know of one." She gave him the name and location of a nice place where she'd gone with a date once. "About an hour?"

"See you then."

She didn't plan to change clothes, so the only purpose of the hour's delay was to show him she wasn't available on a moment's notice. It also gave her time to develop a severe case of jitters over seeing him again. He couldn't possibly be as devastating as her memories of him. She'd see him, be disappointed, and be able to get on with her life without constantly thinking about him. There was nothing romantic about loving the wrong man.

He was waiting at the bar in the lounge, his suede jacket, jeans, and boots looking right at home with the restaurant's western decor. Standing with one foot on a brass rail, his elbow leaning on the mahogany bar, he could've been on the movie set at Old Buckhorn. Two men in business suits looked overdressed and insignificant beside him.

When he saw her by the door, he drained his draft beer and walked slowly toward her, hatless but still taller than she'd remembered him.

"Hi."

His voice started a chain reaction down her spine, and she had to check an impulse to throw herself into his arms.

"Hi, Craig. I hope you'll like the food here."

"Looks great to me." He wasn't talking about the restaurant. "I got here early, so I reserved a table." He smiled at the hostess and touched Libby's arm to guide her to a table, pulling out a heavy, leather-padded chair to seat her.

"You've done something to your hair. You look terrific," he said, sitting across from her.

"Just a trim, thank you. Your beard is gone."

"But not my mustache."

"I'm glad." She couldn't tell him where she'd liked to feel it tickling her at that moment.

"Would you like a drink?"

The cocktail waitress lost no time getting to their table. Libby was sure Craig never had trouble getting good service from waitresses.

"Some wine, maybe. White, not too sweet."

"I'll have another draft," Craig said, not taking his eyes off Libby.

Under his walnut-brown suede jacket he was wearing a silky cream shirt—an unusual combination with jeans, but he pulled it off with natural grace. He'd never looked more appealing. Whatever she'd expected, it wasn't this kicked-in-the-midriff weakness and tongue-tied shyness she was feeling as she stared across at him.

"How've you been?" He made it sound like the most important question in the world.

"Rehearsals are going well. My character is the kind who tries to run the world so she won't have to face up to her own shortcomings."

"When do you open?"

"Next month."

"What I really meant was, how are you?"

"Fine, I suppose."

"Libby"—he paused as though trying to formulate words for some difficult concept—"I missed you."

"I'm glad—to see you," she replied hesitantly.

"Are you?"

He reached across and opened his palm, waiting for her to lay her hand on his. She didn't disappoint him, watching as his long, strong fingers caressed hers, a gesture almost too intimate for a public place.

"So tell me," she asked with forced briskness, "what is this film?"

"Just as I said, a spaghetti Western."

"But you're playing the lead."

He shrugged. "I needed a change of scenery and the money's good. I don't expect much to come of it."

She shouldn't have agreed to see him. A few hours of his time would only make her want him again with the same crazy intensity that had sprung up between them on location.

"The Spanish women will love you."

"There hasn't been anyone since you," he said softly.

The cocktail waitress delivered a tall glass of dark beer and a goblet of wine to their table.

"Your waiter will be here to take your order in just a few minutes," she said.

"No hurry," Craig said, absentmindedly sipping, using his tongue to flick the foam from his upper lip. She was sitting in a nearly full restaurant with the most attractive man in the world, and she felt a sudden stab of loneliness, knowing how little of his time she'd have.

"I've found out something," he said seriously.

"What?"

"I want to be with you."

Her laugh was artificially brittle, masking a spark of hope she didn't dare nourish. "I thought you made that pretty clear once or twice."

"I'm talking about being lonely because I'm not with the person I want to be with."

Just then the waiter arrived, clean-shaven but swarthy, in a red cotton jacket that made him look handsome by any woman's standards. But Libby wished he'd disappear. This was no time for interruptions. He presented them with large, leather-covered menus and recited the specials of the day, then promised to return in a few minutes to take their orders.

"What would you like?" Craig opened his menu and started reading, deciding quickly in spite of the multiple pages of selections. "I'll have the porterhouse, I guess. Dinner on the plane last night wasn't much."

"You got in last night?"

He hadn't rushed to phone her, that was sure.

"Around eight." He didn't give any reasons for not having called her then.

"Craig," she asked hesitantly, not sure if she wanted to hear the answer, "did you plan to call me?"

He sighed and laid the menu aside. "I've spent days trying to decide. Last night I still wasn't sure."

"Well, what made you decide in my favor?"

"I couldn't make myself go overseas without seeing you again."

"I see." She didn't really, at least not in the important sense of knowing how he felt about her.

An expression flitted over his face, reminding her of a man who realizes he's already said enough to hang himself.

"Have you decided what you want?" He picked up the menu as though he intended to change his mind.

"The chef's salad, I guess." She hadn't bothered to see if this item was on the menu. "Oil and vinegar on the side."

After relaying their orders to the waiter when he returned, Craig smiled and said, "Well, this is your city. What do you think I should see?"

"There's so much!" She wanted to ask how much time he had—how much she had—but he cut her off.

"I'm already seeing what I want to see: you. Suppose we just walk some?"

"Fine." She nodded her head, wondering if his planned destination was her apartment or his hotel.

His steak was served on a hot metal platter sitting on a board; her salad was large enough for two, with long strips of ham, turkey, and cheese spilling over the sides.

"I can't believe we're having this for lunch," she said.

"Guess I have my working appetite back."

He did look a little gaunt, as though he might've dropped five or ten pounds he didn't need to lose. When he looked down at his plate, his lashes were a thick fringe shading his eyes, and she wanted in the worst way to feel them tickling the skin above her upper lip.

"Have you worked since the movie ended?" she asked.

He finished chewing a bite of juicy steak. "The worst kind of work for me—talking to agents, firming up contracts, all that bull. I had an interview on Marve Graham's show. Did you see it?"

"Sorry, no. I don't watch much TV." She would have gotten up in the middle of the night to see Craig being interviewed. "What did he ask you?"

"The usual. Are stunts really dangerous? How do I feel about doing them?" He obviously took a dim view of these questions.

"What did you wear?"

"Don't you want to know what I said?"

"You said the stunts aren't dangerous if they're done right, and it's just a job."

"Pretty close." He grinned a bit sheepishly. "Do you know me that well?"

"I think there's an awful lot about you I don't know."

"I guess I wore about what I have on now."

"Silk shirt?"

"No."

"You only wear silk shirts on special occasions?"

171

"My sister gave it to me for Christmas."

"Your sister has good taste."

"Are you trying to give me a hard time?" He sat back in his chair and eyed her narrowly.

"Yes. Am I succeeding?" She felt an impish urge to pull his mustache.

"You know you are!"

He really did want to walk.

"We could cut across to Central Park," she said, "unless you'd rather see Greenwich Village or Broadway or—"

"The park sounds fine."

They sat on a bench, holding hands and saying little as they watched kids playing Frisbee. Then they wandered on a crowded walkway.

"The whole town's out today," he said.

"Hardly, but I've never seen a prettier day."

He ran his thumb over her inner wrist, not seeing the two young joggers who passed them for the third time.

"Those girls have their eyes on you."

"Don't do that, Libby."

"What?"

"Make it sound as if I pick up groupies like filings on a magnet."

"Do I do that?"

"Yes, and it's damned silly."

"Some men like to be admired!"

"I can do without that nuisance."

"How old do people have to be before you start approving of them?"

"Age has nothing to do with it."

"It must. You don't like children."

"That's not true," he said, his voice low and angry.

She headed toward an exit, not wanting to be mocked by

the tranquillity of the park when the mood was shattered for her. Nothing had changed since Old Buckhorn, even if Craig had admitted missing her. She was tense and edgy, expecting him to suggest going to her apartment.

"Libby." He caught up and put his arm around her.

"Maybe it was a mistake for us to see each other," she said.

"No, it wasn't. There is one sight in this city I want to see."

"What?"

She was so sure he'd say her apartment, she didn't believe his answer.

"The Statue of Liberty."

"Really?"

"I know we can't go out to see it now, but I'd like to get a glimpse."

"We can go down to Battery Park," she suggested.

"I'll get a cab."

He stepped out into traffic with his arm outstretched and had no difficulty hailing one.

In the backseat of the cab he kissed her for the first time that day, beginning at the corner of her mouth and gently nibbling with his lips until she felt like melting on the warm leather seat. The driver transported them to the southern tip of Manhattan.

Looking over the water toward Liberty Island, their sides together and their arms around each other, they weren't aware of anyone else in the world.

The breeze was cool by the waterside, and Craig, mistaking her shiver for a chill, slipped out of his jacket and put it around her shoulders.

"I'm not cold, but you will be with just a shirt."

"No." He held the heavy jacket in place on her shoulders, seemingly oblivious to the wind that whipped against his arms and shoulders.

She didn't want his jacket, but she wanted to be held by those arms, so strong under the silk fabric. When he laid her head against his chest, she couldn't stop herself from sliding her fingers between two buttons to touch his bare skin. A small tremor shook them both, and Libby thought love must be a fatal condition. Her heart was going to burst if it swelled any more.

He caught a tiny tear at the corner of her eye.

"Libby, are you crying?"

"No, of course not. The wind blew something in my eye."

She hated herself for not having the courage to tell him how she felt. They were some pair, two secretive singles longing to be together but afraid to admit it. How could such sweet feelings lead nowhere?

"We'd better go," he said.

It took a few minutes to get a cab, and she insisted he take back his jacket. Hopefully she looked cold enough to justify what she was going to do.

In the cab she didn't suppress a momentary chattering of her teeth.

"You *are* chilly," he said.

"All I need is some hot coffee, and it's probably the best thing I make."

"I'm not so sure of that! The stuff you made for me one morning in Old Buckhorn made my hair stand on end."

"That had something to do with being kicked out of bed."

"I just didn't want you to fuss over my aches and pains."

"I knew that. Are you going to give the driver my address?"

He looked at his watch, but it was only a gesture. "I was going to drop you off and go on to Kennedy."

"Oh." She felt like crying.

A line creased on his forehead as he scowled at his watch and gave the driver her address. Holding her tight with his

174

arm across her shoulders, he asked, "How long does it take to get to Kennedy from your place?"

"I'd allow an hour, just to be sure."

"Hell, I don't want to sit around an airport when I could be drinking your coffee. I've got a little time to spare." He kissed her cheek. "Driver," Craig called, "let's swing by the Howard Johnson's first." After he picked up his luggage and checked out in record time, their cab headed toward Libby's.

"So this is where you live," he said when they'd stopped in front of her four-story brownstone long ago divided into apartments. He paid the driver, and they walked up the two flights to her apartment.

"Bright, I like the colors," Craig said as he entered. The colors made the place seem even smaller than it was. "Is this all there is to it?"

"Kitchen alcove around the corner. I like to keep it blocked with a screen. Bathroom through the door, closet behind you. This couch is a Hide-A-Bed."

"I thought my place in L.A. was small."

"I was glad to get my own place. The roommate I had when I first came here had some strange friends."

"Do you have a special friend?" He'd never asked before.

The temptation to let him worry was great, but she didn't. "No, no one special right now. I'll start the coffee."

He followed her into the alcove, watching while she measured four scoops of aromatic grounds from a fresh one-pound can she had to open.

"I'm making too much, I guess." She'd already poured cold water into the automatic coffeemaker. "You won't have time for more than a cup or so."

"I'm sorry I didn't call you last night." He stood behind her, lightly kneading the back of her neck, an exquisite form of torture because she knew how short their time together would be.

175

"So am I."

There was more sadness than sexual longing in his kiss, a long, slow joining of their mouths that made her heart melt.

Pouring the coffee into flowered bone-china cups that used to be her grandmother's, Libby carried them to the round maple table in the dining area, then put the only snack food she had, a packet of graham crackers, on a pink glass plate.

"I haven't had these in a long time." Craig took one and bit into it. "Got any peanut butter?"

She brought a half-empty jar, the grainy kind ground from fresh peanuts in a neighborhood health-food store, watching while he spread a thick layer and made a sandwich of two graham squares.

"Tell me more about the movie," she said.

"I play an outlaw with a heart of gold."

"Robin Hood with spurs?"

"Something like that." He didn't sound happy about it.

"How long will you be gone?"

"Six weeks if I'm lucky, maybe a couple of months."

His jacket was hanging on the back of the chair, and his arms looked more powerful than ever under the soft silk. His throat was still deeply tanned in the *V* where the top buttons were open, and he seemed to bring the Arizona desert into her snug little room.

"That's a long time."

"Almost longer than I can stand." His voice sounded strained. "The past few weeks . . ."

He looked away, pouring himself another cup of coffee from the pot she'd set on a ceramic trivet.

She wanted to tell him they'd seemed like an eternity to her, but a veiled look slipped over his face, warning her against it. "I hate going!" His words were vehement, and he punctuated them by standing quickly and going to the window overlooking the street.

176

"It's a good opportunity," she said, failing to sound enthusiastic.

"Sure." He looked at his watch.

"Maybe I should call a cab for you." She walked over to him.

"No, I'll just grab one."

"You won't have much time. . . ."

They didn't have much time! He held her against him, his fingers laced in her hair.

"I don't want to leave you," he said, sounding miserable.

His kiss was as quick as the flutter of a hummingbird's wings, and it wasn't enough, not nearly enough, to say good-bye. She pulled his head to hers, opening her mouth for the full, swelling thrust of his tongue, pressing against him as though any untouched part of him would dissolve and be lost to her forever.

Lifting her until her toes dangled above his boots, he crushed his mouth against hers, finding sweet response and keen regret that told him his absence would mean pain and emptiness for her too.

When they parted for a moment, they both saw the two soft-sided, bulging bags sitting just inside her door, a reminder that he should leave.

"If I carry them on the plane, I can stay a little longer."

"They're pretty big, and it's an international flight. Shouldn't you check them?"

"I'll see if I have time. If not, I can stuff them in the overhead rack." They came together with a mutual eagerness that took their breaths away, kissing frantically, touching and holding as though this were their last moment on earth.

"Darling, Libby, darling. I don't know how I'm going to make myself leave you."

She held on, not making it easier.

"If you didn't have a play . . ." He didn't finish, kissing her instead with anguished fervor.

For a long, memorable moment they just hugged, arms circling each other, her head nestled against him.

"I can't believe I wasted last night," he said regretfully. "I tried to talk myself out of seeing you."

"I'm glad you didn't succeed."

"I never had a chance." He kissed her with heavyhearted slowness.

"You do have to leave."

Her fingers were tucked under his wide leather belt, moist and warm against the silk covering his back. She pulled out the shirt, nestling her fingers against his skin, wanting to keep him with her.

"You're making it awfully hard." He pulled off her heavy sweater and laid his hands on her breasts, bunching the cotton of her blouse. "I'll have to carry those bags on my lap. I can't seem to think of anything but how much I want you."

"Oh, Craig!" She regretted so many things, most of all his stubborn reluctance to say the things she wanted to hear.

"I have to go."

He kissed her soundly and walked to the table to retrieve his jacket.

"Have a good trip," she forced herself to say.

"I'll let you know where I'm staying."

He didn't ask her to join him there.

"Yes, well, you'd better hurry."

Please hurry, she thought desperately, *before I break down and tell you I can't live without you.*

"Yes, I will."

"If you walk a block to the right, it'll be easier to get a cab."

"Libby . . ."

He took her in his arms one more time, smothering her in

his embrace, holding nothing back in his urgent, hungry, regretful kiss.

Then he was gone. Her apartment felt chill and empty, and the late-afternoon sun mocked her with a cheerful pattern of light on the floor. Suddenly in a panic because she might miss seeing him go, she ran to the window and pressed her face against the glass just in time to see him hurrying along the sidewalk, one bag bunched under his arm and the other in his hand on the same side, the way he'd carried her bags into her bedroom on her first day in Old Buckhorn. He was only in sight for a few seconds, darting around an elderly man walking a little black dog on a leash; then she lost sight of him.

How could he leave her! Two months seemed like forever, and in that time he'd probably take up with another woman and forget all about her. She was positive he cared, but he'd left so many things unsaid. Even at the last moment when he'd desperately wanted her, he hadn't held out any hope for the future. Why was he so reluctant to accept his feelings for her? Did he think she was baiting a marriage trap or scheming to change his life-style?

Without thinking about it she carried the empty cups to the drainboard, rinsing hers but holding in her hand the one Craig had used. She ran her thumb over the delicate china rim that his lips had touched, and then it slipped out of her hand. She watched it smash into a hundred tiny pieces in the stainless-steel sink, and she started to cry—not because she cared about the cup but because Craig was all that mattered to her.

CHAPTER ELEVEN

Acting lessons didn't cover the performance Libby needed to give: convincing her parents everything was wonderful in the big, wicked city. They called only minutes after she'd finished gathering the shreds of broken china from the sink, cutting her finger in the process. She blamed the edginess in her voice on her having broken one of Grandma Sloan's cups but doubted her mother was satisfied with this explanation.

"We're coming for opening night," Betty Sloan assured her daughter. "Dad dropped out of the tournament."

"Mom, you moved to Florida so he could play golf all year. You can see a later performance."

"Let our daughter open on Broadway without being there? We wouldn't think of it! Anyway, we want to see the kids before the weather gets bad."

The kids were her brother Dave's children, Tammy and Christopher. Libby was relieved when the conversation turned to Tammy's big first day in kindergarten, which she'd already heard about from her sister-in-law, and Christopher's antics in preschool nursery. Her mother loved being a grandmother, and Libby was delighted when her hyperactive parent's attention turned in that direction. Her mother was her best friend in many ways, but she didn't want to tell her about Craig. As a woman who had gotten a college diploma one week and a marriage license the next, she was sure to ask questions Libby couldn't answer.

Her dad talked for a few minutes before laughingly handing the phone back to his wife.

"I'm going to an antique show next weekend," her mother said. "Which cup did you break?"

"The one with purple violets and tiny yellow flowers."

"Be sure to save the saucer. I'll see if I can find a replacement to fill out your set."

"Mother, don't do that. I've never used all twelve at once. Don't go to any trouble."

"It's not trouble. I love looking for things."

Libby hung up, feeling so despondent that she missed her parents. Even when they tried to interfere in her life, it was done with so much love, she couldn't resent it. Family life was her rock; would she ever have a family of her own? What terrible irony it was that the first man she loved to distraction didn't seem interested in children.

She stood staring moodily out the window, wishing someone would get rid of the huge flowerpot of dying flowers sitting on a stoop across the street. The season for blooming was over; why try to prolong it by leaving a withered, brown plant in sight?

Why pretend that her relationship with Craig was more than a beautiful but brief flowering of love, destined to die just as surely as the brilliant flowers in her neighbor's flowerpot?

She should have gone to the airport with him. The whine of jets, the crush of travelers, and the urgency to catch a plane would have made parting easier. He was, after all, only taking a trip, and the longest trip had a beginning and an end. He couldn't go home without passing through a New York airport again. The fact that he'd called her meant something;

at least she had hope after three weeks of rock-bottom despair. Craig did care for her.

How had she planned to spend the evening? There were a dozen single friends, men and women, she could call to go to a movie, but she preferred solitude so she could savor each of Craig's words and gestures, remembering his smile, his eyes, his mouth on hers.

Soaking in a hot tub, she almost drowned in melancholy thoughts, trying to unravel the mystery of why people fall in love. What made Craig so special to her? Why couldn't she feel the same way about John or Tony or Gregg, or even the accountant who did her tax forms or the waiter at the steak house? In twenty-eight years she'd never been so obsessed with one person. There had to be a reason why people fell in love. Was she just a little girl at heart, needing someone to tell her to drink milk? Libby rejected this explanation, knowing how highly she valued her independence and self-reliance. She hadn't been floundering, desperate for a man to take charge of her life. On the contrary, a romance at this time wasn't at all convenient. She needed to devote all her attention to the new play.

Warm and pink all over from the hot soak, she slipped into a long flannel nightgown, white with little blue nosegays, and fuzzy blue slippers, then brushed her hair until it crackled. It was too early for bed and too late to bother eating. She couldn't sit still to read, and nothing in her apartment really needed doing. When all else failed, there was always work. She found her script, the corners already dog-eared. Using the center of her single room as a stage, she started reading her part aloud, imagining the other characters' responses. She was finishing the second act when her buzzer sounded. The security in her apartment was good; an intercom system enabled her to speak to her caller before releasing the downstairs lock.

"Yes?"

"Would you believe I missed my plane?"

"Craig!"

She buzzed him in, then opened her door, waiting for him to race up the two flights. He ran, carrying his luggage as though it contained only feather pillows, throwing them ahead of him into her apartment and scooping her into his arms.

He couldn't be here! It was too wonderful to be true. She lost one slipper in the rush to his arms and braced herself with her bare toes on top of his boot. He kissed her heatedly, then banged the door shut.

"I've never done anything so dumb and been so glad about doing it!" he said between kisses.

Locked in his arms, she thought she'd burst with happiness. An evening that had stretched ahead like a prison sentence was suddenly transformed into the most exciting of her life.

"How did you miss it?"

"Come here. I'll tell you."

He led her to the couch, cuddling her until she felt like a little flannel doll nestled on his lap.

"I had trouble getting a cab—don't you dare say I should've called for one!"

"I wouldn't do that!"

"Well, I still could've made it, but there was an accident that held up traffic. I felt like an ass rushing in just about the time the plane took off, then I thought about it and decided I was the luckiest guy in that airport. I could come back to you."

"I'm glad you did."

"You told me to leave an hour early." He kissed her chin, then took her full, pink lower lip between his, caressing it with his tongue.

"I'm not an I-told-you-so," she said when she had a chance, still dazed by his sudden reappearance.

She didn't ask if he'd booked another plane or how long he could stay. Being in his arms made her complete; she could live the rest of her life snuggled against his wonderful, strong chest. The sound of his heartbeat was music enough for the universe, and she'd never willingly stray from the circle of his arms. Nor would she ever again question whether she loved him.

They necked. Like two kids in the backseat at a drive-in movie, they couldn't get enough of each other. His kisses were gentle and chaste; she innocently stroked his chest, feeling the hairiness under the slippery silk. Her lips were swollen from the quantity, not the force, of his kisses, and even the knot in the lower part of her body was a sensation to be savored. In his arms she felt like a whole person, needing nothing else.

"I didn't stop to get a room," he said, stroking her knee under the soft cotton flannel.

"The hotels are probably all full." This little white lie would never trouble her conscience.

"Then I'm in quite a fix."

"You must have friends in a city this big."

"I hope I have one." He kissed her with slow relish, holding her head between his hands.

"You do," she whispered, squirming as his hand crept up her thigh and kneaded her hip.

"Let me love you," he said.

"I'm not prepared here either," she admitted.

"That pleases me immensely."

"But you said—"

"I stopped at a drugstore on the way here."

"You took me for granted!" She only pretended to want to get away from him; he subdued her squirming with a gentle kiss.

"I'll never do that, but you can't blame me for hoping."

She only blamed him for the long, empty nights since they'd last been together, for the days that had passed without a word from him. Her lingering remnant of anger was extinguished like a candle in a hurricane when he kissed her in earnest, pushing her back on a new tangerine pillow and taking his time in exploring her lips and mouth.

"I'm so happy to be with you," he whispered.

She fingered his mustache, fascinated by its bristly perfection. She couldn't imagine him without it.

"I'm so happy to have you here."

"Mind if I take off my jacket?"

In the circumstances, his question made her giggle. "Please do."

He took off his shirt, too, turning on the table lamp beside the Hide-A-Bed.

"This thing opens into a bed?" He looked skeptical.

"Sure, just take off the cushions—"

"I think I can figure it out."

"You were waiting for an invitation?"

"Yeah, I guess I was."

He reassured her with a long, deep kiss, then tackled her couch, whipping it into a bed in less time than it usually took her to remove the upholstered cushions. She got the bed pillows from the closest shelf while he went into the bathroom, returning with traces of moisture on the hair by his forehead. Dusty ash-blond hair the color of his mustache clung to his scalp, but on top the sun had bleached lighter streaks. No matter how many times she saw him, she'd never stop loving the way he looked: lean, strong, dynamic. Barefooted, wearing only his jeans, he looked as he had at their first meeting. The uneasiness he'd stirred in her then had become chronic; he was still the most exciting man she'd ever seen.

Without words they both knew they couldn't wait any

185

longer. He stepped out of his remaining clothing and lifted her nightgown, smiling as he drew it above her head.

"Do you always wear granny gowns?"

"Is that what it's called?" She was in his arms, hardly believing how wonderful it felt to be there.

"Should be. No woman under eighty should wear one."

"I get cold."

"You won't tonight."

How easily he promised to take care of her needs! On fire with expectation, she still felt a deep tinge of sadness, knowing he wouldn't always be there.

"Did you book another flight?" she asked.

"Let's not talk about it now," he murmured, silencing her in the most effective way known to man.

When they were stretched out side by side, her toes only reached to his calves, but she had the cozy feeling of having been made for him. Clinging and touching, they both trembled with eagerness. His breath tickled her throat as his kisses made a shivery trail downward, lingering at her breasts until she clutched at him with anticipation. His skin smelled so nice, reminding her of the hot, wind-scoured desert, and the hairs on his body were charged with electricity, giving her delicious little shocks as she rubbed against him.

For a moment she was afraid she was only imagining him, conjuring his image because she desperately wanted him. Then he hovered over her, large and powerful, and she knew he was real and, for the moment, hers.

Something was different, very different, from the last time they'd made love, but she was too involved in what was happening to think it out. He was gentle but quicker, suckling her breasts to throbbing hardness while his hands fondled her to a state of frantic arousal.

He wanted her so much, he was racing out of control; that was the difference. This was no idle sexual encounter, no

186

leisurely evening of pleasure. Craig was wildly excited, wanting her, Libby, not just seeking satisfaction. He said her name over and over, calling her "baby" and "sweetheart," telling her she was wonderful and beautiful, crooning an ageless ode to passion and meaning every word.

She was a hollow shell until he filled her, a confused emptiness, a mass of unfulfilled longings. He made her feel complete. Nothing had ever felt so right.

The window was open a few inches but the cool night air didn't touch them. Slippery from exertion, their bodies hotbeds of sensation, they couldn't touch enough, straining for that one perfect moment when two people are one.

She loved him so much, it hurt, not with pain but with expectation.

Their physical climax didn't trigger an emotional one; they wanted each other as fervently after the shuddering culmination of their lovemaking as they had before. Locked in each other's arms, more exhilarated than tired, they exchanged hungry kisses and hugs. Above her bed an Art Nouveau poster showed a beautiful woman with long, flowing tresses that fanned around her like a border of vines and tendrils. Libby wished her hair were long enough to wrap Craig in a cocoon; she wanted to bind him in silky strands and keep him with her forever. When he filled his hands with curling locks and pressed them to his face, she trapped him with her arms and legs, weaving her hair around him in her imagination.

"You are something. . . ."

Libby strained to hear his satisfied murmurings, lying by his side now, raising her head to lick the strong column of his throat, her tongue growing moist as it tasted his salty skin.

Tingling in places she couldn't even name, she cuddled even closer, slipping into a euphoric dream state too perfect to call sleep.

The cold woke her, a biting chill that nipped at her toes and made her thighs and bottom shiver. She tried to close the window and cover Craig without waking him but wasn't sorry when she failed. His way of thanking her for the blanket generated more heat than the furnace that serviced six apartments, and she burned with pleasure, again pushing aside thoughts of the day to come. This night would last forever; she couldn't imagine lying alone after sharing her bed with him.

He slept again but she didn't, preferring to study his shoulders and arms in the gray light of dawn, seeing the tiny freckles, almost invisible when her nose wasn't inches away. His back was turned, and she fitted her length against his, rubbing against his back and bottom, succeeding in getting his sleepy attention.

"What time is it?" he mumbled.

"Not quite six-thirty."

"Come here."

She did.

They didn't fall asleep again, and she waited with a knot of dread in her stomach to hear how much time he had.

"I have to go, you know," he said at last.

"When?"

"I was lucky to get on a morning flight to Paris. From there my route is complicated, but I'll make it eventually."

"Will you be late?"

"Yeah, and I don't think I'm going to like working with the director."

"Why not?"

He shrugged and kissed her.

"Why not, Craig?"

"He has a reputation for taking shortcuts. People get hurt when things aren't planned right."

"Not you?"

"No, I can look out for myself. Don't worry."

188

"When do you have to leave?"

"This time I'd better allow a little more time to get to the airport."

"I guess so. When does your flight leave?"

"Soon. I just about have time for a quick shower, darling." He sounded deeply regretful.

"I don't have a shower."

"Oh, I didn't notice."

"You can take a bath."

"That's not my first choice."

"Sorry! Do you want to wait while I ask my landlord to install one?"

"I don't want to leave you. But saying it doesn't help."

"Not a bit." This wasn't wholly true.

He stood, the perfection of his body bringing tears to her eyes. Before, she'd wondered if a night together would make their parting any easier. It didn't.

"I'll get my shaving kit." He bent over one of his bags, finding the things he needed. "I have a contract. I have to go."

"Of course you do." *Damn it, say something important,* she wanted to scream.

Water ran full force into her tub while she slipped into a fleecy pink robe and started a pot of coffee. She tried not to imagine Craig in her tub, a nice modern blue one but undoubtedly too short for him to enjoy. Would he like her to wash his back? Today there wasn't time, and she didn't know if there'd be another chance.

Coffee was sitting on the table when he came out of the bathroom in Jockey shorts and a fresh tan shirt.

"Do you have time for coffee?"

"One cup."

He pulled on jeans, standing beside the chair where he'd draped them. His hair was wet, making it look darker, and he combed it out of his face impatiently, not bothering to look in a mirror. He drank the coffee standing, swallowing it hotter than she could stand.

"I could go with you to the airport."

"How long will it take you to dress? I'm in a hurry."

"Forget it. It wasn't a very good idea."

"Libby." He sounded miserable. "I don't want to go."

She nodded her head, afraid she'd cry if she tried to answer.

"It's not forever," he added, not sounding convinced.

"No."

"As I said before, it's a small world."

He put on his suede jacket, and for a minute she was afraid he was going to say thank you. Instead he held her for a moment and brushed her forehead with his lips.

"If I kiss you properly, I won't leave."

"And you do have a contract."

"Good-bye, Libby." He touched her lips with his and was gone. He hadn't even said he loved her. She believed he did, but that wasn't the same as hearing it. How was she going to live without him? If she had hope, it would mean all the difference in the world; but Craig had left vaguely suggesting that they'd see each other again although he'd promised nothing. She needed much more: a future with him.

In the weeks that followed, her daydreams lost their luster. She saw a little house with a maple in front, two children, and maybe a dog, but she had a terrible time putting Craig into this fantasy.

One postcard came, a pretty scene of a cathedral with blue sky that reminded her of Arizona. He wrote in big script and said little, only that he'd arrived and was busy. Reading it made her miserable, but she put it with the picture side showing on her refrigerator, holding it there with the ladybug magnet.

Most Likely to Succeed opened to a full house that included her parents, both brothers and their wives, and enough friends to make her feel as if she were back in a high school play.

They took her out for brunch the next day; it turned out to be a consolation gathering. Reviews of the play were uniformly indifferent; she could hear Craig saying, "It's been done before." She did get one line of praise: a major reviewer cited the "poignant humor" in her interpretation of the part.

The play didn't close immediately. Both leads were fresh and funny, and the playwright tried some changes in the hope of saving it, even though most cast members believed it was a case of too little too late. As was often true in the theater, the best part of the play was getting to know the other cast members. *Most Likely to Succeed* was unusual in that almost all the actors were in the same age group; after the weeks of rehearsal and the disappointing opening, they felt like brothers and sisters.

Bill Jenson, the lead, asked her out for supper after a midweek performance in a half-empty theater. He was brown-haired and earnest, the kind of actor who was always in demand for small parts like the boy next door or the kindly big brother.

"What will you do when we close?" he asked, giving voice to the question that most concerned the whole cast.

"I don't know," Libby admitted. "Prod my agent, start running to auditions. Who knows, maybe I'll get hungry enough to make another movie." Until that moment she hadn't considered trying out for another film, but there was a lot to be said for guaranteed employment.

"I've got a shot at an Oscar Wilde revival. When they start auditioning, I'll give you a call," Bill said.

"Thanks, I'd really appreciate it."

Bill was a friend; he wouldn't expect any particular reward for recommending her.

She emptied her mailbox every day with more eagerness than she'd felt since her early teens, when her passion had been writing to movie stars asking for their pictures and autographs. Craig's second postcard pictured a Spanish girl with an embroidered skirt. Libby was surprised that the skirt was done with real thread sewn into the top layer of cardboard and covered with a postcard back. Unfortunately one corner was badly bent from passing through the mail; the message was even more disappointing.

Dear Libby,
    Working hard but running behind schedule. Some slow-ups. You'd enjoy the sun.

                                        Regards,
                                        Craig

Regards! What kind of word was that to end a note with? He wouldn't even use the word *love* on a picture postcard. On this card, as on the other, he hadn't included a return address. Was he living at a hotel or in a trailer on location? The name of the town in the postmark wasn't familiar to her. Maybe the whole village was so small, the actors had to board with local families. Craig would probably draw lodgings with a beautiful woman who went weak in the knees whenever he smiled. Thinking this way made Libby dislike herself; jealousy wasn't a trait she admired, especially when there was no known reason for it.

Even more worrisome was Craig's comment about not liking the director. From what he'd said, he'd be doing his own stunt work as well as playing the lead, with an Italian voice to be dubbed in later. Accidents happened even with top professional stunt coordinators like Bert Halloway. Just because Craig was uninjured when the card was mailed didn't mean nothing had happened while it was en route.

The play hung on through another week, but the audience count was going down. It was only a matter of time before the backers pulled the plug.

Bill relayed the bad news to Libby on an afternoon when she stayed home in bed to kick a head cold.

"Saturday's the last night," he said on the phone.

"I guess we all knew it was coming."

"Well, it'll look good on our credits even if *Most Likely to Succeed* had a short run," he assured her.

She was almost too sick to do the last performance. Instead of going away, her head cold got worse until she was on the brink of a dilemma. If she took cold capsules she'd be too groggy to perform well; they dried her throat and made speaking on the stage difficult. Without medication her nose rivaled Rudolph's and her eyes watered constantly. She compromised and took one capsule instead of two; her throat was dry and her eyes still watered.

After the last performance the producer threw a party in the green room, an attractive room decorated not in green but in shades of beige and burgundy, where the cast relaxed before, during, or after the shows. It wasn't a champagne celebration, but they did have a nice buffet and a chance to say good-bye to each other. Libby went even though she felt rotten; anyone who was going to catch her cold probably already had, and she didn't want to be alone that night.

Bill offered to see her home, but she used her cold as an excuse to say no. He was a great friend, but they were at a point where he couldn't understand why a good-night kiss didn't please her. Craig had spoiled her for casual friendships. Being in love was like carrying a fifty-pound weight on her back. She wanted to be her old self again. Certainly her feelings for Craig weren't doing her any good. The problem was that she just didn't know how to fall out of love.

CHAPTER TWELVE

The mail brought two pleasant surprises: a letter from Sandra and a crayon drawing from Danny. Sandra was taking a few months off to be with her son; then she was scheduled to do a spy thriller that ended with a wild chase scene through the snow-covered Rockies. There was no way Danny could go on location for that film, even if he could miss school. She was hoping to find a suitable baby-sitter.

Danny's drawing was done in bright red, yellow, and black, showing him on a horse, wearing a cowboy hat. Libby was pleased she could use her new magnets to hang it on the refrigerator in a place of honor between Craig's three postcards. In a card store she found a foot-high greeting with a comic cowboy; the inside message said, "Howdy, pardner," so she bought it and mailed it to Danny along with a note for Sandra. She missed them both.

After several unsuccessful auditions, when she was beginning to feel convinced that there was nothing for her in New York that season, she got a phone call from Bill.

"The auditions for *The Importance of Being Earnest* start next week."

"I don't know, Bill. Won't I have to sound verrry, verrry British?"

"Not when you're auditioning. I have the part of Algernon sewn up, and I'll be struggling with the accent along with everybody else. Cecily's part has been cast, but Gwendolen is still up for grabs. Should I tell the director you'll be there Tuesday at nine?"

"Sure, why not, what have I got to lose?"

She didn't have any trouble locating a dilapidated copy of the Oscar Wilde play in a used-book store, and preparing for the audition was a better way to spend the weekend than moping. The play was dated, of course, but unexpectedly, she found herself enjoying the witty lines even though a world of lords and ladies, manservants, manor houses, and five-o'clock teas wasn't quite her cup.

By Tuesday she found herself wanting the part, if for no other reason than the potential for great costuming. She could see herself as Gwendolen in a little short jacket with big puffy sleeves and a great, filmy bow. She'd love to flit across the stage in long gloves with a parasol, perhaps wearing a yard-long chain of pearls. Reading Gwendolen's speeches aloud, she imagined the swish of petticoats and the flounce of a long, perfumed fur stole.

Arriving at the converted movie theater for the audition, she felt more like her old self. The theater was a monument to the movie craze of the 1920s, an Italian sculptor's daydream with chunky plaster cupids suspended on the loges shooting imaginary arrows at the stage. The high ceiling was a fake sky, twinkling with tiny starlights. The stage was ample for the needs of live theater; if the magic of the play was working, the audience would forget the frayed, discolored upholstery on the seats, the threadbare carpeting in the aisles, and the yellowed, sooty statues set in recesses midway to the ceiling.

Libby read for all she was worth, throwing lines to a cocky Eager Eddie type without giving him the slightest edge. When it was over, she felt good about herself; whether she got the part or not, she had confidence in her ability to handle it.

After three anxious, hopeful days of repeating to herself that "no news is good news," she was called back for another reading. It went splendidly, and the part was hers.

Another postcard came from Craig, this time with a view of a monastery nestled in the mountains. The buildings were too distant to show whether they were deserted or occupied, but she liked to imagine Craig spending his nights alone in one of the ancient little cells. She didn't want him to suffer on a hard, narrow cot with only a threadbare blanket in a damp stone cubbyhole, but the part about being as lonesome as a monk was satisfying. His message told her little.

Dear Libby,

The horse has the best lines. We may finish by Columbus Day—the five hundredth anniversary, that is. I'm staying at a bed-and-breakfast sort of family hotel. Here's the address if you want to write.

Best regards,
Craig

"Best regards" wasn't any better than plain regards! At first she didn't understand about Columbus Day; the holiday had already passed when Craig wrote the card. Then she remembered a silly little ditty her father used to say: "Columbus sailed the ocean blue, way back in 1492." The movie must be dragging, if Craig joked about it lasting until 1992.

She wasn't magnanimous enough to hope he was having an uplifting, meaningful experience; it served him right for leaving her if the horse was the star!

On her way to rehearsals the next day she bought an "I Love New York" postcard that showed the Statue of Liberty.

It took her all evening to think of just the right message to send him by airmail.

Dear Craig,
Thank you for the postcards. I'd like to hear your horse's lines in Italian. Our movie hasn't been on TV yet. Are there any monks in the monastery?

Hail Columbia,
Libby

She had to squeeze the words in the last two lines, but darned if she'd write a letter when all he sent were postcards.

Rehearsals were fun except for the director. Summerfield Hawkins looked about sixteen with smooth, pink cheeks rarely touched by a razor. Plump and benign-looking until he opened his mouth, he had a Captain Bligh complex, flogging them through scene after scene with unrestrained sarcasm. The cast united against him, forging a tight little clique in self-defense. Fortunately Summie was also brilliant, a prodigy-on-the-way-up, his assistant and chief apologist assured them. Their modest little revival of a dated comedy was shaping into a real classy production.

It was the most exciting professional experience Libby had had in New York. She wished her whole heart were in it; part of her still carried Craig everywhere she went, longing for him with a sharp, unremitting pain. It wasn't fair that love made her so miserable. Romance was supposed to mean hearts and flowers and sweetly whispered sonnets, not a constant nagging, empty feeling. Romance meant two people loving each other, and she was never quite sure how Craig felt.

Feeling just a bit guilty, she didn't invite her family to the opening. If the play was successful, they could see it later.

She'd felt a little suffocated by their forced enthusiasm over *Most Likely to Succeed*. This time she wanted the reviews to be in, figuratively speaking, before she made a big deal out of having them see it. Of course, an off-Broadway revival wouldn't get that much attention from the press or anyone else, but she still wanted to wait until it was safely launched.

Opening night was a success and good word-of-mouth reviews were selling tickets; they weren't packing the theater, but receptive audiences gave the players continual encouragement.

Danny sent her another drawing, this one mailed in a big manila envelope he addressed himself. There was no note from Sandra, but Libby loved the picture of a Pilgrim man and woman. They were short with big, round faces that reminded her of Grace Drayton's Campbell Kids, and Danny showed them leading a chunky brown turkey on a string. She give his picture a place of honor on her refrigerator, rearranging it to make room for her postcard collection too.

She had to wait another week for word from Craig. Postcards were a lovely way of keeping in touch but woefully disappointing coming from the man she loved. She stared at another view of the same monastery, this one taken from the air, showing a pile of rubble at one end. She'd like to lock Craig in one of the remaining cells to keep him safe from harm and temptation until she could fly to him. She missed him too much to be ashamed of this fleeting fantasy. Turning over the card, she read:

Dear Libby,
   Got your card. They're giving the horse top billing. Another week should do it

Fond regards,
Craig

Now his regards were fond! She wanted to strangle him! He wrote the worst postcards in history. Compared to his messages, "Having a wonderful time, wish you were here" was meaty. There was no date; how long did an airmail postcard take? The week might be up now, unless he meant it would take another week after the card arrived. Did that mean he'd soon be calling her? Would he stay in New York between flights? Did he want to see her? She hoped he was living in a bare little cell, because he was making her nights miserable with longing, and now he was torturing her by not telling her any of the things she really wanted to know. When would she see him?

Usually Libby only hooked up her answering machine when she was expecting call-backs from auditions, but the thought of Craig phoning drove her crazy. He might go on to California if he failed to get her. Her single postcard to him hadn't mentioned the new play. He still thought she was in *Most Likely to Succeed*. There was no way he could reach her at work.

The first evening she put her answering machine back on, all she heard were recorded messages from a friend who wanted to borrow a blouse and a publisher's service selling magazines. Libby couldn't find a red felt pen in the kitchen drawer she used for writing supplies, so she put a big X with carmine nail polish across that day's date on her calendar. When there were seven in a row, she'd know Craig had gone back to California without calling her.

Brushing the second red X on the calendar made her so anxious with anticipation that she cleaned cupboards until three in the morning. After putting the third carmine X across the date, she was sure she could never, ever, forgive Craig for the agonizing suspense.

The fourth X was demoralizing in the extreme, and the fifth stood out like a bolt of lightning, vivid and frightening. Maybe he'd never intended to stop in New York; maybe his stay in Spain had accomplished his goal of forgetting her.

She could hardly make herself paint the sixth *X*, sure now that it was a silly waste of good nail polish. After staring at the row of carmine *X*s she'd never want to wear that color again.

The seventh *X* was too much. She threw away the polish and cried herself to sleep.

Success didn't soften Captain Bligh; Summie called a special rehearsal on Monday, their day off, insisting that the timing in the second act was poor. Libby was the only cast member who wasn't angry. She didn't care what she did; almost anything was better than sitting at home, knowing the right phone call might never come. Afterward most of the cast went out and partied, spending a noisy, bibulous evening together as a reward for finally winning a grudging "it's okay" from their boy-genius director. Libby stayed until the end of the party, the very late end, getting a little tipsy and letting Bill kiss her in the cab on the way home. She hadn't had enough sloe gin fizzes to let him come upstairs with her.

It was late, and she didn't want to hear a bunch of silly messages from magazine salesman, so she undressed, got into bed, and turned off the light, only to lie wide-eyed, totally awake. No one could be as sleepy as she was and stay awake! Still her eyes kept flipping open, focusing on nothing at all in the dark room.

She couldn't sleep without checking her answering machine.

Muttering, failing to find one slipper, she shuffled in the general direction of the kitchen alcove and snapped on the light. The machine, on a little table by the phone, annoyed her. If she hadn't bought it, she'd be sound asleep, as any semidrunk, jilted female should be.

His message was the second one, following another call from a friend about a blouse she'd borrowed from Libby.

"Libby, this is Craig. I'm calling from Kennedy. If I don't reach you tonight, I'll call tomorrow."

That was all. Did he mean he'd be in New York tomorrow, or was he on his way home, planning to call her from Los Angeles?

Pacing up and down the floor of her studio, wearing only one slipper, she didn't even notice that the toes on her bare foot were icy cold. She'd missed him! A machine was worse than useless when the caller left Craig's kind of obscure message. That was it! She'd had it with a man who did nothing but let her dangle. If she never saw him again, it would be too soon.

If she never yaw him again, she'd die! There might be a second call from him. She'd been too stricken to check. Disappointed because the only other message was from her dentist, reminding her to make an appointment for a checkup, she flopped down into bed, torn between screaming and bursting into tears of frustration.

The phone was miles away, across a glacier field, beyond the frozen tundra, echoing so faintly that the effort of trying to answer it seemed doomed to failure. Then she remembered Craig and came fully awake, bounding across the room, knocking over the bamboo screen that separated the kitchen from the main room of her apartment.

"Hello!" The dial tone mocked her.

How could she have slept through Craig's phone call? Not for a moment did she doubt that he was the early-morning caller. The little teapot-shaped clock on the kitchen wall showed why she'd been so slow in responding to the ring of the phone. It wasn't even seven A.M. Digging her toes into fuzzy slippers left by the bed, she tried to talk herself into staying awake. Craig might try again. After making coffee she gave up. Her eyelids wouldn't cooperate, and she'd never be able to breeze through Gwendolen's lines with only two hours of sleep. She was out as soon as her head hit the pillow.

The room was bathed in bright sunlight, and this time it was the harsh sound of the door buzzer that insistently roused her from an engrossing dream. Her apartment looked warmer than it felt, as she groggily responded to the summons.

"Who is it?" she called into the intercom.

"Craig. Are you going to let me in?"

"Yes, of course!"

Her response had been automatic. A moment later she wished she'd asked him to wait. She raced to the bathroom and quickly brushed her teeth and dashed cold water on her face, hearing his knock before she could struggle into her robe. With one flannel-sleeved arm caught in the armhole of her robe, she rushed barefoot to the door and threw it open.

His face was deeply tanned, and the hair that fell forward in an unruly tangle was streaked with light silvery-blond. Stepping through the doorway, he brought the summer back into her life.

"Did you miss me?" he asked sheepishly.

Her answer was a headlong rush into his arms. She met his mouth with a fervor stored up through too many long, lonely nights.

He dropped his bags, kicked the door shut, and gathered her against him in one lightning-quick movement.

After a single breathtaking kiss, he held her away at arm's length.

"Where the devil have you been?"

"Did you call me early this morning?"

"Yes, but I didn't get an answer." Looking rather fierce, he kept his hands on her shoulders. "You weren't here last night at one o'clock, and this morning I managed to find out that your play folded a long time ago."

A flash of resentment stiffened her spine. "You can't expect to know everything that's going on in my life when you're gone for months."

"Not that many months! Where were you last night?"

"I have a new play."

"How late does it run?"

"Don't you want to know what it is?"

"After I find out why you were out all night."

"Hardly all night! Our director is a real slave driver. He made us rehearse on our day off, so most of the cast went out and partied last night."

"Until seven this morning?"

He was jealous! She didn't feel nearly so eager to explain, taking a moment to get all the way into her robe and snap it up the front.

"Libby?"

"It was a long party."

"I'll bet it was!"

Anger clouded his face, and she discovered that his unhappiness made her feel bad.

"I heard the phone this morning, but I was so sleepy, I didn't get to it before it stopped ringing. Look, I knocked over the screen trying."

He picked it up. "You cracked one of the bamboo poles. I'll glue it for you later."

"Do you want to hear about my play?"

"Everything about it, but not before we say hello."

He hadn't forgotten how to kiss. His face was cold from being outside, but his lips warmed quickly, pressing against hers with delicious urgency.

"Ummm, you must have been practicing," she murmured.

"I'm so out of practice, I may've forgotten how this boy-girl stuff goes." He warmed his hands on the back of her fleecy robe before sliding his fingers under her hair.

204

"You mean the movie didn't have a beautiful schoolmarm?"

"No, I just rode off into the sunset. I told you the horse had all the good lines." He nuzzled her ear, tickling the inside with his breath.

"You didn't tell me much! I didn't even know your address until you were half done."

"The first part we shot in some rough country. I sent you an address when I had one in town. Not that you wrote much when you knew it."

He stepped away to take off his jacket, the same suede one he'd worn the day he left for Spain.

"Didn't you bring a winter coat?"

"Just a nylon windbreaker. I didn't think about rotten New York weather when I packed."

He was wearing a white turtleneck sweater, a heavy cable-knit that made his face look even darker.

"Any coffee?" he asked.

"Yes, I made a pot when the phone woke me this morning. I'll reheat it."

"Did I get you out of bed just now?"

"You know you did!"

"Pity. You didn't have time to make your bed." He grinned broadly, following her into the kitchen.

"When you're in the kitchen, there's no room for me."

This was true. Everywhere she turned, he was there.

"You're trying to get rid of me?"

"Oh, no!" She answered too quickly, letting a note of panic get into her voice.

"I hope not."

He was caressing her with his eyes, peeling away her robe and nightgown, drinking in her loveliness with his imagination. It was the first time she'd experienced such a thorough mental X ray, and it was surprisingly exciting.

"The coffee should be hot."

"Among other things," he said dryly.

Just having him across from her, sharing a pot of coffee and a plate of Dutch rusk, made her feel bubbly and crazy.

"I do want to hear about your play." His eyes never left her, taking in the smallest gesture, the slightest change in her expression.

"*Most Likely to Succeed* didn't do very well."

"The idea was too tired," he said, taking a dry bite of rusk. "Do you have any jam?"

"Sorry, no."

"The best actors can't do much with a weak script. I know. I've been trying for two months, and I'm no actor."

"I wonder about that."

"So your play closed right away?"

"We struggled for a while, but it was no go. Then I got Gwendolen in *The Importance of Being Earnest*."

"Shaw or somebody like that?"

"Oscar Wilde. It's just old-fashioned enough to work. He wrote terribly clever lines, even if the idea behind the play is corny."

"What is it?"

"These unbelievably innocent young things want to fall in love with a man named Ernest, so there's a lot of silly pretending and—"

"And pretending always leads to trouble." He was still looking at her in that way that gave her goose bumps.

"I promised myself I'd wait thirty minutes," he said.

"For what?"

"For you."

His words rippled down her spinal cord, making her tense with longing.

"Is that an arbitrary time limit?"

"Very arbitrary. I thought it was enough time to tell you that I've thought of nothing but you since I left for Spain. If

206

that damn movie took one more week, I was going to let them finish without me.''

''You were the hero!''

''Was I?''

''Well, you should know. I wasn't there.''

''Come here.''

''I don't know,'' she teased. ''If you've really gone without—''

''If!''

''Craig . . .'' She walked into his waiting arms, sinking down on his lap, hiding her face against his shoulder because extreme happiness made her weepy.

He covered her face and throat with eager kisses, whispering her name over and over. ''I missed you like crazy.''

''I missed you too.''

He stood, taking her with him, unsnapping her robe and letting it drop to the floor. Her nightie, the old white flannel with blue flowers, was open at the throat, and he slowly undid the other two buttons. Touching her breast was awkward through the small opening, but he never did quite what she expected. With the calm deliberation of a man opening a package, he tore the facing below the last button, then slowly ripped the gown down to the hem, splitting it open so that it fell away as easily as the robe had.

''You ruined my nightgown.'' All she felt was surprise.

''If you have to sleep in clothes, I'll get you something else.''

''Something to keep me warm?'' She was torn between shock and excitement about standing in front of Craig in only her slippers.

''No. Have I been here half an hour?'' he asked, pulling off his boots.

''I haven't timed you.'' She touched the top of his pants, a tightly woven tan twill instead of his usual blue jeans, and

207

opened the belt buckle, a tooled silver medallion she'd never seen before. Releasing the catch above his fly, she inched the zipper downward and left the trousers hanging precariously on his hips.

"All the time I was gone, I thought about you." He reached out and covered her breasts with his hands.

"I got your postcards."

"I saw them on your refrigerator." He didn't comment on Danny's pictures.

"You didn't say much." *Talk to me*, her heart was begging; *say something important, not just lover's sweet talk*.

"What is there to say on a postcard? I could see your mailman's reaction if I'd written about what I'd like to do now."

He watched as she slowly unbuttoned his shirt and pulled the cloth over his shoulders and let it drop to the floor.

Running her fingers through the hair on his chest that she loved to touch, she swayed against him, tiny electric charges passing from his golden hairs to her throbbing flesh. Then she pushed his slacks downward and he stepped out of them.

"Make me feel good, baby," he whispered, holding her so close that she felt pangs of desire stirring hot in her loins.

As he lifted her to the edge of the table, she wanted to tell him what he was doing was impossible, but she forgot how to talk. Neither of them heard a small crash. Thrown off-balance by his passionate thrusts, she clung to him with all her strength, digging her fingers into his unyielding muscles, gasping at the impact of his need, not feeling the slap of her bottom on the polished maple tabletop, not hearing her own throaty cries. She shook like the last leaf to leave its branch in a winter gale, digging her nails into his back until they tumbled together onto her soft imitation Persian rug.

He was laughing but his eyes had tears in them, looking as

moist as gemstones under water. She smothered a cry against his throat, slowly trying to prop herself up on one elbow.

"Are you all right?" he asked.

"Yes. Surprised."

"I haven't thought of anything else for forty-eight hours, but I didn't plan anything like that."

"No one could plan that!"

"You're probably right." Getting to her feet, Libby saw there was one casualty: another of Grandma Sloan's cups had bit the dust, having fallen from the far edge of the table where the carpet didn't cover the hardwood floor.

"Your cup. I'm sorry."

"Ten is a more even number than twelve."

"What do you mean?"

She didn't explain.

"Do you have to work today?" he asked, lifting her in his arms.

"Not for hours and hours."

"I was terrible to wake you so early."

"Terrible."

He lay down beside her on the bed, holding her in his arms until, floating with joy, they napped, woke, and napped again.

"I couldn't have planned a nicer homecoming," he said, blowing on her eyelids to wake her yet again.

"Homecoming," she repeated. It was a beautiful word, but she wasn't quite sure what he meant by it.

"Can you get me a ticket tonight?" His lazy drawl sent shivers down her spine, even after their long day in bed together.

"For my play?"

"Unless the Jets are playing tonight. Of course your play!"

"You mean you'd rather see football than me?"

"If you believe that, you just haven't been paying attention! Do you eat before the play?"

"No, afterward. I'm always too nervous."

"I'll try to last until then."

"I have some . . ." She really didn't have anything to feed a man with Craig's appetite. "Well, there's not much here, now that I think about it. You could fry an egg."

"Just leave a ticket for me at the box office."

Her euphoria was fading; the thought of cooking for him made her face reality. How long would he be with her? Maybe he'd already booked a flight to L.A. Nothing he'd said gave her the slightest clue, and she was too proud to ask.

Insisting that she take a cab instead of the subway to the theater, he kissed her good-bye and promised to be at the theater on time. She left, excited because he'd be in the audience but sad because nothing had changed. He was with her now, but where would he be tomorrow?

CHAPTER THIRTEEN

"Good job tonight," Summie said, his mouth puckering with distaste at the indignity of paying a compliment to an actor. Libby got this scrap of praise because he prided himself on being tough but fair, the U-boat captain who sinks the ship but pulls survivors out of the sea. It never occurred to him that he and the performers were on the same side.

She hung up her gown and petticoat, sitting in front of the mirror in pantyhose and chemise to remove her makeup. One nice thing about the drafty old theater was its size. When it was remodeled for live productions, plenty of dressing rooms had been added. She had one to herself for a change.

Engrossed in doing her face, she didn't know how long Craig had been watching her from the curtained doorway. She caught a glimpse of his lanky shape in the mirror and pretended not to see him, preening shamelessly under his watchful eyes. Something about him was very different.

"You were wonderful," he said quietly.

"Did you really like it?" She stood and came to his arms.

"The play, no. But you were fantastic. You kept me spellbound."

"You're wearing a suit!" No wonder he looked so different.

"I had it made in Spain."

He was also wearing leather shoes polished to a high sheen instead of scuffed boots. His suit was a dark mahogany worsted worn with a white oxford-cloth shirt, the collar buttoned down beside a gold-and-brown-striped tie. Somehow he managed to give the impression of sartorial elegance and still look casually comfortable.

"I love it!"

"Good, because I bought it for you. Along with one other little thing."

"A present?"

"Wait and see. Are you ready to go? I'm hungry."

"Almost. Wait outside and I'll get dressed."

He chuckled. "Why outside?"

She shrugged, not knowing why she had sudden attacks of modesty in front of him. "Stay, then."

Her old standby red wool dress with long sleeves and a square neckline didn't seem special enough to go with Craig's new look, but she was too hungry herself to suggest going back to the apartment to change.

He was the one who found the perfect restaurant. The tables were small, but there was ample room between them in a cozy brick-walled room intimately lit by candles on the tables. Their knees touched under a corner table for two, and the waiter's low-key attitude promised the maximum of service with a minimum of interruptions. Craig insisted on champagne, even though Libby knew he'd rather have beer. She persuaded him to try bouillabaisse, and he pretended to like it, although he was a bit curious about the ingredients. He did refuse to share an appetizer of *moules provençale* when she explained that they were hot, garlicky mussels.

His prime rib was pink and juicy, and her duck with black cherry sauce was a gourmet specialty of the house. A crock of butter sat on the table to go with hot rolls and corn sticks, and they even managed to share an order of carrot cake.

"Many meals like this and my waistline will never recover," she said, intoxicated by the loving expression on Craig's face.

"Don't worry, the Italians don't pay that well."

Did that mean he'd be off on another job soon? Being with him was like standing on the edge of a deep crevasse, marvelously challenging and exciting, with disaster looming only a step away.

"Let's go home and unpack my bags," he said softly.

"Does that mean you're staying?"

"If you'll have me."

"I don't know what to say."

"Tell me to leave, and I will."

"Oh, no!" She wasn't strong enough to do that, not when being with him meant more than anything in the world. "I've been so worried about when you'd leave."

"I'm glad it didn't affect your appetite." His gentle teasing made him even more lovable.

"How long will you stay, Craig?" It was the hardest question she'd ever asked.

He hesitated for what seemed like ages, finally holding out his hand for hers.

"I don't know," he said slowly, "but I can't imagine not loving you."

Hard cords of tension seemed to snap in her neck, shoulders, and arms, leaving her as limp as a marionette whose performance is over. In her heart she'd known Craig loved her, but she'd desperately needed to hear him say it. He loved her! Nothing else mattered.

Almost floating as she left the restaurant and got into a taxi, she shivered against him because winter was coming early.

"I'm going to freeze without my flannel nightgown," she said, pretending to scold him.

"Tonight it'll be summer in New York," he promised in a

whisper, totally oblivious to the world outside the cab as he kissed her with unhurried fervor.

When they entered her apartment, his bags were nowhere in sight.

"It looks like you've unpacked already," she teased him.

"One bag was all dirty clothes. I dumped it in your hamper."

"If you think I'm going to do your laundry . . ."

"I don't mind washing. I'll do yours too."

"Craig, what will you do here?" She was too concerned not to ask.

"Look around. I have your word that this is quite a city."

"And when you're done being a tourist?"

"I can probably pick up some work on commercials. Did you see the one I did for motor oil?"

"Not that I remember. Was it long ago?"

"Eight or nine years, maybe. I was prettier then."

"You were never pretty!"

"You are." He lifted her against him and kissed her. "There's one thing I didn't unpack. Give me your coat."

He hung her camel-colored winter coat in the closet; he was still coatless himself.

"You've got to get a winter jacket."

"I've got a good sheepskin-lined one at home."

"Can you have it sent?"

"Don't worry about that now, darling."

He took a package wrapped in blue tissue paper from an otherwise empty bag. "Close your eyes," he ordered.

She did, tingling with suspense, hoping he hadn't bought an album for the postcards.

"Okay, open them." He was dangling an exotic black lace nightgown from his thumbs, looking more ill at ease than she'd ever seen him.

"Oh, it's beautiful! Thank you!" She touched it, fingering

214

the soft, almost silky lace, so much finer than machine-made. "Mr. Wicklow, I almost believe you're blushing."

"Do you like it?"

"I love it. I love you!"

She hugged him, crushing the gown between them.

"I love you, Libby, darling."

She was so filled with emotion, she had to choke back tears.

"Try it on," he urged.

She changed in the bathroom, insisting he see it all at once. He was going to see quite a bit of her too. The floor-length gown was as revealing as it was gorgeous, made of nothing but lace and shiny satin ribbons with a few scraps of reinforcing nylon.

His loud, throaty whistle told it all. As he stood by the closet, hanging his suit but still wearing shorts and dress shirt, his eyes grew cloudy with passion and his lips tightened.

"Is it Spanish?" she asked.

"No, I bought it in Paris. I had a long layover there trying to get to Spain after I missed the plane here."

"Thank you," she said softly, welcoming him with open arms.

"Darling," he said, sounding too serious for what she had in mind, "will you get yourself some birth control pills?"

"I suppose I can." She wasn't altogether convinced they were good for women.

"Please. I don't want to worry."

It hurt her that the thought of her getting pregnant worried him so. She walked to the kitchen, pretending to want a drink of water.

The beautiful lace gown didn't seem as sexy as it had a few minutes ago. She wandered over to the TV, turning it on and sitting on the couch without turning it into a bed.

"Darling, I haven't lived with anyone in a long time. It won't all be easy." He sat beside her, taking her hand and holding it against his thigh.

"I've never lived with anyone," she admitted ruefully, meaning that she'd never lived with a man.

"I couldn't make myself get on a plane for L.A."

"I don't want you to."

"Can we take it a day at a time? See what happens?"

Was he hoping to get over being in love by living with her for a while? She couldn't imagine going through life feeling the way she did now, excited by the sound of his voice, the scent of his after-shave, the sight and feel of his hand covering hers on a restaurant table. Sitting beside him, feeling his shirt-sleeve on her bare arm and the bone of his ankle against hers, she was aroused to a state of quiet hysteria. No two people could be together all the time without losing some of that. She needed him there so she could begin living a normal life again, untormented by continual longings; she couldn't condemn him if he felt the same way.

"I'm glad you're here," she said sincerely.

It was the right thing to say. He took her in his arms, telling her how lonely he'd been in Spain without her.

"Did you agree to do a movie there because of me?"

"Maybe. I'm not sure." He held her head against his chest, wrapping her in his arms. "Things were going too fast with us. I didn't believe I could feel this way for more than a few weeks. I wasn't sure I wanted to."

"Thought you were over the hill, huh, pardner?" She moved closer to him, loving him with her whole being.

"Way over."

"Do you want me to talk to my agent for you?"

"I'd better talk to mine first. We have a contract."

"You and your contracts!"

216

"I hate them," he said.

She wondered if that included marriage contracts.

"We'll have to decide who takes out the garbage," she said.

"I don't suppose you have a maid?"

"On my pay? With this apartment?"

"It is pretty small," he said grimly. "I'll need a place to work out."

"There are lots of health clubs. You can shop around."

"I hate to think of jogging here in the winter."

"Sometimes we go for months with lovely, crisp days. You just need the right clothes." He'd find out about the snow all too soon.

"How long will your play run?"

"All winter, I hope. It depends. If Summie—our director— annoys the producers as much as he does the cast, who knows? Actually it depends on the ticket sales."

"I can't figure out who wants to see a play about some guy abandoned in a suitcase."

"There's a lot of satire, you know, jabs at the privileged classes and all that."

"I read the program, but the whole thing seemed silly to me."

She giggled. "Didn't you like it when Cecily talked about the great moments of physical courage men have?"

"I've heard snow jobs before!" He fingered the lace on her thigh, finding tiny finger holes in the design.

"What about my lines? Did you like any of them?"

"All of them, but only because they were coming out of the loveliest mouth I've ever seen." He fingered the pattern of lace on her breast. "Are you through fishing for compliments?"

"I just want you to like me!"

"Libby, I do! More than I ever thought possible. I love you."

Was this how honeymoons were, free of the anxiety of parting? They petted on the couch, feeling no urgency because the days stretched ahead without the pain of separation. She was afraid to trust such bliss, but Craig reassured her with long, sweet kisses and playful caresses.

"I'm glad we live now," he murmured, "instead of when that play was written." He found a supersensitive place below her ear and showered lovely little kisses on it.

"Men were gentlemen then!"

"I'm not?" He was fascinated by the wispy black lace against her breasts, caressing it with the tips of his fingers.

She was losing the impulse to tease. "You really don't need a plum velvet smoking jacket like Algernon."

"I should hope not!"

Awaking beside him in the morning was the nicest part of all. He used his tongue to arouse her nipples, then drew her on top of him, letting her make love to him until her thighs were shaky. Suspended over him, her breasts were like ripe fruit, his own personal ambrosia, and her gown was a lacy veil hanging on the bedside lampshade. They came together, their pleasure so intense, it was close to pain, forgetting about the existence of the rest of the world.

His groan of pleasure turned to one of pain after Libby collapsed in her arms. "How do you sleep with a steel bar across your shoulders? This folding bed is murder."

"It's harder with two." She didn't know why; the Hide-A-Bed was an ample queen-size.

"Maybe if we put our heads at the foot, it'll feel better," he suggested, lazily nuzzling the top of her head, brushing aside a lock of hair that was tickling his nose.

Stricken by a sudden flash of precognition, she was sure

her apartment would be too small, too confining and uncomfortable for him. They could look for a bigger one, but that would mean planning ahead, making a commitment to be together for a while. She'd promised to live one day at a time, but it wasn't going to be easy.

The bathtub crisis came a few days later. They stayed in bed until noon after a late night of dancing that didn't begin until her play was over.

"I can't face it," Craig said, sounding alarmingly gloomy.

"What?" Slipping into her robe, she hurried across the room to turn up the thermostat. Craig didn't like the apartment hot while he was sleeping.

"That miniature bathtub. I have to sit with my knees under my chin."

"You're exaggerating."

"Not much."

"I could get one of those shower heads with a hose that fits onto the faucet of the tub."

"That would be about as handy as hosing off an elephant in the kitchen sink."

"I'm sorry!" She really wasn't. "Go dirty!"

"Be serious."

"Would you like it better if I scrub your back?"

"It can't hurt to try."

She loved his back, the skin unblemished and smooth, and he did enjoy his scrub. She squeezed water over his shoulders and let it trickle over his chest, then bedeviled a little wrinkle of skin on his tummy, the closest thing to a fat spot that he had.

"Don't let me buy any more beer. I'll turn into a tub sitting around this place," he grumbled.

He joined a health club the next week, but it wasn't a convenient one in her part of town. She sent him off for the subway almost every day, and one gloomy Friday he wasn't back after three hours. It was time to leave for the theater, so she left a note with lots of Xs for kisses and a tuna casserole he could warm for his dinner.

Summie was on a rampage, finding fault with everything from Bill's timing to the size of the cookies they served as biscuits in the first act. He called a special meeting in the green room after the performance, not even giving Libby a chance to call Craig.

Winter was thundering through the streets, pelting her with snow, when the irate director finally let them go. Bill came out stomping his loafers in the slushy accumulation and offered to share a cab, but not even a two-block dash on the slippery sidewalks brought one within hailing distance.

"I guess it's the subway," he said with no noticeable enthusiasm.

"That or freeze."

The yellow glow in her window was a welcoming beacon dimly visible through the swirling snow. Her feet were soaked and so cold, her toes felt like ice cubes. The thought of Craig's arms had never seemed more inviting, but they weren't open and waiting when she reached the second floor, still breathless after rushing there from the subway.

"I was getting worried." He sounded irritated, not relieved, to see her.

"That insufferable director called a meeting afterward." She shook her coat and hung it up. "Then you might know, I couldn't get a cab."

"How'd you get here?" He was wearing a navy sweater with faded jeans, his feet warm-looking in thick, white wool crew socks.

"Subway," she said absentmindedly, taking off her wet shoes.

"I don't want you riding the subway alone at night!"

"Oh, Bill was with me. He goes two stops beyond mine."

220

"Well, that makes it safe," he said sarcastically.

"We couldn't get a cab. Anyway, no muggers are out on a night like this."

"Next time call me and I'll meet you," he insisted.

"Did you enjoy your workout?" she asked to change the subject.

"It was okay. My parents are making a big deal out of Christmas this year, and they'd like me to spend it with them in Texas."

"Are you going?"

Her feet were warmer, but the cold had moved inward, making her insides feel chilly with dread. In the few weeks they'd been together, they'd never talked about plans for the future; she didn't want to now because she was afraid of anything that might separate them.

"Can you come?"

"I'll only have the one day off. I don't see how I can."

"Then I won't go, of course."

She dreaded the time when he would start going places without her. They settled the problem of Christmas without a crisis, but Libby didn't feel elated. Craig didn't complain, but she knew he was restless. His morning jog ended earlier now as the weather worsened, and several hours at the health club didn't begin to tap his energy. They saw New York together, but each evening it became harder to leave for the theater, knowing he was bored in her absence. Going to a hockey game with her landlord seemed to make him gloomier; he missed being in the center of action himself.

January was a blustery month with snow and cold that made any outside activity a test of endurance, and February wasn't much better. Craig gave up jogging and spent more time working out at his club, but Libby was relieved when he got a job making a series of commercials. He joked about

221

being a boob-tube salesman but wouldn't tell her what he was selling.

Sitting on the bed with her knees pulled up and the covers tucked under her chin, she watched him dressing. "You can tell me what company it is, can't you?"

"Nope."

"Craig!" She sent a pillow flying in his direction, but it missed and fell to the floor.

"It's no big deal."

"Just tell me if you have to do any stunts."

"Not to speak of."

When his drawl was thick enough to bottle, she knew he was putting her on.

"If you don't tell me, I'll die of curiosity."

"Dog food." He sounded disgusted.

"You're making a dog-food commercial?"

"The greyhound gets top billing. First horses, now dogs."

"Darling, you don't have to make commercials."

He shrugged. "It's something to do."

He was playing a racing-dog handler, he told her that evening when she got home from the theater. What he didn't say was whether the day's work had gone well. She was afraid to ask.

Danny sent her another picture, this time a scribbly sketch of a cowboy in a black shirt and hat that wasn't at all like his usually careful drawings. She put it on her refrigerator, making a special effort to write to him right away, also sending her little friend a small gift, a book with illustrations that popped up. His mother was on location again, and Libby wished he could be with her instead of with another new sitter. The poor little guy's world was constantly being upset.

Craig finished the commercials just in time to enjoy an unseasonable break in the weather, several dry, moderate days that allowed him to jog in comfort. Libby ran with him

222

for a couple of mornings, but she gave it up, knowing she held him back after the first mile. She was basically a sprinter and couldn't hope to match his staying power.

Something was different when she came home from a discouraging Saturday-evening performance with nearly a third of the seats unsold. Craig was working on another mailing for the environmental committee, laboriously signing, folding, and sealing the letters, this time not asking for her help. Preoccupied as she was by the play, it took her a minute to realize that the refrigerator had been stripped clean of drawings and postcards.

"What happened to Danny's pictures?" she asked, trying to keep her voice level and unchallenging.

"Oh, I wiped off the stove and refrigerator just for something to do."

"But where are the things I had on the fridge?"

He looked up, a picture of innocent surprise. "The pictures were getting dog-eared, so I threw them out with the garbage."

"Craig, I wanted them."

"How was I to know?"

"You could've asked."

"You weren't here. It seemed like a good idea to clean up the kitchen. I have to do something while you're out playing the Victorian lady."

The resentment in his voice bothered her more than the loss of the pictures.

"Oh, I put the postcards in the drawer with the bills and stuff," he added.

"You saved the cards but threw away Danny's pictures?"

"I didn't expect you to get mad." He left his letters and tried to take her in his arms, but she was too upset.

"It's just the idea, Craig. I like getting Danny's artwork. You could've asked me before tossing them out."

223

"You've already told me that. I'm sorry." There wasn't a trace of apology in his voice.

"I'll bet you are! You just don't like Danny."

"That's silly."

"Is it?" She walked away.

"Do you want me to see if I can retrieve them?"

"Covered with carrot scrapings and tomato skins? No, thanks."

"I forgot we had salad for lunch."

"Just forget it."

He might dismiss it as unimportant, but she couldn't. It really hurt that he didn't want any reminders of Danny in the apartment. Not inclined to made a big issue over something that couldn't be remedied, Libby didn't say anything else, but Craig's attitude hurt. He was rarely childish in any way, so it made her doubly distressed that he so obviously rejected Danny.

The next time she went shopping alone, she bought Danny a set of watercolor paints and mailed them to him. If he sent a drawing in return, it would get a place of honor in her apartment. She might even frame it.

Summie called another green-room conference on a Thursday night, this time berating ungrateful producers, money-hungry creditors, and unappreciative audiences more than the cast members. She left the late-night session feeling drained, not refusing when Bill urged her to join some of the others for a quick drink before going home. She only had two glasses of wine, but the gathering became a consolation party; the play would probably close soon, and it was a bad time to look for work.

There was no welcoming glow in her front window when the cab brought her home, and even the stairway seemed darker than usual, the metallic-green walls badly in need of painting and the light on the second landing burned out.

Craig was asleep; she could tell by his even, deep breathing. Using the light from the bathroom, she undressed quietly, getting ready for bed without disturbing him but hoping he would wake up. She needed to be hugged and cuddled; without his arms around her the world seemed cold and hostile.

Shivering in the cold apartment, she found her black lace nightgown, ignoring the goose bumps on her arms and thighs while she slipped into the Parisian creation. Under the covers with Craig she'd be more than warm enough.

Sleeping on his side with his back toward her, he still showed no signs of waking. She cuddled, spoonlike, against him, pressing her cold legs against his, warming herself against the bare expanse of his back and bottom until he stirred sleepily, half sitting to look at the luminous numbers on the alarm.

"You're late."

"Yes, Summie called another meeting."

"I appreciate your calling," he said sarcastically. "What did you do, run through the whole play?"

"No, it looks like we may close. I went out with the rest of the cast for a drink afterward."

"I hate it when you're running all over town at this time of night." He corrected himself. "Morning."

"I'm sorry. I'm just not used to checking with anyone."

She hadn't forgotten to call. It had just seemed easier not to. Feeling a bit guilty, she knew he would have told her to come right home. His invitations to bed were as hard as ever to turn down, but sometimes she needed to assert her independence. Their arrangement was too informal for him to make the rules.

"I think you work late enough without hanging around bars with a crowd of actors."

225

His tone of voice was infuriating, but she wanted him to hold her more than she wanted to argue.

"Now that I'm here, are you happy to see me?"

She rubbed her leg against his, loving the firmness of his calf and the fuzziness of his skin.

"I would've been happier two hours ago."

He turned his back to her again, fluffed the pillow, and pulled the covers over his shoulders. He was going back to sleep.

Needing him badly, she ran her hand over the swell of his hip, caressing his thigh and bottom until she couldn't lie still. He didn't turn to take her in his arms.

"I'm going back to sleep," he said gruffly.

His rejection hurt. Craig not wanting to make love was a man she didn't know.

"You're angry with me." She moved away to put space between their bodies, but the backs of her fingers still touched his side.

"I'd just like to get some sleep. I hate staying up half the night waiting for you to get home."

"It never bothered you this much before."

"If you want to argue, we can do it in the morning."

"Why do you have to jog so early? You could go out anytime."

"Rub it in! I don't have a darn thing to do all day."

"I didn't mean it that way."

"I like mornings. I'm used to being up early." He still didn't turn toward her.

"Get up at dawn for all I care!"

She turned her back with a maximum amount of squirming and rearranging of covers, even more furious when, only minutes later, his breathing told her he was sleeping again. Lying there without touching him, she thought of all kinds of things to say. It wasn't her fault he'd done nothing but

226

dog-food commercials since coming to New York; she'd repeatedly urged him to work with her agent. Every spare minute she spent entertaining him; if he wanted to see anything from belly dancers to a U.N. debate, she went with him. Her friends had given up calling her, and when they did go out with people she knew, Craig was usually eager to get home.

She lay wide awake, piling up grievances like a baby with building blocks, constructing a shaky pyramid of complaints, then demolishing it in one quick mental swipe when she turned again and cuddled against Craig's backside. Nothing really mattered as long as they were together.

At daybreak little teasing kisses woke her, and she reached for Craig automatically, not choosing to remember his coldness of the night before.

"Are you still in the mood?" he whispered, starting to make sure she was.

Reaching under her lacy gown, he laid a warm hand on her tummy, making lazy circles that kept getting wider and more exciting. He parted her lips with his tongue, testing the edges of her teeth before plunging in to sample the slippery closeness of her mouth.

Pushing her gown higher, he fondled her breasts, all the while sliding one leg against hers. He was a conductor tuning his orchestra, getting responses from every section before beginning the symphony.

Remembering last night's rejection, she became evasive, removing his hand when he became more audacious, turning on her side and curling up, muttering utterly false protests. He gave her rear a love tap and pretended to get up, springing on top the moment she uncoiled from her protective position.

"Got you!" he hooted triumphantly.

"Stop!" she cried, but if he had, she would have been very disappointed.

She was addicted to his tender, exhilarating lovemaking. When he praised her pretty face and vibrant blue eyes, she became more beautiful for him. His anger was worse punishment than a lash, and his unhappiness made her miserable. Their winter together had made her love him more, and she tried to forget the little differences that were troubling both of them, again receiving him in her arms and her heart.

His morning lovemaking was slower and more intense than the evening encounters, carrying her to dizzy heights with unhurried caresses and deep kisses. Every part of her was as familiar to him as his own body, but he explored with fresh wonder, making her feel mysterious, desirable, and above all, cherished. He had the rare gift of making the inside of her arm or the arch of her foot totally erotic, bestowing worshipful kisses and penetrating caresses with a generosity of spirit that made her want to give him total happiness.

Coming together under the covers when the cold air in the room made them both shivery, they began the world's oldest dance, the rhythmic joining of two lovers devoted to giving and receiving pleasure. Playful without being coy, they let the good feelings build, patient but expectant, not disappointed when the tempo increased and built to a deep, thrilling climax. She closed her eyes, willing the aftershocks to go on and on, wanting him to love her forever.

"This doesn't mean," he teased, "that I'm not angry."

"You have no reason to be mad at me!"

"Out drinking with a bunch of actors until the early hours. Ha!"

"I rarely do that!" She cuddled against his chest, rubbing her nose when his hair tickled.

"Don't do it again. Please."

"Just because we live together doesn't mean we can't have some life apart," she said earnestly. "You have your health club and your running. . . ."

He snorted, sounding so disgusted, she wanted to drop the subject.

"I'm not used to being penned up in a little hole all winter."

"A hole! I worked hard to make my apartment look nice!"

"It's nice—what there is of it."

"You wouldn't spend so much time here if you were more aggressive about looking for work."

"Aggressive! If you mean I should fawn over a bunch of—"

"That's not what I mean! My agent could do a lot for you if you'd give him a chance."

"I don't trust him."

"Why not? He's done all right for me."

"Haven't you noticed that ninety percent of his clients are women and the other ten percent wish they were?"

"That's the silliest thing you've ever said. You're just making excuses for sitting around all winter!"

"You think I'm lazy?" He got out of bed, pulling off the top blanket to wrap around himself.

"You're giving a pretty good imitation of it."

She didn't want to say these things! Sometimes the man just goaded her beyond reason.

"I'm going to take a bath, if you can call sitting in that kiddies' tub taking a bath!"

It wasn't their first fight, but she'd never felt so bad. They were arguing about minor things to avoid the real issues, and both knew it. How much longer could Craig stand being idle in a city he didn't like? How could she tell him to go to L.A. and find stunt work when losing him would break her heart? Could they continue living together? Could they exist apart?

Not unexpectedly, *The Importance of Being Earnest* closed. No one could feel too badly since it had lasted through most of the winter, but, in spite of Summerfield Hawkins, the play was special to the cast members. Sometimes in the theater the right people come together in the right play, and the result is a stellar production. Some of them might never work together again, but they'd all remember the Wilde revival. An *enfant terrible* had somehow managed to direct them in a bit of theatrical history with the help of energetic young talent. In a sentimental mood the cast chipped in and bought their director a plaster bust of Shakespeare as a closing gift. His face puckered so much, Libby was sure he'd cry, but he disappointed no one when he snarled an ungracious thanks and put his winter beret on the bard's head. No one wanted to remember him as a weeping man-child.

Craig came to the closing performance; Libby glowed under his attentiveness but felt a little guilty that she'd never invited her family to see the play. The reason was simple: her parents and brothers wouldn't be thrilled with her living arrangements. They might like Craig as a fiancé or husband, but as a roommate they wouldn't. Her brothers were apt to be more protective than her parents, but her mother would be deeply hurt. Cohabitation wasn't what she wanted for her only daughter.

When the cast party started to turn into a wake, she and Craig left. He'd been unusually quiet all evening, but it was three days later when she learned the reason.

"I have a job offer," he said over dinner at a neighborhood café where they often went when neither felt like cooking.

Dread, not surprise, kept her from responding.

"It's on the West Coast. I have a few days to think it over."

"Do you need to?"

He looked uncomfortable but didn't evade her question.

"No. I need to work, Libby. I can't hang around here forever."

"I guess not." Her throat was so tight, she could hardly speak.

"It's a good offer. I'll be assistant stunt coordinator, something I've wanted for a long time."

"You won't be doing the stunts yourself?"

"No, and I have some ideas on how to make the work safer for those who do them."

"That's good." She wanted to cry but choked back the tears.

"Darling, you can come along."

She didn't think he planned to abandon her, but she didn't have a ready answer.

"Your play's closed. You don't have anything else lined up. What is there to keep you here?" he asked urgently.

"I don't know, Craig."

"You have a few days to decide before I leave," he said. His voice was devoid of expression, but she could still hear the hurt in every word.

Nothing more was said about either of them going West. By unspoken consent they kept busy seeing and doing things that were still new to Craig. She even persuaded him that a trip to the Metropolitan Museum of Art would interest him and felt rewarded by his fascination with the displays of medieval armor. He didn't press for an answer about her going with him, but she knew the offer was still open.

He'd asked her to "come along." It wasn't enough! In California she'd only be his mistress, a hanger-on in his life.

Slowly she realized that she wasn't being honest with Craig. How could he know her feelings when she kept them to herself? He couldn't possibly realize how strongly she felt about permanent commitments, about sharing the future with the one person she loved.

She could never love anyone the way she did Craig, but without more honesty and openness in their relationship, she couldn't be sure that he felt the same way. After two long, painful days of pretending they were playful, carefree lovers, she knew what had to be done. Before she could make a decision about going with Craig, they had to have a good old-fashioned showdown.

CHAPTER FOURTEEN

"I have to make plane reservations. Do I need two seats or one?" Craig asked as they lingered over coffee after a late brunch.

She'd been rehearsing what to say for two days, but approaching Craig was much harder than performing for an audience in a theater.

"When do you have to be there?" she asked.

"I'm supposed to sign the contract by the end of next week."

"Oh, then there's no hurry." She pretended to be relieved, but it was bad acting.

"I've been waiting long enough. Do you want to come with me?"

"It's not that simple! There are things to—"

"Yes or no, Libby?"

"I can't walk away from my life here on a moment's notice."

"Last time I looked, you were unemployed. Your family doesn't live here. What's the problem?"

"There's my apartment. . . ."

"You can sublet it."

She stood and walked to the front window, finding it immensely difficult to be evasive with him.

"There's more to it than that, isn't there?" He followed, standing behind her with his hands on her shoulders.

"My apartment doesn't have anything to do with it." She couldn't lie, not now when their future was at stake.

"Do you love me?" he asked.

"You know I do."

"Then everything should be simple. We belong together."

"If you believe that," she said, turning to face him, "why don't you ask me to marry you?"

"So that's the trouble," he said slowly, taking a deep breath.

"Don't say it like that!"

"Like what?"

"In that patronizing voice. You're thinking: *Isn't that just like a woman, wanting a piece of paper and a ring?* Well, that's not my point at all!"

"What is?"

"I want to make plans for the future."

He looked down at her, his face guarded. "Go on."

Help me, Craig, she was crying inside, but when she spoke, her words sounded stiff and formal. "When two people love each other, is it so terrible to make commitments?"

"You're talking about a contract, not love."

"No! Not the kind of contract you mean. You're deliberately trying to misunderstand."

"You want to get married. That's not complicated."

"I want you to want marriage!"

"I don't." He shook his head gravely.

"Craig, I'll be twenty-nine. If I'm ever going to have a husband, a home, children, now is the time. I've discovered I want these things very much."

"You can have a great career."

234

"It's not enough!"

"Not when I'm with you too?"

"You don't understand!" She walked away from him, but he followed.

"I understand, but I don't agree. Putting it in writing won't make our love any stronger."

"You don't know that."

"Don't I? I've been married before, Libby."

"And in all the time we've known each other, you've never told me your ex-wife's name."

"Kim. Her name was Kimberly."

"I don't care about her name!"

"You want to know why our marriage failed. You think it's the reason why I don't want to try again."

"Is it?"

"Yes—no. I don't know!"

"Do you love me, Craig?" She whispered, fearing his answer.

"Libby!" He crushed her against him. "I love you so much!"

His words seemed to make everything right when he was holding her, but she pulled away, unwilling to give up so easily.

"It's having children that you don't want, isn't it?"

His face went white, and for a long moment he seemed unable to answer.

"Yes," he said heavily.

"You really don't like Danny or any other child." Hearing him admit it was like a knockout blow, forcing her to sit on the edge of a kitchen chair.

"Liking children has nothing to do with it!"

Scarcely hearing his denial, she said, "I didn't want to believe it, but you never pretended otherwise. You didn't want Danny near you. You didn't want his drawings in our apartment.''

"You don't understand.'' He stood halfway across the room, his fists clenched by his sides.

"I'm beginning to. You made sure we always took precautions. You insisted I go on the pill. The only thing I don't understand is why you haven't had a vasectomy.''

"Before you, it'd been a long time since I'd met a woman who didn't protect herself. I had my fill of surgery on my knee. You're wrong about my not liking children. It's not that way at all. . . .'' His voice trailed off and he walked to the window, staring down at the street.

"You don't want children of your own.'' She repeated it, trying to make herself face the truth.

"Does that mean you don't want me?'' He looked over his shoulder at her for just an instant, not long enough for her to be sure if his eyes were moist.

"It doesn't make me stop loving you.'' Her chest felt as if a heavy weight was pressing against it. "But I need to understand, Craig. I thought you cared for your family. Would it be so terrible to have a family of your own?''

"I had a family of my own!'' His words came out like the crack of a whip.

Stunned, she couldn't ask what he meant.

"I had a son,'' he said, his voice close to breaking. "He died.''

"Oh, no.''

The pain on his face brought tears to her eyes, but she didn't know what to say about such long-buried sorrow.

"He died before he was three,'' he said, forcing every word through a constricted throat. "He was born with a congenital cardiac defect and some other severe complications. When he got pneumonia, he just wasn't strong enough.''

"Craig.'' She walked to him and laid her face against his

236

back, putting her arms around him, feeling wholly inadequate, hearing the torment in his voice.

"My wife and I went through hell," he said. "Afterward she wanted another baby right away."

"You didn't?"

"No."

She didn't need to ask about his unwillingness to risk that kind of pain a second time. By the time he met Danny, his defenses were rigidly in place. He didn't want to be vulnerable to a child's suffering again.

"Maybe our marriage wouldn't have lasted anyway." He stayed in the circle of her arms, looking vacantly out on a gray day. "We got married too young. She hated my work, especially when I went on location. Losing Josh just made us realize it sooner."

"I'm so sorry," she whispered.

Her sympathy seemed to upset him. He freed himself and went to the closet, putting on the tan quilted jacket he'd finally bought for winter in New York.

"I'm going to work out at the club for a while."

"Don't go yet."

"I won't be long."

She cried when he left, great gulping sobs of frustration because she didn't know how to take away the naked pain he'd let her glimpse for the first time. How could two people be as close as they'd been and still conceal so much? No matter what happened next, they could never go back to being lovers in the superficial way they had been. Either this was the beginning of a deeper relationship or there was no hope for a future together.

Libby cried herself sick, stopping only when the throbbing pain above her eyes became unbearable. It was after dark when Craig returned.

They didn't try to make small talk.

"I went to a travel agency," he said.

"For plane tickets?"

"One ticket."

"You don't want me to come with you?" She didn't know how much more pain she could stand.

"Yes, more than ever, but I won't let you."

"Isn't that my decision?"

"Libby, I know what you want. Nothing's changed with me. I'm not marrying you. I'm not going to be the father of your children."

"All I want is you." She forgot what pride was.

"Now you do, but you deserve to have it all, a wedding, babies, a white picket fence. I'm not going to spoil it for you."

If only her head would stop pounding, she might be able to think clearly. There had to be a solution, a compromise, a way to keep him in her life.

Even when he started packing, hurriedly stuffing clothes into his two bags, she couldn't believe this was the end. If he loved her half as much as she loved him, he couldn't possibly leave without her.

He came out of the bathroom carrying his shaving kit and the black velour robe she'd given him for Christmas. Remembering their long walk through the snow on Christmas Eve brought big wet tears to her eyes.

With his coat on he took her in his arms, bending to kiss her pounding forehead. "I know how much it hurts, baby, but someday you'll thank me."

"No!" She blindly shook her head, her knuckles white as she bunched his jacket with her fists.

The moment when he walked out the door was the emptiest of her life.

As soon as he was gone she thought of a dozen urgent things to say. She had to make him understand that they could

238

take a chance together; she loved him enough to help him risk the pain that could come with having a child. He was a reasonable man; she'd make him understand that most children grew to healthy adulthood. The joys of a new family would help him forget poor little Josh.

This couldn't be the end of them! Love like theirs was the rarest of gifts, the blessing of a lifetime. They had so much to give each other.

An hour passed and then another. She clung to the faint hope that Craig might change his mind at the airport and come back to her instead of getting on the plane. Pacing until her apartment seemed like a prison cell, she wouldn't leave, not as long as there was one chance in a million that he'd return.

It was after midnight when her hope died. If she ever saw him again, it would be fate or coincidence. He wasn't going to come back to her.

The normal early-morning street commotion, the hum of the refrigerator, and the noise of other tenants leaving for work weren't enough to break the unnatural stillness in her apartment. It felt like a place where people used to live.

She made coffee and toast, carrying them to the couch, which was already made up so she wouldn't look at it and remember Craig's tousled hair on the pillow. Only yesterday they'd sat across from each other at her kitchen table, and the sight of it brought back memories of the morning he'd returned from Spain. She was drinking coffee from a battered old smiling-face mug rather than use the bone china as she always had with Craig, but little changes in habit were no help at all in erasing his aura from the apartment. There was nowhere she could look without triggering a memory. Her toast was smeared with strawberry jam he'd bought, and the coffee was strong the way Craig liked it. Impatient with her misery, she turned on the television, staring doggedly at the small black-and-white screen. Game shows didn't appeal to her, but she preferred the nervous-looking contestants and squealing winners to silence. She hadn't anticipated the dog-food commercial.

Craig was on-camera with a greyhound, both of them looking like lean thoroughbreds. Even shown a couple of inches tall, he had a stage presence that made her heart melt. Speaking with a lazy drawl, he sounded entirely sincere, as natural as any director could wish. Only his own lack of inclination was keeping him from success as an actor, but she knew he preferred the physical challenges of stunt work to the subtleties of acting. Was his unwillingness to act a way of containing his emotions, keeping them under tight rein? Was it his way of locking his feelings inside? Now that she knew about his son, she wondered if physical activity were his way of combating depression. Acting would force him to reach deep inside for emotions he wanted to repress.

What if she'd known about Josh from the beginning? Would it have changed their relationship in any way? She couldn't imagine loving him less; if she loved him any more, she wouldn't be able to function as an independent person.

The hurt wasn't going to go away. She tried distraction, calling her agent to prod him into finding something for her, then cleaned her apartment with compulsive thoroughness, crying when she found Craig's after-shave in the bathroom cabinet and again when she dusted a little glass horse he'd given her as a humorous reminder of his trip of Spain.

The hardest decision was whether or not to call him. At last, late in the evening, she dialed his number in L.A. He answered after three rings, but when she heard him say "hello" in a deep, husky drawl, she couldn't speak. Replacing the receiver without a word, she knew she wouldn't call again. There was nothing to say. Separating had been his decision.

Her agent counseled her to be patient when she called the next day. Her friends seemed like strangers because she couldn't share Craig's tragedy with them. This was one of those times when only family could help.

Without realizing it her parents came to the rescue just as she was floundering, not knowing what to do with her life.

"We'd like to give you a round-trip ticket to visit us for your birthday," her dad said. "Florida's mighty nice this time of year. No piles of gray snow."

"I'd love to come."

Making a decision, even one that only involved a vacation, was a first step to recovery, she told herself. She didn't have any hope that the pain would go away, but having a plan of action made it endurable. She tackled all the little chores of leaving home with frenzied eagerness: reserving her plane seat, making arrangements to have her apartment checked, canceling the newspaper, getting clothes ready. Because she didn't know how long she'd stay, she even filed a change of address with the post office to have her mail forwarded.

Maybe she'd stay in Florida forever. There was always summer stock, or she could go back to college and try for a job teaching drama. The day before she was scheduled to leave was spent mulling over her possibilities, trying to generate enthusiasm for a new job. Positive thoughts were constantly shot down by the painful longing she felt for Craig. All she could do was go to her parents and hope the healing process wouldn't take forever.

Her bags had been packed the night before, but there was no point in leaving for the airport before noon. She did her nails, then gave the apartment a last-minute dusting, not exactly doing things in logical order as she waited to leave.

No mail came. If Craig had sent any message, even a postcard to let her know he'd gotten back safely, it would be forwarded to Florida. She hadn't read a newspaper in days,

241

and the TV remained dark. Seeing Craig's commercial again would only set back her recovery.

Her heart stopped every time the phone rang. This morning she was reluctant to answer. It would be terrible timing if a job opportunity came her way on the day she was leaving.

Curiosity won out; she answered it.

"Libby, this is Freeman Cartwell. I didn't see you at the funeral, so I was afraid you might not have heard."

"Funeral?"

Her blood stopped flowing. If the AD was calling to tell her Craig was dead, she'd die on the spot.

"You didn't hear about the accident, then?"

Not even Freeman could talk rapidly enough to put her out of this misery. "Whose funeral?" she interrupted.

"Sandra Faraday's. You seemed like pretty good friends when you were making *Freedom Gulch*, so I thought you'd want to know."

The shock was so great, she felt only a hundredth of a second's relief that it wasn't Craig.

"What happened?" She reached for the kitchen counter, afraid her shaking legs wouldn't support her.

"She and two others were killed on location in the Rockies."

"Yes, her new film," Libby said woodenly.

"They're still investigating, but the crux of it is that she was buried under an avalanche that shouldn't have happened. Maybe it was too late in the season. Maybe the vibrations of a helicopter had something to do with it."

"I can't believe it. Sandra said the worst injury she'd ever had making a movie was an infected hangnail."

"It's tough. Half of Hollywood was at her funeral. I didn't know if it got much media coverage in the East."

She didn't bother to explain that she'd stopped the newspaper and avoided the TV.

"Who was the stunt coordinator?" she asked urgently,

242

remembering the many times Craig had talked about the need for putting safety first.

"Howard McFee."

"I've never heard of him."

"His reputation isn't the greatest. He does great sequences, but he takes a lot of chances."

"One too many this time," Libby suggested bitterly. "What about Sandra's son? What about Danny?"

"I don't know," Freeman said. "I'm sorry to tell you such bad news. I just had a hunch you might not know. It's a real bummer. This one will go to court for sure."

"I still can't believe it. Thank you for calling, Freeman. I'm glad you told me."

Libby made it to a chair, sitting stiffly on the edge, reeling under a new kind of pain. It was unbelievable that such a sweet, caring woman was gone. What would happen to Danny? Sandra didn't even have a relative who could watch him for short periods of time while she was on location. Who would care for him now that he was all alone?

Blinded by tears, she let her grief boil up and overflow, needing a few minutes of crying to vent her terrible sorrow. Life seemed so unfair, and she'd never needed comforting more.

Blotting her eyes on a tissue, she cut short her weeping. It was terrible to lose a friend, especially one who was so young and had so much to live for, but Libby knew what Sandra would want her to do. She had to find out if Danny was all right. If he were shuttled from one foster home to another, or even worse, put in some kind of institution, it would be horrible. She had to know where he was and what was happening to him. If there was any help or comfort she could offer, she wanted to be there to do it.

Her first impulse was to call Sandra's apartment; a friend or distant relative might be there. Unfortunately Sandra had been too well known from her film work to have a listed number. No amount of cajoling succeeded in prying the unlisted number from the phone company's information service.

Her luggage was ready, lacking only the last-minute addition of a few toiletries. She'd packed to run away from her loneliness and hurt. Now it seemed she'd have to postpone that trip.

Her mother was in a rush, readying the condo for an afternoon bridge party, but the sorrow in Libby's voice immediately gained her full attention.

"Mother, a friend of mine was killed in an accident. I have to go to California instead of visiting you and Dad."

"Of course, you do what you think is best."

Her mother was always the first to offer a casserole to a bereaved family and a shoulder to comfort mourners. Libby hung up after a whispered thank-you, immensely grateful for a mother who knew when to ask nothing.

There was no point in trying to change plane reservations by phone. She was going to California if she had to fly by way of Newfoundland. Four hours later she was on a plane flying west.

CHAPTER FIFTEEN

What could she say to a young child who had lost his only parent? Libby agonized over Danny during her flight to California, coming to the realization that words would mean little to him. Nor could she make a brief appearance in his life without doing more harm than good. Whatever his situation, whatever legal arrangements were being made for his care, she had to be available as his friend. If this meant a long stay in California, she was resigned to it. Her movie money was largely untouched, thanks to the salary from *The Importance of Being Earnest*. She'd stay close as long as she could help Sandy's son in any way.

A wild little hope sprang up unbidden: adoption. Libby had to face how hopeless the idea was; the chances of a single woman, an unemployed actress, adopting Danny were probably nil. Prospective parents had to have something to offer in the way of a home, and she wasn't even a resident of the same state. The best she could expect was the role of big sister, honorary aunt, or friend.

Los Angeles was alien territory, or so it felt when she landed at L.A. International Airport with only a vague idea that she needed to go north from there. On impulse she rented a car for a week, reasoning that ready transportation was a necessity until she knew what Danny's situation was. This was no time to be skeptical about her own driving skills, even though she'd hardly driven since using her parents' car in high school.

It was past the hour when people were driving home from work; she couldn't imagine where all the cars were headed. Did Californians live on the freeways, endlessly driving to and fro without destination or cause? That was the way it seemed to her. She missed her turnoff because she was in the wrong lane and couldn't get over in time. By the time she cautiously changed lanes, she didn't know how to get back to where she wanted to be.

Even if Danny was staying with someone in Sandra's apartment, her chances of finding the place in the dark were poor. She stopped at the first motel with a vacancy sign, too exhausted to do anything else. Practically prying her hands from the steering wheel, she was surprised at how tightly she'd been gripping it. Her legs felt weak, and she desperately needed a rest room. Her only consolation was that, wherever Danny was, he was probably sleeping by now. Tomorrow was Saturday; she'd find him if it took all day.

Thanks to a helpful desk clerk she found Sandra's apartment complex without too much difficulty the following morning. The Lockwood Apartments were set in a green oasis, beautiful to behold after traveling in the concrete desert surrounding it. A security guard stopped her, taking her name and destination, then calling the apartment for clearance. She was greatly relieved to learn that someone was there to okay her. It meant she wouldn't have to play detective trying to trace Danny's whereabouts. Her biggest fear had been that he might be a ward of the court, held in some grim institutional home. She should've known Sandra's many friends wouldn't allow that to happen, but she wasn't sorry for coming. She

246

loved Danny, and anything she could do to help him took precedence in her life.

The guard directed her to follow a road to the right; Sandra's apartment was at the rear of a two-story building of gleaming white stucco. Libby parked beside a silver Corvette, but she was too intent on seeing Danny to do more than glance at the sleek sports car. She didn't know what to say to her young friend, but she desperately wanted to do what was best for him. Taking a minute to compose herself, she vowed not to cry if it killed her. A big emotional scene was the last thing the boy needed.

The door chimes had a melodic sound, audible from where she stood on an imitation-grass mat outside the door. Huge red, yellow, and green Mexican pots flanked the entrance, each filled with a variety of thriving plants. Sandra had once mentioned having a green thumb; plants liked her, she'd claimed. So did people.

The man who answered her ring came to the door in jeans and a faded blue sweatshirt, carrying a dish towel in his hand.

"Libby!" Craig looked as dumbfounded as she felt.

"I didn't expect to see you here." Never before had she uttered such an understatement.

"I guess it is the last place you'd look for me. Come in."

"Thank you."

"You heard about Sandy?"

"Yes, Freeman called me."

"I'm sorry I didn't. You only worked with her on one film, but I should've known you'd be worried about Danny."

"Where is he?" Her heart seemed to have lodged in her throat.

"I took him to his lesson—he has a Saturday swimming class. We thought it would be best to stick to his routine as much as possible. Keep him in his own home. Let him go to the same school. My apartment is too far away for that."

247

"We?"

"The lawyer who's handling the estate—a friend of Sandra's. And Brad's aunt. She's the one who really has the say."

"Craig . . ." She started crying, unable to contain everything she felt.

"I know, baby." He did the natural thing, taking her in his arms and letting her cry against his chest.

"It's so unfair. Sandra loved Danny so much."

She pulled away and found a tissue in her purse; there wasn't any comfort for her now in Craig's arms, and she had questions that begged to be answered. "I don't understand why you're here."

"Shooting on the new picture won't start for another six weeks. I go to the studio for planning sessions, but I work them in when Danny's in school."

"Do you mean you're taking care of him all the time?"

Everything pointed to it, but she found it too incredible to believe. Craig had never wanted anything to do with children.

"It was that or throw the poor kid into the court system."

"But why you?"

"Brad and Sandy were good friends. Danny's only relative is Brad's aunt. She's in very poor health, too old to assume responsibility for his care, but she's agreed to give me temporary custody of Danny until adoptive parents can be found. I'd met her before, and she remembered me as a friend of her nephew's." He shrugged and walked away.

The bright, airy room reminded her of Sandra. The walls were creamy ivory and the dark wooden floor was highly polished. Green plants hung in baskets in front of the windows and threatened to become top-heavy enough to topple their stands. The couch and matching chair were forest-green velvet with a floral pattern in shades of gold and cream, and a Chinese jade carving of a horse sat on the glass-topped coffee table. The kitchen and a small office were to the right;

beyond the living room was a room that served as Danny's playroom, casually cluttered as any boy's nook should be. The only thing that didn't fit in the apartment was Craig's presence.

"Are you living here?"

"Temporarily. It seemed the only practical way."

"That's your car?"

"The Corvette, yes. You drove here?"

"From the airport. I rented a car there."

"I didn't even know you could drive."

"After being on the freeway, I'm not sure I can. When will Danny come home?"

"I have to pick him up in about twenty minutes. Do you want to come with me?"

"Do you mind if I just wait here?"

"No, whatever you prefer. Should I tell Danny you're here?"

"Do you think you should?"

"Yes, he'll be delighted. He talks about you and about being at Old Buckhorn."

"I'm glad." She had to choke back a fresh onslaught of tears.

"Coffee? I just made some."

"Oh, yes, please." She'd just caught herself clenching and unclenching her hands and was desperate for something to do with them.

"When did you get here?" he called from the kitchen.

"Last night. I'm staying at a motel not too far from here. I was afraid I wouldn't find this place in the dark, and I wasn't sure Danny would still be here."

"You came all the way to California just to see him?" His voice was expressionless.

He carried two mugs of coffee on a tray, setting it on the

low glass-topped table. He didn't need to ask if she used cream or sugar.

"Yes, I was so worried about what would happen, where he'd be sent. I guess I didn't need to be."

"It's wonderful that you were. He needs all the friends he can get. Will you stay long?"

"I don't know. A few weeks, maybe. I'm still out of work."

"Have you thought of looking for something here?"

He sounded like a polite stranger, standing to drink his coffee while she sat on the edge of the couch.

"No, no, I haven't thought very far ahead at all. I guess I'm taking things a day at a time. What's the name of your new movie?"

"The working title is *Seven Days to Sundown*. I hope they change it."

"Is it a Western?"

"A modern one of sorts. Cattlemen who can't make it in today's market. Lots of good outdoor action."

"You'll be going on location, then."

"Some, when the shooting starts."

"Craig, you know about these things. Did Sandra die because someone was careless?"

"The courts will have to decide that," he said slowly. "I'd settle for ten minutes alone with Howard McFee."

She'd never heard him sound more grim.

"It's so unfair. How is Danny? How's he taking it?"

"You can see for yourself. He's a game little kid, but it's rough. You will be here when we get back, won't you?"

"Yes, of course."

As soon as Craig left, she did a terrible thing, or so it seemed to her. Feeling uneasy in the strange house, she climbed to the second floor, wanting a private moment to say good-bye to her friend. There were three bedrooms, one

250

obviously Danny's with horse posters on the wall and a bright red-and-white bedspread. Craig had taken over a guest room, his luggage standing in one corner. She went to the third that had to be Sandy's, a very feminine room with a peach satin comforter and a pair of boudoir chairs in Wedgwood-blue crushed velvet. Her clothes were still in the closet, and Libby wondered if Craig would want help clearing out the personal possessions. Maybe nothing could be done until the estate was settled. A movie star's clothing had some market value, but she hated to think of her friend's garments being sold at an auction.

The specter of stolen years tormented her; Sandra loved her son so much, and now she'd never see him become a man. It was too sad for tears.

Libby was pacing in the living room, trying not to think of the time she and Craig were wasting, when he returned with Danny. Seeing Craig again was like balancing on a high mountain peak. She felt threatened and confused, afraid to say anything for fear it would be a false step. He'd left her; if he still loved her, the first move should be his.

"Libby!" Danny bounded across the room and into her arms, hugging her soundly.

She'd worried for nothing about what to say. Danny seemed to be accepting his mother's death as well as possible, perhaps partially conditioned by her frequent long absences. He very seriously told her about the accident and the funeral, and, although Libby had a hard time not crying, she realized that Craig had handled Danny's trauma very sympathetically and skillfully. Maybe, because he was no stranger to loss himself, he was able to relate to Danny. What she couldn't understand was how he could encourage such openness in Danny when he bottled up his own grief. Was she giving him more credit than he deserved?

251

Danny had dozens of questions, and Craig left the two of them alone, going into the kitchen to prepare lunch.

"Tuna fish, yuck," Danny said when Craig returned with a platter of sandwiches. "All Craig can make is tuna fish."

"We had dinner at McDonald's last night, didn't we?" Craig was unruffled by Danny's opinion of his culinary skills.

"I like Quarter Pounders." Danny was trying to scrape the filling out of his sandwich.

"What else do you like?" Libby asked, even though she had a pretty good idea after eating with him many times at Old Buckhorn.

"Hot dogs."

"Hot dogs are junk food," Craig said blandly. "You don't want to eat a pig's snout, do you?"

"Really!" Libby protested.

"Sorry, I guess we men get a little crude living alone without a woman's touch," Craig said softly to her.

"Tell me what you both like, and I'll fix dinner," Libby offered.

After several minutes of debating they agreed on fried chicken, but only if she made biscuits and gravy too.

"You're pushing my culinary skills to the limit," she warned him.

"You offered," Craig said, giving Danny a comical wink.

Her chicken was burned on one side, but with the black layer sawed off, it didn't taste too bad. The gravy was a bit lumpy, and the biscuits a trifle doughy in the centers, but both Danny and Craig enjoyed the meal, if only because they could give her a hard time about her cooking.

"What is this, pick-on-Libby day?" she asked defensively, winking at Danny behind Craig's back as he cleared the dishes before desert.

No one complained about her desert: ice cream with chocolate fudge sauce and ground nuts.

"After that we need some exercise," Craig said.

"Miniature golf," Danny suggested excitedly.

"Miniature golf it is!"

Even Danny beat her by a dozen strokes, but Libby was glad her horrible putting was a source of amusement. Part of her felt awkward about enjoying the outing so soon after Sandra's death, but she understood what Craig was doing and throughly approved. Danny needed some happy moments in his life right now. Neither of them could guarantee what his future might hold, but they could keep his apprehensions at bay for short intervals.

They tucked him into bed together, but Libby had to leave the room quickly when he said a prayer aloud for his mother. She couldn't stop the hot stream of tears from rolling down her cheeks.

"You did good." Craig came up behind her in the living room, putting his arms around her.

"No." She shook her head. "You deserve all the credit. You're wonderful with Danny. I feel awful for saying you didn't like him."

"Just drop it," he said wearily, walking away to slump down on the couch.

"I'll be going now."

"If you'd like to stay here, save the motel cost, there is an extra room."

"No, I don't think so."

He didn't press her."

"Can I see Danny tomorrow?"

"Of course. You don't need my permission."

"What do you have planned?"

"He goes to Sunday school. I planned to take him to an ice cream parlor for lunch. They also serve sandwiches. You're welcome to join us."

"Yes, I'd like that."

"Good. Afterward we'll go to the zoo, I think."

"That sounds like something Danny will like."

"He's not too hard to entertain."

"But it has to be hard on you, spending all this time with him when you have a new job."

"I'm only the assistant stunt coordinator on this one, but I have a lot to learn. You can do me a favor: pick Danny up after school Monday and take him for a haircut. It's hard getting away from the studio and out here by the time his school is out."

"Yes, I'll be glad to do that."

Sunday was a full day for the three of them, but being with Craig became more and more of a strain. He talked to her through Danny, avoided eye contact with her, and remained cordially formal no matter what they were doing. Libby returned to her motel as soon as Danny was in bed for the night, wondering how much longer she could endure being so close to Craig when he treated her in such a distant manner. Her feelings for him were unchanged; if anything, his kindness toward Danny only made her love him more.

To make her visits easier Craig secured a parking pass and a key to the apartment for her. He took Danny to school Monday without seeing her, planning to work late and return to the apartment before bedtime. They only exchanged a few words about Danny before she went back to her motel that evening. Without much conversation about it they divided the responsibility for taking care of him, an arrangement that lasted through the school week.

On Friday Libby knew there had to be some changes. The motel wasn't as cheap as she'd let Craig believe; she couldn't afford to stay there indefinitely, nor could she afford the car rental for an extended period of time.

Questioing Craig about Danny's future didn't make planning her next step any easier.

"These things take time," he said. "I can call the lawyer for a progress report, but I doubt if anything's happened. Placing a child Danny's age is never easy, and then there's the problem of the estate and his great-aunt's wishes. She's actually his legal guardian according to Sandy's will."

"But she's too old to raise him."

"She realizes that, but she takes her responsibilities very seriously. I have to check in practically every day to let her know how he's doing."

"I have a problem—two, actually. The car has to be returned tomorrow."

"Let me call around. If you don't mind an older car just to get Danny after school, I can probably get a cheaper rental. I'll take care of it—it's worth a lot more to me to be able to work later. I just didn't have the heart to start foisting him off on strange sitters so soon."

"I want to help Danny," she said firmly, refusing to let Craig make her feel like an assistant sitter.

"What's your other problem?"

"The motel," she admitted. "It's getting a little expensive staying there."

"You're welcome to stay here."

"I wouldn't feel right moving into Sandra's room."

Did he really expect her to stay in the same apartment with him? They might be acting like nodding acquaintances, but she couldn't stand the thought of lying in bed knowing he was only one door away.

"I may have a solution. We can pack up her clothes and things. I've been meaning to ship them to Brad's aunt; they're her responsibility. Then we'll turn that room into a playroom for Danny. You can use the back room downstairs. That is, if you want to. It would help Danny—and me—a whole lot."

"I don't know."

Craig was in her thoughts continually, no matter where she

slept. Would using the little downstairs room make any difference?

"Let me talk to the lawyer about moving Sandra's things. Then we'll take it from there."

There was no logical reason to disagree with the plan, and before she could muster an effective argument against it, Craig had professional movers packing the contents of the room. Danny helped them move his playthings upstairs, excited when he heard Libby would be staying there.

"It's only for a little while," she warned him.

"I understand," Danny said gravely, his round brown eyes studying her.

Living together, Libby and Craig were almost painfully polite, each of them deferring to the other to make their joint care of Danny as smooth as possible. Their reward was his well-being, but they couldn't deceive themselves about his state of mind. He was often too quiet for a boy his age, and he seemed to prefer his own company to that of school friends, refusing several invitations to stay overnight with classmates. The only times he showed much animation were when the three of them were together, which reinforced Libby's determination to be there for him as long as possible.

Danny made quite a big deal out of her move, but Craig pretended it was as ordinary as taking in the mail. Sandra's cleaning service still came twice a week, so there was little for Libby to do during school hours. She made a few cautious forays onto the freeway but preferred to explore areas that were accessible by back roads. The third day after her move she did receive a surprise: Craig invited her to lunch, asking her to meet him at a restaurant she could reach without tackling a major expressway.

Her Florida wardrobe was holding up well in California, the only excess baggage being the winter coat she'd still needed in New York when she went to the airport. Just to remind Craig that she wasn't just a live-in baby-sitter, she wore her most sophisticated dress, a silky, silver-gray, silk-blend chemise with big pockets and a deep slit revealing one leg to the middle of her thigh. Simply styled, it fit to perfection with buttons at the shoulder and cuffs. She added a bright yellow-and-gray silk scarf, one of her prizes from Second-Hand Rose's. Whether Craig liked it or not, he was going to have to treat her like a woman, not a nanny.

"You look nice." He was there ahead of her, waiting in the lounge, reminding her of their lunch at the steak house in New York, a memory that was painful to her now.

"So do you," she said.

This was only partially true; he was wearing a linen-textured suit, a rather conservative navy, with normal street shoes and a deep-red tie, but he looked tired, his eyes shadowed with gray and the line on his forehead more deeply creased.

"Meeting with some of the big bosses this morning," he said when they were seated. "I'm glad it's over. I didn't realize how much a stunt coordinator has to play politics."

"In what way?"

"Skirting a balance between economy, safety, and the kind of thrills the producers want. I'm glad I'm only the assistant on this one."

"You haven't changed your mind about being a coordinator?"

"No, I think that's where I'm needed. You're needed, too, you know."

"By Danny?"

"Yes, and by me. I don't know what I'd do without you. It's just too soon to start leaving him with strangers."

"Yes." She agreed almost absentmindedly, not liking the big round table-for-four where the two of them were sitting. Craig seemed half a block away physically and a thousand miles mentally.

257

"I thought you needed a day off," he said. "I can pick up Danny this afternoon, and you can go shopping or something."

"That's nice of you."

It wasn't what she really wanted. She read the menu but decided to order her usual: a chef's salad.

"How've you been?" he asked after the waiter took their order and collected the menus.

"Fine." She gave the conventional answer, not thinking of it as a lie.

"I have no right to say this, but I've missed you, Libby. Missed you a lot."

She stared at him, moistening her lips with the tip of her tongue, afraid to open the floodgate of her own feelings. To say she missed him would be the understatement of her life. At a loss for a casual way to return his admission, she said nothing.

"I saw Carl McDowell yesterday," he said.

"He's a good director. I like him."

"He said to say hello to you."

"That's nice."

She felt like a boxer, skirmishing before the first exchange of punches. Why did Craig want to talk to her here instead of at the apartment? They were living together again, although not in a meaningful way.

"Why did you ask me here, Craig?"

"For the reason I said."

She could stand up to him, but she couldn't stare him down, feeling flushed under his steady gaze. A disconcerting image flashed through her mind: Craig hovering over her in bed, his features softened by passion, his lips parted, his eyes seeing only her. She wanted to ram through the barriers separating them, forget his desertion, and make a new beginning. It saddened her immensely to realize that he had no such intention. Being kind to Danny didn't mean he'd

258

changed. He still wasn't the man to star in her most important fantasy.

The luncheon was a dismal failure. The conversation was stilted, the food tasteless, and their differences unresolved. Craig walked to the car he'd rented for her, a three-year-old blue Chevy, opening the door for her.

"This wasn't fun for you. I won't ask you out again without Danny," he said.

In spite of the reserve between them, she hadn't expected him to say something like that.

"It's not fair to you," he added with obvious unhappiness. "I intended to ask you to sleep with me again."

A mule couldn't deliver a harder kick to her midsection.

"But you didn't."

"I can't do it to you." He sounded as miserable as she felt.

"You're telling me nothing has changed."

"That's right."

"I appreciate your honesty." Really, she hated it!

"I'm asking a lot, expecting you to help with Danny."

"I'm doing it for him—and for Sandra. I planned to stay before I knew you were taking care of him."

"I know that."

"Thank you for lunch."

"I'm sorry, Libby."

"I hope you are. I really hope you are!" Her voice broke on the last few words.

She couldn't drive away quickly enough, tears blurring her vision. But as soon as she saw a place to park, she stopped, too shaken to remember the way back to the apartment. Craig was a fool! Why couldn't he see they needed each other?

During the weekend all three of them were together. Craig was a great planner, knowing just the right way to entertain a boy, driving them in the rented car because the Corvette was designed for the comfort of two people. They drove along the

Pacific Coast Highway, picnicked in a state park, and returned road-weary but pleased with themselves. For one long, lazy day they'd put the future on hold.

On Sunday they played Frisbee, gave miniature golf another try, and ate junk food until Danny thought the day was nicer than a birthday. They returned home just in time to bundle Danny off to bed, so he wouldn't be too tired for school the next day.

"That was a good day," Libby said when they'd tucked him in and returned to the living room.

"It could be even better." Craig's eyes explained exactly what he meant.

The nervous energy that had carried her through the day in high spirits seemed to evaporate. She was tired and her resistance was at a low ebb. Craig was standing close, a pleasant, fresh-air smell clinging to his casual cotton pullover, his hands stuffed in the pockets of his jeans, pulling the denim taut over his hips. Wanting him so much that she felt jumpy, she wavered, not protesting when he lifted her hand and lightly kissed her inner wrist.

"You're so wonderful," he murmured, tracing the outline of her lips with the tip of one finger. "I don't know how I'd survive without you."

He rested his hands on her waist, slowly running them over the swell of her hips. Wearing one of her few pairs of jeans, she'd felt rumpled and grubby only moments ago. His words turned her into a princess, a transformation as beguiling as Cinderella's. She was melting, floating off in her own fantasy world as the last of her resistance dissolved. Craig reached under her loose rose-colored rayon top and released the snap on her bra, filling his hands with the full, silky warmth of her breasts. Kneading them until her nipples were erect, he slid his leg between her thighs and enveloped her in his arms, doing things to her mouth that he'd never done as her lover.

"In your room?" he asked with hoarse urgency, unbuttoning the waistband of her jeans. He slid his hands down the back, squeezing soft, pliant handfuls of her bottom until she dug her nails into her shoulders and demanded all that his mouth could give. Forcing his fingers between her thighs, he inflamed her to the brink of desperation, lifting her in his arms when a familiar moan told him the time had come.

"Libby!"

Danny was shouting from his bed, but his voice was loud enough to sweep the clouds of passion from her mind.

"It's Danny," she said needlessly, freeing herself from Craig's arms when he showed no willingness to let her go. "I'll see what he wants."

"No, he called me."

Panicked by another loud cry, she rushed up the stairs, bursting into Danny's room with barely enough breath left to ask what was wrong.

"Danny, what is it?"

He was sitting upright, looking so scared and vulnerable, she automatically took him in her arms.

"I had a bad dream!"

"Those hot dogs get you every time," Craig said from the doorway, not sounding especially concerned.

"Do you want to tell me about it?" Libby asked.

"There was a black thing. It was going to get me."

"Danny, nothing's going to get you. There's only Libby and me here, and we'll see that you're safe," Craig reasoned in a reassuring voice.

"Don't leave me," he whimpered, his fear breaking Libby's heart.

"Don't worry, honey, I'll stay right here," she said.

"You're a big boy, Danny. You just go back to sleep, and everything will be fine," Craig said.

"He wants me to stay," Libby insisted.

261

"He'll be all right," Craig said just as urgently.

Danny lay down but didn't release his grip on Libby's fingers.

"You go back to sleep. I'll stay here until you do," she said, ignoring Craig.

Either the nightmare or the attention made Danny lose interest in sleep. He started to tell her about another dream he'd had, one that she suspected was sheer fantasy invented for her benefit. Craig told him one more time to go back to sleep, but she couldn't bear to leave him alone, not after all he'd been through.

From dreams he went to TV programs, then he had to tell her about a movie he'd seen with his last sitter, a woman he usually referred to as "the grumpy one."

Craig took a shower and put on his robe, looking in on Danny one more time with a none-too-friendly warning to stop fooling around.

When she finally came downstairs, Craig was watching TV in the dark and drinking a beer in the eerie glow of the set.

"He's old enough to go back to sleep alone," he said crossly.

"He's been through a lot," she said defensively.

"He's also smart enough to con you into staying just to fool around."

"Well, that's the second time I've been conned in one evening, isn't it?" she said angrily, liking Craig less as the autocratic father-figure than she ever had before.

"Just what do you mean by that?" He reached for her hand and missed, getting up to confront her.

"Exactly what I said!"

"Look, Libby, calm down. We'll talk about it."

"You're the last person to discuss anything reasonably. The only way to find out what's in your head is to take an X ray."

"There was no secret about what I was thinking before Danny yelled."

"There's never been any mystery about that. How convenient for you that I can't bring myself to leave Danny." She was bitter enough to say anything, wanting to wound him with falsehood if the truth wouldn't do it.

"You'll have to leave him sooner or later."

"It probably can't be too soon for you!"

"Why do you say that?"

"Tonight you were just as mean as ever to Danny."

"All I expect him to do is settle down and go to sleep."

"His dream frightened him. A little comforting can't hurt."

"Libby, I'm sure there aren't any parents in this country who at one time or another haven't had to lay down the law to their kids about going to sleep. My father thought a whack on the rear was better than psychology or a sleeping pill."

"Next you'll be hitting Danny!"

"Don't be silly."

"I know the real reason why you suddenly got so strict."

"Oh?"

"Danny interrupted your fun!"

"My fun? Not our fun?"

"I'm going to bed by myself!"

"If that's the way you want it."

Of course, it wasn't the way she wanted it, but she'd never tell Craig that.

She hated the narrow child-size single bed! Every time she turned, a hand or foot dangled off into space. The kind of nightmares Danny had would be welcome to her. Her wakeful thoughts were much less endurable. Craig would never change. He might go to work in a sport jacket and spend a Sunday afternoon picnicking, but in his heart he was a rover; domestic tranquillity was only an interlude, like being involved in a new movie. He was eager to see Danny permanently settled with some capable couple. He'd never see himself as part of that couple.

Two days later a social worker interviewed Danny, coming to the apartment by appointment but insisting that she speak to him alone. Libby felt helpless, knowing she had no say whatsoever in his future.

Just for her own information, she contacted several social service agencies and made a trip to the closest library to learn something about California adoption laws. She was only giving herself false hope; the chances of a single, unemployed woman adopting a child were very slim. The fact that Danny had a comfortable legacy coming from his mother could only complicate matters. There were all kinds of financial issues to settle before he could have a secure future.

She couldn't leave Danny while he needed her, but living in close proximity to Craig was a constant strain. He seemed to avoid her as much as he could without neglecting Danny, but both of them relied on their acting skills to preserve the illusion of a happy household.

On more than one night Libby heard pacing above her head, but there was no need for her to investigate it. The footsteps were too heavy to be Danny's. It didn't give her any pleasure to know that Craig's nights were as troubled and sleepless as hers.

Craig had to make a trip to the ranch where most of the movie would be shot in order to supervise some arrangements for stunts. He'd be gone three or four days and he wanted her to bring Danny and come with him.

"He has school," she protested.

"A few days off won't hurt."

"Craig, it's not Danny. I don't want to go with you."

"That's plain enough."

He sounded hurt, but she didn't think he had a right to expect any other answer.

"I've been thinking of getting a job myself," she said.

"Out here?"

"Only a temporary one. Until Danny's permanently settled."

"Do you want me to ask around?"

"No, I'll do it myself. I have plenty of time during the day while Danny's in school."

"Would separate motel rooms change your mind about coming along?"

"No, nothing would change my mind."

Danny was moody and irritable while Craig was gone. He didn't like to have the people who were important to him out of his sight, Libby realized. For the first time since she'd arrived she felt inadequate as his substitute mother. Both she and Danny were relieved when Craig returned.

CHAPTER SIXTEEN

Every day Libby eagerly awaited the time to claim Danny at his school, a private one that Sandra had chosen because the staff paid special attention to the needs of children whose parents were in the entertainment business. Craig had arranged things so her domestic duties were light, and he did most of the planning for activities the three of them shared. She didn't feel needed until she picked Danny up from school in the afternoon. The hours they shared were precious, all the more so because they might be taken away at any time. Because the lawyer was a special friend of Sandra's, he was expediting things as much as possible. No one was quite sure how the inevitable lawsuits would affect the estate, but steps for Danny's personal welfare were being taken with dispatch.

Libby's life was a strange mixture of tension, boredom, and suspense, relieved only by the carefree hours spent with Danny. When Carl McDowell, her director on *Freedom Gulch*, called, she was ready to listen to any proposal.

"I may have some work for you," he said on the phone. "Can you come in and talk to me about it?"

She wrote down the directions to his studio office, agreeing to an appointment at his earliest convenience. His big, pleasant face and no-nonsense directness would be as welcome as

266

a spring rain on the desert. No matter what he had to propose, she looked forward to seeing him.

Allowing plenty of time after dropping Danny at school on Friday, a job she did for Craig about half the time now, she located the studio and was checked through to see Carl.

"What happened to Sandra was a tragedy," he said.

"Yes."

She felt closer to Carl because they'd lost a mutual friend. It was only with Craig that sorrow didn't seem to work this way.

"This is a nice office, Carl." She looked around and commented on the most unusual thing she saw. "That's quite a gun collection. Is it yours?"

"Yes, I used to keep them locked up at home, but I thought they'd make a nice conversation piece here. They're mainly types used in Western movies. It's been a hobby of mine for years, buying them whenever I have a chance. I guess you have an idea why I asked you here."

She smiled. "Should I have contacted my agent?"

"You might want him to look over this contract." He shoved a sheath of papers toward her. "I liked what you did with Cassandra Rose. This part isn't very big, but I think it's one you'll like. You'd play a rancher's wife, not one of the leads, but it's fairly worthwhile. I have a script here."

He gave her a minute to look at it.

"Seven Days to Sunset," she read slowly, recognizing the title of the movie Craig was working on.

"We may have a title change. Take a look at the contract too."

"What's the time frame on this?" she asked, feeling as if she'd just been asked to make a momentous decision.

"I need your answer by next week. If you're interested, we'll send the contract express to your agent—unless you're thinking of getting a representative out here."

267

"I haven't given it any thought. I'm not sure I want to stay here."

"You're not turning down the part without reading it."

"No. No, I definitely want to read it. My life is pretty unsettled right now."

"I heard you're helping with Sandy's kid. That's only temporary, isn't it?"

"Yes, only temporary. Can I take the script with me?"

"Of course. You'd be perfect for this part. I hope you'll take it."

"Thank you, Carl. I really appreciate the chance to look at it."

Contracts, scripts, nothing mattered but the fact that it was Craig's movie. Was this an astonishing coincidence, or was he behind it?

Passing the glass-fronted case where Carl's gun collection was mounted, she could almost hear a whole series of little gears clicking into place in her brain. Stopping to stare at the assortment of rather awesome weapons, she let the germ of an idea start to crystallize, doubting only her own nerve to pull it off.

"Some of these are so big," she said. "I guess that's why they invented the holster. They wouldn't fit in anyone's pocket."

"Something like that." Like any dedicated collector Carl was incapable of ignoring any interest shown in his collection.

"Which one is the oldest?" Libby's mind was racing, buying time with idle questions.

"This Colt." He unlocked the case and lifted one out with his handkerchief, not touching the well-preserved metal, showing her by the way he handled it that she was privileged to get this opportunity to examine it closely. "Samuel Colt invented the many-chambered, rotating breech pistol—a revolver. This is one of his early ones."

Guns scared her, but no way was Carl going to learn this.

"Are there any other Colts?" She didn't want to be responsible for even touching such an old relic; it was obviously precious to him and probably very valuable.

"There's a .45 caliber automatic—it was made after 1900. It became the official military sidearm after 1911."

"Danny would be thrilled to see one. He's so cowboy-crazy."

"You'll have to bring him here sometime."

"He's in school all day, then there's homework and swimming lessons. You wouldn't believe how busy a little guy can be. I'd love to take one home to show him."

"I don't know, Libby." He replaced the valuable piece rather protectively. "Guns aren't toys. I'm not sure that's a good idea."

"Well, it was only a thought. If you don't trust me with one . . ."

She tried to stuff the script into her purse, but it couldn't possibly fit; it was only a delaying tactic.

"It's not that I don't trust you. There are a lot of regulations about firearms. You need a permit. . . ."

"You have one, don't you?"

"My collection is perfectly legal."

"All I'd need would be a box with a studio stamp and a note from you saying I was taking it out for repairs. It doesn't matter which one I take. The least valuable would be fine."

What she really wanted was the biggest, most dangerous-looking one in the case.

"A little kid wouldn't be too excited about a pocket automatic like this Browning, I suppose."

"No, that wouldn't look like a cowboy gun to Danny."

"I suppose I could loan you this double-action Colt revolver on the bottom shelf. It's defective; no one could fire it if they wanted to. I haven't had time to have it fully restored."

"That one certainly looks impressive."

269

"I don't know about showing guns to kids, Libby."

"This one will be shown with a very stern lecture. Danny idolizes that cowboy-shootout stuff so much, I think it would be good for him to see a real gun. He needs to know that pretend fighting is entirely different from real violence."

"What do I know?" Carl smiled, pleased by her interest in spite of his misgivings. "I have three daughters."

The gun was heavier than she'd expected and so threatening, she hated to touch it. For a defective gun it was marvelously shiny, the dark gunmetal oiled to a sheen.

"You're sure it won't go off?" She needed an extra bit of reassurance.

"Look, no bullets," he said, showing her. "Even blanks aren't anything to fool with."

"Yes, I read about the young actor who died from firing a blank at his own head."

"Terrible," Carl said. "If you can teach a kid that guns aren't toys, it's worth my lending it to you."

"Danny will never see this gun as a toy," she promised.

In fact, he'd never see it at all, if she could help it.

She felt so conspicuous walking out with a gun wrapped in paper towels in a corrugated cardboard box that she nearly took it back to Carl. What if a policeman stopped her? She could easily break a traffic rule in this crazy state; the cars went so fast, she didn't have time to remember all of them. Nothing she'd done in years had made her quite this nervous. She drove home with the caution of a refugee escaping from East Berlin.

Behind the closed door of her little room, she took the gun out, handling it warily because it was the first time she'd touched a real firearm. The Colt scared her; only high stakes could induce her to keep it in her possession. She picked it up by the barrel, using a piece of paper toweling the way Carl had used his handkerchief.

The room didn't suggest any clever hiding places. The single closet was shallow, the curtains were short and semitransparent, and the furniture was functionally modern with no concealed nooks or crannies.

Danny was usually courteous, not coming into her room uninvited, but boys were curious creatures. What if he decided to explore a bit while she was in the shower or busy in some other way?

Falling back on a traditional hiding place, she rewrapped the gun in a terry-cloth hand towel and slid it between the mattress and springs of her bed, putting it near the foot and hoping the lump wouldn't keep her awake. To her relief no bulge showed under the woven rust-and-brown coverlet.

Danny greeted her with an excited babble, finally calming down enough to tell her the reason for his unusual after-school mood. Tomorrow, Saturday, he was invited to go to Knott's Berry Farm with Marc, his best friend at school. Marc's mother would call that evening to make sure he could go.

"They have cowboys and they rob the train. It's a real train, and we're going to ride on it," Danny said, talking nonstop all the way home.

It was the first time he'd shown any enthusiasm about doing something with a friend his own age, and Libby was delighted for him. Marc's mother called shortly after dinner and asked if Libby could drop Danny off at their house in the morning; picking him up was quite a distance out of the way, and she wanted to get an early start. Libby agreed readily, making the decision because Craig was still at the studio.

She had persuaded Danny to go to bed early so he wouldn't be tired for his excursion, and he had been sleeping for several hours when Craig came home.

"Good day?" she asked.

"Grueling. You?"

271

"Just a routine day."

She didn't mention her trip to see Carl, his job offer, or Danny's invitation to Knott's Berry Farm, the big recreation park that rivaled Disneyland. She escaped to her room shortly after Craig's arrival.

When she heard him go upstairs, she pulled out the firearm, running the tip of her finger down the hard steel of the barrel, frightening herself with the deadly potential of the weapon.

Her fear didn't go away after she had rewrapped the gun and slid it under the mattress. What she was planning was reckless, foolish, and probably doomed to failure. Conscious that tomorrow she would risk everything, Libby lay awake with cold perspiration on her forehead that had nothing to do with the pleasant breeze coming through the window.

Her alarm was set, unnecessarily, since she was awake long before it rang. She crept upstairs barefoot and woke Danny, cautioning him not to wake Craig.

"I want to tell him I'm going to Knott's Berry Farm," Danny insisted in a whisper loud enough to rattle the windows.

"Tell him when you get home tonight. He had to work very late, and he's tired. Now, do you want to wear your red shirt or the green?"

Somehow she got Danny to eat a toaster pastry and drink a glass of milk without turning the Saturday cartoons up full blast. Insisting that he take a jacket, although it really was warm enough to go without, giving him some money, and shushing him for the hundredth time, she finally got him out to her rented Chevy and off to his friend's without waking Craig.

The drive took over half an hour one way, and she had to talk with Marc's mother, Darla Peters, for a few minutes. She was a pleasant woman in her mid-thirties with a daughter besides her son Marc. She knew about Sandra and was concerned about how Danny was doing. Any other time Libby would have loved talking to her. This morning she left as

272

soon as she was assured that Darla and her husband would bring Danny home, probably around nine o'clock in the evening if that wasn't too late. If Libby's plan worked, it was perfect; if it didn't, time wouldn't mean much one way or another.

Railing at the unfamiliar streets, she made a wrong turn and lost precious time. If she didn't get back soon, she might lose her nerve.

The apartment was silent when she got home, but she tiptoed upstairs to make sure Craig was still sleeping. Just as she reached the top step, she heard the shower go on. If he wasn't in a hurry, he might stay under it ten minutes. She raced downstairs, not cautious about noise now, and ran to her room, immediately setting her plan in motion.

Her black lace nightgown was on top of her lingerie in the drawer, and she whipped it out with lightning haste, letting her street clothes fall where they would until, naked, she slipped the revealing garment over her head and gave her hair a few frantic brushes so it fell enticingly over her shoulders.

The next part was much more difficult. She reached under the mattress, extracting the bulky bundle hidden there.

Imagination made the firearm seem icy cold; just touching it made her jump; it seemed to sear her skin like dry ice.

This wasn't going to work; she'd never make it up the stairs. Suddenly the shower shut off, and she knew the time was now or never. Craig always shaved before his shower, and it wouldn't take him long to dry off and tidy the bathroom.

Running on bare feet, she padded up the stairs and into his room, going to the far side of the unmade double bed, automatically reaching down to smooth the burgundy-, black-, and white-striped sheets. She wasn't there to make his bed! she reminded herself. Running her fingers up and down the gun barrel one more time, she tucked a bare foot between the mattress and springs, leaned forward, and rested her right arm on her thigh above her bent knee. In the position she'd planned, she pointed the gleaming, sinister weapon at the doorway.

He didn't come.

Pointing the gun for one anxious minute after another, she felt it grow heavy. Her hand and wrist ached, and her finger warily touched the trigger. If he didn't come soon, she was going to bolt through the door out of his life. She couldn't endure the suspense another second!

He came through the doorway drying his hair with a bright-red towel, an identical one secured at his waist. Watching him before he noticed her, she was too petrified to swallow, struck dumb by the depth of her love for him. The towel was clinging wetly to his hips, outlining the swell at his groin and ending in the middle of strong, hairy thighs. His perfectly formed legs were marred only by the cruel knee scars, and his feet were endearingly bare.

He gave his head one more rub and draped the towel around his neck, looking in her direction at last.

"Libby, what . . ."

"Reach for the sky, Wicklow," she said in the most authoritative voice she could manage.

"You're kidding." His eyes traveled the length of the peephole lace gown, coming to rest on the Colt she was pointing directly at him.

"Reach!" she repeated sharply, holding her breath until he slowly raised his hands above his head.

"Where did you get a thing like that?" He was frowning, trying to decide how serious she was.

"That's my business."

Calamity Jane couldn't have said it better.

"Where's Danny? He wasn't in his bed when I woke up."

If she let him talk, she'd forget everything she planned to say.

"He went to Knott's Berry Farm with his friend Marc. Don't move another inch!"

He'd advanced nearly a foot closer to the bed, and she didn't for an instant trust his quick reflexes.

"Honey, guns are nothing to play with. If you'll just put it—"

"Keep your hands up and be quiet!" She wished Carl had taught her how to make the gun click.

"You're the boss—for now," he conceded.

"Then you listen to me, Craig Wicklow. We've got a score to settle." She felt as melodramatic as she sounded.

"Oh?" He moved his right foot, inching just a tiny bit closer to the bed.

Alarmed now by the threat in his eyes, she stood upright and edged away from the bed, backing up against the dresser. There was no retreat for her; she had to go through with her plan.

"Stay there. Put your hands up higher!"

"I won't be accountable for this towel if I do." He complied, glowering at her fiercely enough to make her shiver. "I take it this isn't a social call."

"You know it isn't."

"A business call in black lace." A sudden, lewd grin broke across his face.

"You listen to me," she said, trying to sound as tough as John Wayne facing down the bad guys. "I've had enough of your shilly-shallying."

"Oh? That's interesting. What do you mean?"

"You know what I mean! I insist that you make an honorable woman of me."

His laughter caught her off-guard for an instant, and he advanced to the foot of the bed—still a safe distance away, but his move made her furious.

"You'd better take me seriously!"

"Shouldn't your father be here with a shotgun?"

"A hundred years ago maybe. Not today. Well?"

"Well? What do you expect me to say?"

"You know you should marry me! You'll never find anybody as right for you as I am!"

"Give me the gun, Libby, and we'll talk about it."

He slid one foot forward a few inches but not without her noticing his advance.

"I warn you, stop that right now!" She was frantically trying to remember all the reasons why he should marry her.

"You were saying?" A cocky grin flitted briefly across his face, replaced by a stern frown.

"I'm a nice person, nicer than you deserve."

"I can't argue with that." He lowered one hand to lazily scratch his side.

"Hands up!"

"You're too bossy, though, and if you don't stop waving that thing at me—"

"There are more reasons!"

"They'd better be good ones, because when I get that gun, you're in big trouble."

This wasn't the way the scene was supposed to go! If this were an old-fashioned melodrama, they'd fall into each other's arms. Or was this the part where the hero rode off into the sunset with his horse?

"I'm kind," she insisted.

"Do you call it kind, standing there half-naked in your Paris nightie and not letting me near you?"

"I cook better than you do," she insisted, ignoring his comment.

"Not much."

He pretended to sneeze and managed to move another foot closer, halfway across the foot of the bed.

"You like to sleep with me," she stated.

"Do I? It's been so long, I've forgotten."

"Craig! Are you going to marry me or not?"

"What happens if I don't?" He raised one eyebrow, reminding her of Lucifer bargaining for a soul.

"You've had it!" She nervously waved the gun in an arc, then, trying to ignore how heavy it was getting, stretched her arm full length and took aim.

"Below the belt?" Craig asked laconically, as unruffled as she was flustered.

"You're terrible! I don't know why I'd even consider marrying you! You're conceited and selfish and—"

"And so much in love with you, I can't think straight!"

"What?"

Her arm fell, and before she'd realized it, he sprang, grabbing her wrist and wresting the gun from her hand.

"Of all the featherbrained stunts!"

He was examining the gun, making the little clicking noise she'd been afraid to try. "At least it's not loaded!"

"I'm not crazy!"

"Where did you get this? Wait, let me guess. It's from Carl's collection. I recognize it. It's the one he's been meaning to have fixed. When did you get it?"

"I don't see what difference that makes!"

"When, Libby?" He laid the Colt on the dresser, making her realize that she was cornered.

"Yesterday."

"You were in his office?"

"Yes."

"Why didn't you tell me?"

"It never occurred to me you'd be interested!"

"He finally got around to offering you a job?"

"What do you mean 'finally'?"

He put his hand on her bare arm below the fine satin shoulder strap. His grasp was gentle but absolutely unbreakable.

277

"Never mind. Did you accept?"

"You had something to do with it!"

"I may have mentioned you were here."

"Why?"

He shrugged his shoulders and released her.

"Why, Craig?" she insisted. "Tell me, or I'm leaving you forever. You'll never see me again."

"Darling, I'm glad you do the acting, not the writing. We'd all be out of work!"

"Are you saying my scene was corny?"

"You put Iowa in the shade."

"You're only saying that because you don't have one good reason for not marrying me."

"You're absolutely right!"

"You don't like being a bachelor all that much, and you're not getting any younger, you know." She was remembering all the arguments she'd been rehearsing.

"I said, you're absolutely right!"

"You did, didn't you? Does that mean . . ."

"I don't have a single reason for not marrying you."

"Are you saying . . ."

"Yes." His voice was deeply serious. "I'm dead inside without you, Libby. I tried to walk away, but since you came to see Danny, I've been treading quicksand."

"You didn't try very hard to—"

"With Danny in the house and you pouting most of the time?"

"I do not pout!"

"Umm, if you do, I know what to do with your puckered lips."

He reached out, touching her cheek, bending his head for a long, deep kiss.

"That was an engagement kiss," he murmured, gathering her into his arms.

"We're not engaged!"

"Don't you want to be?" He didn't sound alarmed, instead tossing aside the towel draped around his shoulders and gathering her in his arms.

"You won't know until you ask."

"We have to negotiate this contract?"

"Especially the fine print!"

"Sit here." He led her to the edge of the bed, sitting beside her and taking her hands in his.

"Your palm is damp." He brought it to his lips, kissing her knuckles, flicking his tongue between her fingers. "Did it make you nervous to stage your little melodrama for me?"

"You'd like to think so, wouldn't you?"

"Yes, because I've been trying for days to think of a way to take back all the dumb things I've told you about not wanting to marry you." His face was somber, but when he smiled, her heart started singing. "Will you marry me, Libby?"

"Yes, I think I should."

"Should?"

"Must!"

"I love you!"

"Me too!"

"Me too?" He tickled her nose with his mustache, slipping his tongue between her lips and quickly withdrawing it. "Is that the best you can say?"

"I love you so much," she said softly.

"I'm glad the gun wasn't loaded!"

He lay back on the bed, pulling her against him and kissing her.

"You knew it wasn't!"

"When anyone points a gun at me, I assume it's a dangerous weapon."

"You were in grave danger, all right!"

"In danger of losing you?" he murmured. "I've never

279

seen anyone come to a shootout in an outfit like this." He ran his finger over the lacy pattern.

"It's from Paris," she teased, raising her leg, letting the gorgeous lace fall and bunch at the tops of her thighs. "It was a very special present. I think it's beautiful."

"Nothing is as beautiful as your body."

"People say I have a nice nose."

"All of you is gorgeous." He kissed her knee, holding it in his hand and letting his lips work their way up her thigh.

Sunshine seeped in around the edges of the shade, making a golden pattern on her hip as he raised the gown to her shoulders and helped free her of it. Tossing his towel on the floor, he held her against him.

He bathed her with his tongue, inhaling the unique fragrance of her skin and gently massaging her until her whole body was pliant and relaxed. The gentle tickle of his mustache on her breasts and tummy made her writhe against him, tingling until she thought she'd go mad with delight. Feeling like the goddess of love, she slid on top of him, nuzzling his throat, exploring his lips with hers, letting her tongue slither over his until he moaned with pleasure.

Touching him filled her with wonder, and she still couldn't believe they'd be together always.

"Ask me again," she purred.

"Ask you what?"

"You know!"

"I wanted it to be my idea!"

"Is that important?" She kissed him, giving him a moment to think.

"Being with you is all that's important. I was ready to do anything to keep you from going back to New York."

"Even a desperate measure like marriage?"

"Especially that."

His hair, laced between her fingers, was nearly dry from

280

his shower, soft waves of ash blond that had captured streaks of sunshine. The contours of his head, hard under her fingers, intrigued her; she ran her hands slowly through his hair, then rubbed the base of his neck, teasing him into rolling onto his stomach. His shoulders rippled under her touch, and his spine relaxed. The grace of his torso, ending in round, muscular buttocks below almost invisible silky golden hairs made her weak with longing. Moving to her side, she stretched her length against his, moving against him, keeping his lips covered with her own.

With gentle maneuvering he rolled onto his back, catching a lock of her hair as it fell forward over his face. Taking her breast between his lips, he probed with his tongue, moistening the tip, arousing her until she felt feverish. His hand cupped the swell of her womanhood while his mouth played sensual tricks with hers, letting her ride a roller coaster of desire. There was nothing about him she didn't love. She slid her finger over the fuzziness of his navel, inflicting sweet torment.

He inched his hands under her buttocks, lifting her to meet his thrust, holding her as liquid pleasure flowed between them, bringing a sheen to her skin and slippery moistness to his.

She was spellbound by ecstasy; nothing gave her greater joy than his eyes, dark, emerald gems flickering with the intensity of his love, telling her more eloquently than words that she was the wonder, the love, of his life.

He shuddered, and she felt a great, quaking ripple, then a happiness so complete that her eyes were swimming under clenched lids. Resting his head against her breasts, he was her pilot, her guardian, her captain, staying with her as she rode the crests of a swelling sea, shaking as wave after wave pounded against a secret shoreline.

His kisses were almost bashful, and his endearments caressed her soul, telling her that the special moments of her life were just beginning.

"I love you," he whispered.

If he said it a million times a day, she'd never tire of those simple little words.

As they lay locked in each other's arms, their legs entwined, she offered her breast as a pillow, trembling when his gentle suckling kindled new sensations, making her tingle and throb.

"Was that an earthquake?" she murmured.

He disentangled his legs and leaned over her, a pleased smile making him seem almost boyish.

"Carl really did offer you a job?"

"You were behind it!"

"I don't want a wife unemployed. I also don't want her anywhere but where I am." He teased her lower lip with his tongue.

"You really do want to marry me?"

"I hate that jerk who left you in New York."

"No, don't feel that way! I think we needed to be apart . . ."

"To know how we really feel? No, I knew then."

"You didn't want to spoil my chance to have a family."

"I still don't."

A cold finger of apprehension nudged her heart. *Did he really mean to marry her?*

"So will you take that job?" he asked softly.

"In *Seven Days to Sunset*?"

She understood the title now; it expressed the wishful thinking of someone who didn't want night to come.

"No, as my wife!"

"That won't be a job!"

"It will be. I'm a bear to live with."

"Bears don't scare me!"

282

"They should. There's nothing meaner than an old grizzly without a mate."

"This old grizzly has a mate." She tugged on a tuft of hair in the middle of his chest.

"This old grizzly bites," he warned with mock ferocity, covering her nose with a kiss.

"Do you want me to accept Carl's offer?"

"It's up to you. If you're going on location with me, you might as well get paid."

"You did pressure him into giving it to me!"

"No pressure was required. You're good at what you do."

She'd pushed aside her one big worry too long. "Will Danny be settled with new parents by then?"

"I'm sure he will be."

"I don't know how I can leave him," she said, desperation creeping into her voice.

"School will be out. You won't have to."

She sat upright, searching his face for his meaning.

"Don't look so stunned, darling. Most women go through a lot more to become a mother."

"Are you saying we can adopt Danny, you and me together?"

"The courts have the final say, but I don't see any real problems. His great-aunt likes me, and she's sure to love you. She can help us get legal guardianship, I'm sure. It will be a great relief to her to know Danny has a family."

"I don't know what to say." Tears of happiness clouded her vision, but he cradled her against his chest, patting her head and whispering that he loved her.

"Can we tell Danny?"

"We can't promise him anything, but we can tell him we're going to get married and try to keep him with us."

"As soon as he gets home?"

"Let him tell us about Knott's Berry Farm first," he said with a broad smile.

"You're not doing this just for me?"

"No," he said gravely, "I wouldn't take responsibility for a child unless I could give him my love. With your help I'm sure I can now."

"You're not marrying me just so—"

"Danny can have a mother? Absolutely not!" He kissed her with a resounding smack, pulling her into a bear hug that took away her breath.

"You can't believe how happy I am!"

"I can, because I feel the same way."

"When will we get married?" She felt almost timid about asking.

"As soon as we can assemble both families—parents, brothers, my sisters, nephews, nieces, aunts, uncles, the works!"

"You want a huge wedding!"

"No, I want a quick wedding, and I want everyone I care about to meet the mother of my children."

"Your children?"

"Danny will be our first son, but I hope not our only one."

"What if we have all girls?"

"I'll cherish them as much as I do their mother."

His eyes were misty, but he didn't look away.

"Imagine," she said with a smile that came from her heart, "I got my man without firing a shot!"

"You sure did, lady," he said in a deep drawl, wrapping his arms around her.

CANDLELIGHT Ecstasy Supreme

☐ 61 **FROM THIS DAY FORWARD,** Jackie Black 12740-8-27

☐ 62 **BOSS LADY,** Blair Cameron 10763-6-31

☐ 63 **CAUGHT IN THE MIDDLE,** Lily Dayton 11129-3-20

☐ 64 **BEHIND THE SCENES,** Josephine C. Hauber 10419-X-88

☐ 65 **TENDER REFUGE,** Lee Magner 18648-X-35

☐ 66 **LOVESTRUCK,** Paula Hamilton 15031-0-10

☐ 67 **QUEEN OF HEARTS,** Heather Graham 17165-2-30

☐ 68 **A QUESTION OF HONOR,** Alison Tyler 17189-X-32

$2.50 each

At your local bookstore or use this handy coupon for ordering:

 DELL BOOKS -Dept. B651C
P.O. BOX 1000. PINE BROOK. N.J. 07058-1000

Please send me the books I have checked above. I am enclosing $ _____ (please add 75c per copy to
cover postage and handling). Send check or money order—no cash or C.O.D.'s. Please allow up to 8 weeks for
shipment.

Name _____

Address _____

City _____ State Zip _____

Fans of JAYNE CASTLE rejoice– this is her biggest and best romance yet!

From California's glittering gold coast, to the rustic islands of Puget Sound, Jayne Castle's longest, most ambitious novel to date sweeps readers into the corporate world of multimillion dollar real estate schemes--and the very *private* world of executive lovers. Mixing business with pleasure, they make passion *their* bottom line.

384 pages $3.95

Don't forget Candlelight Ecstasies, for Jayne Castle's *other* romances!